THE LAST TRIBE OF LEVI

Richmond, Virginia

BROWN REFLECTIONS

THE LAST TRIBE OF LEVI
Richmond, Virginia

ISBN: 9781944440169

Library of Congress Cataloging-in-Publication Data on file.

MANUFACTURED IN THE UNITED STATES OF AMERICA

THE LAST TRIBE OF LEVI

Richmond,
Virginia

KAREN SLOAN-BROWN

Table of Contents

Priscilla and the Stranger 7

Thomas Edwards Freeman.................................. 11

William Edward Freeman 45

William Edward Freeman Jr. 87

William Edward Freeman III 125

Priscilla 205

Finding the Way Back...................................317

Epilogue 341

Prologue
Priscilla and the Stranger

The sun crept up over the horizon. I had been up all night listening to this strange man who had entered my life uninvited—or what was left of it. He had interrupted my peaceful farewell to a life that, for all practical purposes, had ended months ago when I lost my family in the plane crash. His excuse for wandering into my backyard was to help me restore my faith. He claimed to know me, but I am sure we have never met. After talking all night, he still hadn't told me his name, so I called him Mister.

He asked me to listen to a story, a story that went back to Abraham, the father of many nations and the father of the Twelve Tribes of Israel. He told me that it's my story, that I am a descendant of the Tribe of Levi, the priests designated by God to protect and preach His word, the intercessors and ministers to His people. The story is a long one. Mister began with Aaron and the freed Israelites venturing to the Promised Land, followed by the years in Jerusalem and the Babylonian exile. He told me about Jozadak crossing the Arabian Desert to Saba and then his descendants crossing the Red Sea into Axum centuries later. Among these high priests, there were kings and queens who migrated from Ethiopia to Kenya. The story took a tragic turn, with these descendants being enslaved again, shipped to Jamaica, and then shipped to the United States.

I had listened to Mister's story closer than I cared to admit; and, honestly, it touched something deep inside my soul. I felt a kinship with each of the priests and their families. I was humbled to hear of the tremendous adversity that the generations had to overcome for their survival. I'm sure that was his intention. Apart from that, he was asking a lot. He was asking me to live after I had already made the decision to die. Then combine that with the wariness I was feeling now that the story was moving nearer to my own.

"Can we take a break, Mister?" I asked, sounding like an unprepared student taking a difficult exam. "I'm exhausted in every way possible—mentally, physically, and emotionally."

"We're getting close to the part that would most interest you, Priscilla," he said, determined to continue.

I wanted to tell Mister that that was what I was most afraid to hear. I was confused, and I couldn't think straight. There was a stirring inside of me, between my heart and my stomach, a restlessness, and I was hoping it wasn't a panic attack.

"I don't feel too good," I told him, rubbing the back of my neck. "Maybe a hot shower will clear my head."

"Relax, beloved," he said. "It's a shift in your being. It's a moment of change and acceptance."

"I can't do this right now!" I said, rushing out of the room. The peace I had had with my decision the night before was gone.

Staring in the bathroom mirror, I refused to cry. I had cried enough tears to drown myself. I turned on the shower and undressed while the water warmed. I stood beneath the streams of water, watching them swirl at my feet. If only all the hurt could roll off me and spin down into the drain. Then, suddenly,

I felt exposed and vulnerable. I wrapped my arms around my body. I needed someone or something to hold me together. Instinctively, I got out of the shower before I fell and hurt myself. I pulled on a pair of sweats and a t-shirt and returned to the kitchen.

"Are you feeling better?" Mister asked.

"Not really, but that won't stop you, will it?"

"You'll feel better when I've finished," he said confidently. "Then you'll have your chance to tell me your story."

"Why don't we finish this outside? I need some fresh air."

The stranger nodded. The only other thing we agreed to at this point was that he had gone too far to stop.

Chapter One

Thomas Edwards Freeman

(born 1847)

Charles City County was Thomas's home. His grandpapa had bought his freedom here, his papa had raised him here, and he was going to die here. Most people in Ruthville didn't know it, but Thomas wasn't born free. His grandpapa owned him and his papa, in the legal sense of the word. His life wasn't like that of a typical slave, but that didn't count for much. His family worked as hard as other indentured people in Virginia.

"There are two kinds of slaves," Thomas's grandpapa told them. "The one who is held captive against his will, and the other who holds himself captive because of his ignorance. Both instances are crimes against humanity."

Thomas was determined that he would be neither kind. That's why he wanted to fight in the war on the side of the Union with the United States Colored Troops. A few of his friends chose to serve on the other side, but there was no way he was going to stoop to the side of the godforsaken Confederacy. Unlike some of the others, he was too smart to be duped into thinking it was the only way to save their land.

Thomas's father, Edward Freeman, had spoken his piece on the subject, rebuking him for his foolhardy notion of fighting and dying in the white man's war. Even so, as much as Thomas wanted his papa's approval and his blessing, he was going with or without it. It was his time to be a man in the family. That time came in early May of 1864 when the Union troops marched into Charles City County. Without hesitation, Thomas joined the Colored Troops. The first person he told was his sweetheart, Anna Bell.

Thomas met Anna Bell coming out of the house to gather wood for the stove. She could tell from the look on his face that something was on his mind, and she suspected what it might be. He fell in step beside her, and they walked toward the woods, with only the sound of birds chirping high in the trees and squirrels scampering nearby in the brush. For about ten minutes, she picked up thick dry branches and stacked them in his arms without saying a word.

Thomas broke the silence. "I enlisted with the Union Army," he said, shifting the load of branches in his arms.

Anna Bell took a few more steps before she said anything. "Why, Thomas? You're already free, and your folks aren't starving. You're just gonna get yourself killed."

"No, Bell," he said, pulling at the sleeve of her dress. "I wouldn't do anything that would keep me from coming back to you. You know we gon' get married. I'm gonna take care of you."

Anna Bell stopped moving, but she didn't look at him. "What if you come back with one leg or one arm or blind? How you gon' take care of me? I'm gonna have to take care of you!"

"Everything in my heart and soul tells me that's not gonna happen, Bell. I feel like I got to do something; I got to help the Union win this war. If I don't, then I don't deserve to be free."

"What you talking 'bout, Thomas? Don't nobody deserve to be no other man's slave. What they done to us is evil. We read about that in school."

"You know what else we read?" he asked. "We read what Frederick Douglass said: 'Those who profess to favor freedom, and yet depreciate agitation, are men who want crops without plowing up the ground. They want rain without thunder and lightning. They want the ocean without the awful roar of its many waters. This struggle may be a moral one; or it may be a physical one; or it may be both moral and physical; but it must be a struggle. Power concedes nothing without a demand. It never did and it never will.'"

Anna Bell finally turned and looked Thomas in the eye. "Stop trying to impress me," she said, doing her best not to smile.

"I still know how to get your attention," he said, grinning.

"Why you got to go now?" She whined. "Can't we just get married first?"

"I was gonna go after harvest last year, and then Grandma Caroline passed away. Besides, this is Maria and Stanford's turn to jump the broom. I'm leaving right after they get married on Sunday."

Anna Bell put her arm through Thomas's, and they walked back to the house without talking. There was so much she wanted to say, except it all seemed meaningless at that moment. The only thing that mattered was that she could hold onto him for as long as she could.

***

Blossom, Thomas's mother, had the seamstress make a fancy dress for her daughter, Maria, to get married in, and she spent an hour fixing her hair. All their neighbors and church members assembled in the front yard. Edward did the ceremony as he had done so many times before for other couples, save for the emotion that hung heavy in his throat for his daughter. Although the family joined in the singing and dancing after Maria and Stanford jumped the broom, there was sadness in the air, as if it was Thomas's last supper.

While the guests danced in a circle around the happy couple, Blossom noticed two negro men in a wagon approach the fence. Thomas caught sight of his mother hurrying into the house.

"I'm sorry, Bell," he said, stepping away and trotting toward the house. "What's the matter, Mama?" he asked when he got inside, pulling her hands from her wet face.

"I'm losing my family!" she cried, her eyes tightly closed.

"No, Mama, that's not true!" he said to console her. "Maria got married, but you'll see her all the time. And I'm only gonna be gone for a little while."

Blossom grabbed her son and held him tight, her head pressed against his heart. "Thomas, you know I couldn't take it if something happened to you."

"Nothing is gonna happen to me, I promise."

"I don't want to hear anymore empty promises," she said, covering her ears.

"I've got to go now, Mama."

Thomas hugged her and gave her a kiss, got his knapsack, and then went out to speak to his papa. Edward had come up to the front porch and was sitting in the rocking chair with his long legs stretched out in front of him. Anna Bell was waiting at the bottom of the steps.

"Bye, Papa," Thomas said, standing over him.

"You went against me," Edward said, sounding brokenhearted. "You're the hope for the people around here. If something happens to you, they won't have that."

"God spoke to me, Papa. There's nothing to be afraid of."

"I pray you're right, son," Edward said, standing up to look him in the eye.

Thomas nodded. He walked down the steps, kissed Anna Bell, waved to Maria and Eliza as he walked to the fence, and climbed into the wagon.

Anna Bell stood on the porch next to Blossom. Something inside her wanted to take off running as fast as her legs would carry her, with Thomas chasing behind her again. That made more sense to her than watching him walk away, scared stiff that she might not see him again.

***

Edward was relieved when Thomas's regiment, the 38th Infantry, was among the 1,100 Colored Troops that stayed in Charles City County. Under the command of Brigadier General Edward Augustus Wild, they began construction on Fort Pocahontas. Located on Wilson's Wharf, high on the James River, it was the prime spot for the Union to defend its position.

Proud of his classification as Private Thomas Freeman of Ruthville, Thomas found it didn't mean much, especially since he was one of the younger soldiers. It qualified him to dig in the earth from morning until night to build the rampart or mound of earth surrounded by a ditch.

"You should be happy to have your back bent digging," the sergeant over him said. "Tall as you are, you're a clear target."

Other colored soldiers worked on the abatis, the fortification from felled trees. They sharpened the limbs, twisted them together, interlaced them with wire, and laid them in a row facing south toward the enemy. In between time, the men practiced marching; did musket drills, where they learned to handle, load, and fire their weapons; and trained to fight with the bayonet.

On May 24, before the construction of the fort was completed, the colored troops were attacked. General Wild refused a request for surrender by the Confederates, after which 2,500 Confederate soldiers—commanded by the nephew of General Robert E. Lee, General Fitz Lee—were given the order to charge, starting the only battle in the state fought against nearly all black Union soldiers.

The Confederate battle cry started at 12:30, with their advancing line becoming entangled in the abatis. Wild then gave the order to the United States Colored Troops (USCT) to fire. The crack of the rifles and blasts from the cannons were deafening. Smoke clouded his view, but Thomas could see bodies soaring through the air like acrobats. Amazingly, he felt God's presence as he huddled in the trench with bullets flying toward him in slow motion. Rationally, he knew that was impossible, but he couldn't deny what his eyes could see. There was an invisible shield of protection around his fellow soldiers.

The fighting lasted 90 minutes before the Confederates retreated from the strong defense. An hour later, they fired again on the USCT, which were now being reinforced by two Union gun boats in the James River. The Confederates paused, and another order of retreat was given. The battle ended at 6:00 that evening, after six hours, when General Lee accepted defeat by the Union forces, consisting of almost all colored soldiers. Around 180 Confederate men were killed, wounded, or missing, compared to seven Union soldiers killed and around 40 wounded.

Battles raged in Virginia throughout May and June. General Grant trapped General Lee's army around Petersburg, and the siege went on for ten months. In December 1864, Thomas's troop, the 38th Infantry, paraded through Charles City County on their way to join the other USCT around Petersburg to become part of the XXV Corps of the Army of the James. The large force of black soldiers marching to join the Petersburg Campaign numbered between 10,000 and 15,000 men.

Dressed in the blue Union Army uniform, marching in step with the band, Thomas stretched his neck, searching the crowd, hoping to see his family members among them. He had nearly given up when he saw Anna Bell waving frantically. He could see her mouth moving, but he couldn't decipher the words. Her face looked sad, the look people have at funerals as they stand over the casket when they say their final goodbyes. He mouthed the words, "I'll be back," but marching further away, he doubted that she could see him under the shadow of his hat.

***

The winter freeze around Petersburg cooled most of the gun fire. The Union army, much like the Confederates, huddled into winter camps, waiting for the thaw. In February 1865, military action between the sides heated up again, fighting in the trenches only 400 yards apart. The USCTs participated in six major engagements north of the James River, south of the

Appomattox River, and east of Richmond, with bodies left lying behind them like broken trees after a storm. The harshest reality for them was the fact that most of their casualties were from sickness rather than combat with the Rebels.

Each night, Thomas prayed for the dead and for the protection of the living. Each morning, he said the Lord 's Prayer and recited the same Scripture: "The Lord is my rock, my fortress, and my savior; my God is my rock, in whom I find protection. He is my shield, the power that saves me, and my place of safety. He is my refuge, my savior, the One who saves me from violence. I called on the Lord, who is worthy of praise, and He saves me from my enemies," 2 Samuel 22:2-4.

"Are you some kind of preacher?" one of the men asked, his warm breath turning white in the cold. "You praying all the time."

"No. My papa is though," Thomas answered. "I just know that God is with me, with all of us here, so I have to give Him honor every day."

"I don't need to give no honor. I'm ready to take down as many of them Rebs as they done us," another soldier said. "I'm ready to fight for all the times I been whupped, all the times my daddy been whupped, my mama, my sister, and my wife. I want to have some of that retribution for myself."

Some of the other men spoke out in agreement. Thomas knew how they felt. For so long, he wanted revenge on those white men, too. When he left the farm, he thought he couldn't wait to shoot or beat as many as he could. Except, he took no joy in killing. He didn't want the blood of another man on his hands, on his mind, on his heart, or on his soul. He didn't want to be like his enemies or those who would persecute him. He wanted to be better than them.

The soldier who first spoke to Thomas hit him on his shoulder. "Keep praying, young brother, 'cause we need somethin' to help us make it out dis cold hell we in. We'll be froze like ice if we stay here another week, and it'll save Jonny Reb the bullets."

"My faith is in the Lord. More of them dying than us," Thomas said with conviction. "One thing I know is you reap what you sow."

Thomas was right. The Confederate Army was suffering mass casualties of white soldiers and was running out of options. A notice printed in *The Petersburg Daily Press* in an effort to recruit slaves in the Southern army stated, "To the slaves is offered freedom and undisturbed residences at their old homes in the Confederacy after the war. Not freedom of sufferance, but honorable and self-won by the gallantry and devotion, which grateful countrymen will never cease to remember and reward."

On March 25, 1865, units of the Union Army of the James, which included a division of the XXV Corps and Thomas's infantry, were moved to fill in the Petersburg lines and break the Confederate defenses. Having recruited black soldiers as well, 40 percent of the federal troops around Richmond were United States Colored Troops. A week later, the fall of Petersburg was imminent. The Union army had crushed the Confederate line southwest of Petersburg.

***

On April 2, known as Evacuation Sunday, the Confederate

government surrendered Richmond and fled south on the last open railroad. As the Rebel soldiers bolted the city behind the government officials, they set fires to the armory, the warehouses, and the bridges. With no one left to put them out, the fires spread with the help of flames from burning tobacco storehouses. Much of the city was destroyed, and mobs looted through the billows of smoke.

Twenty-five miles south of Richmond, Thomas sat with the XXV, waiting for the next offensive. The Union band played and marched all night in an effort to sound stronger in number than they were. Not far off, broken by General Grant's forces, the Confederate drums beat a rhythm that said they had more fight left in them. Even so, before daybreak, a bright red hue rose in the sky, not from the sun, but from huge fires burning in Richmond. Smoke swelled and curled above the inferno. Loud explosions followed in succession, and Thomas felt the earth tremors as he huddled in the trenches.

At 5:10 that morning, the troops were told to prepare to advance in an hour because the Confederates were evacuating Richmond. The words they had waited so long to hear didn't seem real. "What if it's a trap?" someone whispered. It's an unbelievable feeling when the circumstance you wished for, prayed for, and fought for has finally become reality. It takes time for the mind to process the change. The troops had less than an hour.

The Union soldiers packed up for the march to the capitol with orders to extinguish the fires; establish order; and protect the women, the children, and the property. The heaviness in their steps was gone. In its place, there was eagerness and excitement that made them feel as if they were walking on air.

Explosions boomed, mixing with the beat of the drummer boy's cadence as they got closer, but they were undeterred.

It was shortly after noon on April 3, 1865, when the black soldiers came over the hill. They were the first Union forces to enter Richmond's city limits. "Richmond at last!" they yelled, throwing their hats high above their heads and hugging one another. Exhilarated, the band played, and the men danced.

Thomas cried, shouting to the heavens, "We got the victory! Thank God Almighty!" By the time the white brigade got there, they were already in formation, with their colors flying high.

A huge mass of black people flooded the streets among the burning buildings, dancing and thanking God, fully aware that with Richmond taken, the war was over. The few whites in the streets had tears in their eyes. Free slaves cheered the Union soldiers as they marched down Main Street to the capitol. When they got there, Union soldiers dragged the Confederate flag down and raised the Stars and Stripes. It was total chaos, confusion, and celebration.

It meant the world to Thomas to be there at that moment, to know that he had had a part in winning the war. Along with the XXV Corps of the Union Army that occupied Richmond, Thomas worked to put out the fires that were still smoldering throughout the city. The following day, April 4, Abraham Lincoln came to witness the devastation in Richmond. The word spread among the freed slaves, and a crowd rushed to greet him, shouting, "Glory hallelujah!"

"My poor friends," the president told the crowd. "You are free—free as air. You can cast off the name of slave and trample upon it. It will come to you no more." On April 9,

1865, General Lee surrendered at Appomattox. Five days later, Abraham Lincoln was assassinated. The papers called him a "modern-day Moses."

***

Thomas was anxious to get back to his life and back to Anna Bell. He had fought for his freedom and the freedom of his people; but after his ordeal, all he wanted to be was a peaceful man of God. Like his papa always told him, he was chosen to be better than a soldier dying in battle. Several times a day, he had to shake his head to clear the visions of all the death he had witnessed. As far as he was concerned, the only good that came out of that destructive war was that no more of his people would be other men's property again. Thomas left the burned-out city of Richmond and went back to Charles City County.

The welcome home wasn't quite the one Thomas expected. When he walked up to the house and yelled, "I'm back home!" there wasn't any rushing about or screams of joy. Eliza was the first to come out.

"I'm glad you're back!" she said, playfully knocking his hat off and then giving him a hug. "We didn't know how long it would take you to get home."

"I got out of there as soon as I could. I'm ready to put all of that behind me."

By then, Edward and Blossom were coming down the steps to greet him. He could see the relief on their faces, but they still appeared stressed. His mother hugged him first and then moved aside for his father to have his chance to welcome him.

"Y'all don't seem happy to see me," Thomas said, bewildered by their half-hearted responses. "How are things going 'round here?"

"Things been tough," Eliza said, speaking up. "We barely had enough to feed ourselves, with the Yankees taking from us one day and then the Rebs the next. White folks and black folks been stealing everything not nailed down. We had some newly freed folks work beside us on the land, hunt, and fish to have a roof over their heads and somethin' in their stomachs. It helped us get through. We was even able to sell some provisions and make a little money."

Thomas looked at the ground. That was his only regret for the decision he made to volunteer. He wished he could have been there to help out his family.

"I know it hasn't been easy on none of us, but the war is over," Thomas said, forcing a smile. "The Lord brought me home safe like He promised, and things are going to be better for us."

"Well, come on inside," Blossom said. "I'll make you somethin' to eat. You look like you need some good home cooking."

"That'll be nice, Mama, but first I got to see Anna Bell," Thomas said, grinning.

Blossom's shoulders dropped. "You just got here. Can't I have a minute with my son?"

"Bring her back here," Edward chimed in. "Eliza will fetch Maria and her folks, and we'll have a big celebration dinner to welcome you home."

***

Thomas found Anna Bell in the backyard of her family's house. She was hanging clothes on the line. He snuck up on the other side of a sheet tossing in the wind and recited a portion of a poem by George Moses Horton.

I'll love thee for those sparkling eyes,
To which my fondness was betry'd
Bearing the tincture of the skies,
To glow when other beauties fade,
And when they sink too low to see,
Reflect an azure beam on me.

Anna Bell pulled the sheet down and started to cry. "You're always showing off!" she said, through her tears. "I was so worried about you!"

Thomas wrapped her up in his arms and rested his chin on top of her head. "I'm home, Bell," he whispered in her ear. "I told you I was coming back."

She pushed him back to check him for injuries. "Did you get hurt?" she asked, looking at him from head to toe.

"No, I'm fine. I saw a lot of bad things, but God blessed me and brought me through. I saw you in the crowd on the day we marched out of Charles City. I saw how sad you looked. Nothing was gonna keep me from getting back to you. I wanna see you smile, Bell!"

A big, beautiful smile spread across Anna Bell's face. "I guess I can stop being mad at you."

Thomas smiled, too. "Put on your prettiest dress, girl! My mama is gonna make a big dinner for me, and I want you there sitting beside me."

"Give me a few minutes!" she said, sprinting to the house.

Thomas laughed out loud, watching her run. It was the most wonderful sight he had seen in a long time.

***

There wasn't as much food on the table as they had had during the holidays or other celebrations, but it tasted just as good. Being at home with family was more satisfying than anything Thomas's mother could have set before them. Even so, Thomas detected a somber tone to the banter around the table and was disturbed that his parents avoided eye contact with each other. Anna Bell was occupied with Maria and Stanford's baby, bouncing her on her lap and squeezing her cheeks.

Stanford finally asked the question Thomas knew they all wanted to know. "Did you kill many of them Rebels?"

"What a soldier does on the battlefield, he leaves there," Thomas answered, and they could hear the edginess in his voice. "Don't none of them want to go through it again talking about it. Believe me, it's a horror you don't want to know nothing about."

"Stanford didn't mean nothing by it," Maria said. "We just glad none of them hurt you."

Thomas softened. "All of us out there was doing what we thought was right."

"Sad part is that a whole lot of them didn't make it back to tell about it one way or the other," Edward said. "You shouldn't have to spill that much blood for men to know what's right."

They finished the rest of the meal in awkward silence. When Maria and Stanford prepared to leave with their baby, Eliza joined them, wanting to have more time to spoil her niece.

"I'm going to walk Bell home," Thomas said, getting up from the table.

"It's going to take a while for you to get used to being back home," Anna Bell said, after they had walked away from the house. "You may not know it, but it changed you."

"Probably so," he admitted. "Everything is different, except for you. Folks don't seem as happy as I thought they would be."

Anna Bell sighed. "Hard times aren't over. For some, things are going to get harder. With the war, there was work for everybody. Now black folks need jobs. Yeah, they free, but some are walking with no place to go and only the clothes on their backs."

"I seen 'em all the way here from Richmond. Lot of 'em heading north," Thomas said wistfully. "We startin' out with nothing, but it's better than being somebody's slave. Trust me, Bell, I'm going to make a good life for us."

"You did the most important thing," Anna Bell said, standing outside her door. "You came back alive. We can do the rest together."

Thomas held and kissed her for a long time, in a way he hadn't done before. "I'll be back around tomorrow," he said happily.

Thomas ran all the way back home. He had so many plans. Now the time had come for all the things he had dreamed about to become real. It didn't matter to him how hard he had to work. He would build a house for him and Anna Bell and make her his wife. He was going to build a proper church for his father. It wouldn't be the grand temple that Solomon built, but it would be one that would surely please the Lord. The first thing he needed to do was increase their land. If he wanted to make bigger money, he had to plant bigger crops; and to do that, he needed more land.

***

Edward was sitting on the front porch smoking his pipe when Thomas got back to the house. Before he could say anything, his father said, "Go on in. Your mama's been waiting to talk to you."

Thomas went inside, wondering what was wrong. "Mama, it feels strange around here. What's going on?" Blossom didn't answer at first. She kept sweeping, even though he could see the floor didn't have a speck of dirt on it. "Mama, what's wrong between you and Papa?" he asked, sitting at the kitchen table.

Blossom didn't stop sweeping, but she finally answered. "I'm leaving, Thomas. I only waited here for you to come back. Now that you are here safe, I'm free to go."

"What? Mama, no!" Thomas groaned, confused and incredulous. "I know things have been hard, but we can all start over. All our lives will be different."

"It's too late, son. It's no use. This isn't the life I wanted. I'm like the rest of the slaves. I've been released, and I'm going away from this plantation."

"Mama, that's crazy! You ain't never been a slave, and this ain't no plantation. This is our family land; we own it."

Blossom stopped sweeping and shook her head. She didn't want to hurt her son, especially when he just got back and was looking to start a new life with Anna Bell. But she decided that some things just couldn't be helped.

"Don't you love, Papa?" Thomas asked, still trying to make sense of the sad news. He couldn't understand how she could just leave.

"I love your papa, and I always will; but I can't make him happy, and he can't make me happy. Around here, I feel like another acre of land. Sometimes I'm needed; other times, I'm just walked over. I need to feel like more than that. I think I can feel like that away from here."

"Does Papa want you to go?"

"No, he doesn't.

"Has he been mean to you or done somethin' to you?"

"No, he hasn't."

"What about the promises you made to each other?"

"Trying to keep my word to him, I broke the promises to myself. What I wanted matters, too."

"What do you want him to do, Mama?"

"I don't blame him, it's not his fault. I should never have married him. I thought he might want to get away from here, that he would help me get the life I wanted. I didn't understand that he needed a woman who would help him live the life God called him to lead. I won't stand in his way, but I can't let him stand in mine. I been seeing everybody in this family doing what they felt they had to do. Now it's my turn."

"I don't see how you can walk away from the family after all this time."

"Eliza wants to get away from here, too. She wants to go to Baltimore or Philadelphia. She can fix hair better than I can. We gonna go together. Your papa and I have already talked it over."

"Before I left here to join the Union Army, I prayed on it, Mama. It was the Lord who let me know I should go."

"Then pray for your mama, son, and pray for your sister."

Thomas dropped his head in his hands. That was all he could do.

***

When the new year began, Blossom and Eliza had been gone for about eight months. Thomas had been worried about how his father would react after his mother left; but, in reality, not much had changed. Edward spent most of his time on the front porch, staring out into the fields, no matter what the weather. His behavior was beginning to worry Thomas because the temperatures had fallen well below freezing, and his father didn't need to sit out there in the cold. Thomas put on his hat and coat and went out to check on him.

"What's on your mind, Papa?" Thomas asked, taking a seat beside him.

"Just thinking about the ways of this world."

"What you mean? Are you sad about Mama?"

"Not really. The Bible says there will be trouble in this world, things we will never understand. I've gained a lot, and I've lost as much; but His grace is sufficient."

"I guess you're right." Thomas said, looking out at the frozen fields, thinking about all the work he needed to do. "I don't know when I'll be able to prepare the seed beds for the next crop with this freeze on. I need to burn a lot of the undergrowth from the other crops y'all grew to sterilize the ground for the tobacco."

"Have you thought about finishing your schooling?" Edward asked, changing the subject.

"What do I need to go to school for?" Thomas asked, trying to shrug off the chill. "I already know how to read and write."

"Black folks don't have to go to school in secret no more. You can get your education like any other proper man. When the time comes for you to be the leader of the church, you should be trained. I'm thinking you ought to go to that school in the city, the Richmond Theological School for Freedmen."

Thomas shivered. "More learning. That's not for me. I want to work the land with you, Papa."

"I want you with me, son, but you have to be prepared to take your place in the pulpit. The men in this family have been appointed by God to stand and preach His word. This goes back for generations. Now that we all free, we need to get you a license. Folks are starting to come back to church. We have to do this right, and God will bless our works."

"You don't have to worry about that. I don't need to go to no school to talk with the Lord. I can do that here. I can't tell you how many times I felt God with me out there fighting on them battlefields. I have no doubt that my hand was in God's hand. Everything we need is right here on the land."

"There was a reason that the Lord didn't want the Levites to have land when he designated them as priests. He didn't want them distracted from the responsibilities to the Israelites."

"Papa, you can see that our people are like newborn babies out here. They not able to support themselves, much less support us. Trust me. I can work this land and preach God's word. Plus, you know I'm ready to marry Bell as soon as I can build us a house."

"If I've learned one thing, you gonna do what you want, no matter what I say," Edward said.

"Come on out of this cold, Papa. You'll get sick sitting out here," Thomas said, standing up and coaxing him to come into the house. "I'll make you some hot coffee. When the freeze breaks, I want you to come to Richmond with me."

"What for?" Edward asked, letting his son help him to his feet.

"I'm gonna deposit my army pay and the money I earned cleaning up the city at the new Freedmen's Savings and Trust Company."

"Why you wanna do that?" Edward said, shaking his head. "I don't trust nobody to hold my money except me."

"A lot of us soldiers are putting money there. It's how the white man gets rich, Papa. They invest in stocks and bonds; the money does all the work while you sit around drinking whiskey."

"I would tell you different, but I know you ain't listening. Just remember, the Good Book say you don't work, you don't eat or drink," Edward said, shutting the door behind them.

***

Edward convinced Thomas to put just half of his money in the bank. With the other half, he bought a little more land. It was a slow process to restore order on the farm. After the freeze, torrential rains flooded the fields, and it would be another year before the tobacco crop was planted. They didn't have money to hire workers, so Thomas plowed the main field for the seedlings behind the mule. Then he planted them and fertilized them. He had the patience to wait for the leaves to grow, but he didn't have the patience to wait to marry Anna Bell.

"Papa, I need your help," he said after a long day in the fields. "I want to build a house for me and Anna Bell so we can get married."

"If you ready to be a man and have a wife, then you must be ready to stand beside me in the church. You don't need to build a house right now. It's plenty room for you and Bell to live here. When times get better, we'll build you a fine house."

"All right, Papa," Thomas said. He didn't have the strength to struggle with the land and his father, too. As long as he was with Anna Bell, he could make it through.

After supper, too tired to walk, Thomas rode the wagon over to see Anna Bell. Seeing he was exhausted, she poured him a cup of cider, and they went outside to talk where her parents couldn't hear. For a while, they sat on the back of the wagon, listening to the crickets, while Anna Bell rubbed the tense muscles in Thomas's shoulders.

Then Thomas blurted it out. "I don't want us to wait no more to get married, Bell. I want to be with you all the time. I know I said I would build us a house—and I will—but in the meantime, Papa says we should stay there in the house. There's plenty of room."

"That's fine with me, Thomas," she said, putting her hand on his. "I would have married you when you first got back. It don't matter to me where we live."

"I'll make you happy. I promise," he said, overjoyed.

She laughed, "I'm already happy, silly!"

***

Thomas and Anna Bell were married on May 11, 1867, in front of the church on a beautiful Saturday afternoon. Maria and the women from the church cooked a big spread, and all of the couple's friends and neighbors kicked up their heels in celebration. Still, with Thomas's mother being gone, there was a slight shadow over the day. What made it all right was that Thomas got to spend the whole night with his wife, Bell, and wake up next to her in the morning.

The next day, during the worship service, Edward announced the news to their small congregation.

"I've been waiting for this Sunday for a long time, the Sunday when my son would stand beside me and bring the Lord's word. I am a happy man today. John 15:1-2 says, 'I am the true vine, and My Father is the vinedresser. Every branch in Me that does not bear fruit He takes away; and every branch that bears fruit He prunes, that it may bear fruit.' It is always a blessing when you plant a seed and it grows tall and strong into a vine. Brothers and sisters, a vine is a special plant. Not only can it climb high, but it can spread across a wide area. It can change to survive in all kinds of conditions, even places where there is no sunlight and little soil. Jesus is the vine, and we are his branches. As you all know, Thomas and Bell were married yesterday. We are so happy for them, and I pray that the Lord will bless their bond to bear much good fruit." The people clapped and shouted amen. Edward turned toward Thomas. "Give us a word, son."

Thomas moved forward. "Good morning, saints of God. Bell and I want to thank you for your kindness toward us. With that, the Lord has already blessed us. We don't have to look far back to see the suffering we have gone through, and we still have a ways to go—all of us do. We're starting with next to nothing, but remember Isaiah 66:9: 'I will not cause pain without allowing something new to be born, says the LORD.' So, I'm asking each and every one of you to hang on to that strong vine because our struggle isn't over yet. But we got a lot to be thankful for. Sing with me, church: 'Free at last!'"

The congregation stood as they clapped, sang, and rejoiced.

***

Things were improving for black people after the war during the period of Reconstruction. In meetings all over the state, they heard powerful speeches; and on October 2, 1867, black men in Virginia voted for the first time. Thomas and Bell celebrated another first on October 17, 1867: the birth of their daughter, Althea. The 14th Amendment was ratified in July 1868, giving blacks the rights of American citizenship.

The following year, on July 6, 1869, Ballard Trent Edwards was one of two black men elected to the House of Delegates. Edwards voted to ratify the 14th and 15th Amendments to the Constitution, a requirement of Congress before Virginia could be readmitted to the United States.

It was a time of jubilee. Black people were going to school, earning wages, buying property, and registering legal marriages. Resentment among whites grew as the newly freed men and women prospered. And like weeds that try to choke off thriving plants, the Ku Klux Klan terrorized black people wherever they went. Using violence and intimidation, the racist group wanted to keep blacks "in their place" and stop them from progressing politically and financially. The KKK even threatened other whites who purchased goods from black farmers. Some were beaten; others were killed. Things deteriorated so badly as a result of the vicious attacks, that even white people were fearful.

On November 4, Thomas and Bell had another daughter, Susanna. The family sat by the fire after the Christmas holiday thinking about the new year.

"Things are going to be tougher next year, Papa. We barely had enough folks to bring in the harvest this year. The families we had working here before are scared to work on the farm. They feel it's safer sharecropping on the white man's farm so they won't get arrested or hired out to work for free. It seems like for every two steps I take forward, I gotta take one back."

Edward puffed on his pipe. "Well, we have to stay in prayer and keep the faith. God has always provided."

"Just surviving is no way to live. I want more than that for my kids," Thomas grumbled.

"You sounding more like your mama, son. Don't forget to count your blessings."

"This ain't about how the Lord has blessed us. This is about how they trying to keep us working as slaves. White planters can't bring they crops in, so they come up with these laws, black codes, to make us work for free."

"Don't get yourself all riled up for nothing," Bell said, trying to calm him down.

"It's not nothing, Bell! These black codes saying we can't buy and lease land. They saying it's a crime if a black man don't have a job or working where they don't want him to. Then if he can't pay their tax, they call him a vagrant."

"Listen to me, Thomas," Edward said, pointing at him. "I know you've seen some things in this world, but I've seen them a lot longer. 'Be controlled and alert. Your enemy the devil prowls around like a roaring lion looking for someone to devour. Resist him, standing firm in the faith,' 1 Peter 5:8-9. This is not a new fight we in; it's been going on for a long time. We fought it back in Africa, Jamaica, and now here in the States. 'The race is not to the swift, nor the battle to the strong, nor the bread to the wise, nor riches to the intelligent, nor favor to those with knowledge, by time and chance happen to them all,' Ecclesiastes 9:11. Don't lose your head or your faith."

"Quoting Scriptures is not going to keep food on our table!"

"Don't be disrespectful, Tom!" Bell said, rocking the baby. "Althea can hear you."

"It's all right, dear," Edward said. "I said the same thing to my papa."

Things got worse with the KKK physically attacking and lynching blacks and destroying their property. They also intimidated them from voting. Part of the Freeman farm had been set on fire. The violence became so horrific that the newspapers that once supported the KKK's vigilante behavior started to condemn their violent actions. Congress passed the KKK Act of 1871, making their violence and political intimidation illegal.

***

Getting a crop from seed to harvest was an awesome feat, but wrestling out a fair price for the yield was another colossal contest. Less workers on the farm meant Thomas wasn't able to bring in large crops, but his saving grace was the quality of the tobacco, which brought him a higher price. Still, there was always one battle after another. Thomas thought that things couldn't get much harder until Bell gave birth to their third child, a son who was born with the umbilical cord wrapped around his neck. Devastated, Thomas worked harder. He took his pain out on the earth. He hammered it and dug deep into it, fighting the urge to give up and give in to the beating life had dealt him.

Thomas would learn how relentless fate could be during the Panic of 1873. The whole country had gotten caught up in expansion after the war ended. Huge amounts of money had been invested by banks in building railroads, even in places where land had not yet been cleared. The Freedmen's Bank was among them. Add to that, mismanagement and fraud, and all the banks were in serious jeopardy.

Thomas trudged up to the house after a hard day in the fields. It was the middle of harvest season. Edward was sitting on the porch reading *The Richmond Planet* newspaper. He folded it up when Thomas got to the steps.

"The papers say there's some bad trouble at that Freedman's bank," he told Thomas. "You need to get your money out now, son."

"The money is protected by the government, Papa," Thomas replied, too tired to entertain his old-fashioned suspicions.

"Have you forgotten about the land given to these folks around here after the war and then taken back by the government? The only place you can put your trust is in God."

Hearing that gave Thomas pause. He exhaled and climbed the steps to go inside.

"First thing in the morning, I'll ride up to the bank and see what's going on," he said, walking through the door.

Thomas got to the Richmond branch early the next morning, but there was already a run on the banks. A crowd of blacks in a state of panic stood outside the entrance. Thomas got in line, resolved to take his papa's advice and withdraw all his money; but he was let down when his turn came. He rode back to Ruthville with only half of it.

"Did you get your money, son?" Edward asked.

Thomas shook head in dismay. "Not all of it. Like you said, there's a lot of trouble going on. They told us we would have to wait until things settled down."

Edward left it alone. No need to pour salt in his wounds by saying, "I told you so."

In March 1874, Edward read in the paper that Frederick Douglass had been elected president of the Freedmen's Bank and had invested $10,000 of his own money as a show of confidence. Unfortunately, it wasn't long before Douglass discovered that he was "married to a corpse" and recommended that Congress close the bank. Depositors lost more than a million dollars of savings. Thomas never got another dime of the other half of his money.

That was only the beginning of the depression. It would last for five years. There were more business failures and more bankruptcies. High prices for seeds and fertilizer slashed profits. Laborer's wages were cut, and farm food prices were falling. Workers went on strike. To make matters worse, the KKK was waging another war of terror on black people.

***

Far off in the field, Thomas questioned his eyes when he saw his mother walking toward the house. He thought he would never see her again on this side of heaven. He dropped the tobacco leaves in his hands and took off running toward the house. He could see his father get up from his chair and come to the bottom of the steps. Thomas's eyes teared up as he got closer. They were tears of joy, but also of heartache. His mother looked older and worn down.

"Mama!" he called out, watching Edward wrap Blossom in his arms.

"Go get your sister!" Edward said.

Thomas didn't look for Bell or the girls. He rushed to the barn, hitched the horse to the wagon, and goaded it to a quick trot. Just a couple miles away, Thomas rolled onto Maria and Stanford's land like a runaway train. When Thomas rode up, Maria was outside boiling tomato jars she had canned. Her daughter Lydia was sitting nearby with Althea and Susanna while they picked green beans.

"Mama's back!" he yelled from the wagon. Maria's mouth dropped opened, but she was speechless. She couldn't believe her ears. "Come on, girls!" Thomas said, waving his arms. "Where's Stanford?"

"He's helping his papa on their farm," Maria said, climbing into the wagon, with Lydia behind her. "How's Mama? Is Eliza with her? Why didn't she write and say she was coming?"

"I don't know. I didn't get a chance to talk to her. Papa just told me to come get you real quick," Thomas answered, turning the horse around to head back. "She just came out of nowhere."

Back at Edward's house, the wagon had barely stopped rolling before Thomas, Maria, and the children were hopping down and hurrying inside. Sitting at the supper table with Edward and Anna Bell, Blossom stood up when they burst through the door.

"Mama, I'm so happy to see you!" Maria said, squeezing her tightly. "Where is Eliza?"

"I'm happy to see all of you," Blossom said weakly, reaching out to hug Thomas. "And who are all these pretty girls?"

"The tallest one is Lydia. She's grown a lot while you were gone," Maria said. "And these are Thomas's daughters, Althea and Susanna."

"Oh, my goodness!" Blossom said, getting emotional. "I have missed you all so much!"

"Sit down, honey," Edward said, guiding her to the chair.

"I'll fix you something to eat," Anna Bell said to Blossom. "You girls go on out and play. Give your grandma some time to catch her breath."

Thomas and Maria sat down at the table. They had so many questions, but they could see their mother was tired.

"Where is Eliza? Is she coming home, too?" Maria asked, trying to contain her eagerness.

Blossom shook her head. "No. She married a fella there named George. They gonna try to make it there. They praying trouble don't last always."

"Are you here to stay, Mama?" Maria asked, and they all listened intently for her answer.

"Yeah, I'm here for good," she answered. "Things got real hard up there in New York when the Depression started. We shared a couple of rooms with another family. Hardly had enough to eat. Some days our meal was at the soup kitchen."

"You don't have to talk about that now," Edward said. "We just glad that you back here."

"No," she said. "I got something I need to say to you." She grabbed Edward's hand and looked him in the eyes. "Forgive me, my love. For some reason, I always thought there was something magical out there, a place where life was fair and everybody got what they deserved. I didn't find that place. And out there, nobody loved me, and nobody cared. I searched for more and ended up with less than what I had. With you, I had someone who loved me and took care of me. I didn't appreciate you, husband, and I'm sorry for that."

"I know that, honey," Edward said. "I don't have no hard feelings towards you for wanting more in this life. I wished I could have given it to you."

"I was too stupid to know I had everything a woman could want," she said, sobbing.

"Hush that crying, woman!" he told her. "We gonna be all right now."

"Yeah, Mama," Thomas added. "Things are going to be better soon."

***

"Hallelujah!" Edward shouted. "There is so much to praise God for this morning. My heart has wings today. Nothing can hold me down. Christian folk, Ezekiel 34:15-16 says, 'I will feed my flock and I will lead them to rest,' declares the Lord God. 'I will seek the lost, bring back the scattered, bind up the broken the sick." Thank you, Lord God, for your mercies and your grace. He blessed me, and I'm so thankful. He's blessed all of us. His grace is sufficient. Hallelujah," he cried out, raising his arms high. "Thank you for Your faithfulness to us. I praise You!" Filled with the Holy Spirit, Edward began to dance.

Thomas moved to the podium. "Brothers and sisters, we have all sinned and fallen short of the glory of God. But if we confess our sins, He is faithful and will forgive us. We only have to trust God in all things, even though most of us don't have nothing left except for the land and our faith. None of us had it as hard as Job. Folks, this is our time of restoration. We are coming out of the darkness. We are laying down our burdens, we are moving forward as a people. Thank God Almighty! Nevertheless, we come humbly before the throne asking Him to continue to bless our works. 'You are the LORD our God, who teaches us what is best for us, who directs us in the way we should go,' Isaiah 48:17."

"Let's sing together, saints," Edward said, putting his arm around Thomas and leading them in singing "Amazing Grace."

It was a joyous time, in spite of the bitter circumstances of the Depression. Their words inspired the congregation; and each week, more people came to hear Edward and Thomas preach. Sometimes they spoke together, like two singers in a duet. It was an awesome sight to behold.

***

Time can be a great healer, renewing faith, hopes, and dreams. Over the next five years, Thomas worked hard, and the Lord restored his crops and his money. The congregation outgrew the small church, and they built a bigger one. He and his father became the pastors of one of the three largest black churches in Charles City County. But Thomas's greatest blessing came when Anna Bell announced she was pregnant again.

"Thank you, Jesus!" he said, raising his fist high before he picked Bell up in the air. "It's time for me to build that house I promised you."

"You don't have to do that, Tom," Bell giggled. "We have plenty of room here. All I want is for this baby to be healthy."

"I'm not worried about that, sweetheart," he said spinning

her around. "God spoke to me a few weeks ago. I heard Psalm 30:5 echoing in my ears: 'His favor is for life, weeping may endure for a night, but joy comes in the morning.' Everything is going to be all right."

"We know better than to boast about tomorrow," she said cautiously, pushing him to put her down. "Let's take the days one at a time."

"Can't I just enjoy this moment?" he asked, smiling.

"Sure," she said. "We have a lot to be grateful for."

Nonetheless, time can be a destructive bandit, breaking us down and robbing us of our health and vitality. Despite all the prayers and nourishing meals Bell prepared, Blossom never fully recuperated from the years she had lived in New York. The doctor said that it was tuberculosis. Five years after coming back home to the farm, after the Thanksgiving holiday, Blossom died. At her funeral, Edward preached and sang, "Nobody Knows the Trouble I've Seen." Tears streaked down the faces of every man, woman, and child in the church. Edward's pain filled the room like fog.

Blossom's eulogy was the last sermon Edward preached, and he never explained why. The next day, he started working in the fields again. He was up before dawn and worked late after sunset.

"Papa, you need to slow down. You're pushing yourself too hard," Thomas told him after a few days. "It takes a while for your body and your back to get used to being out here."

"Look here, son, you don't need to tell me how to work this land. I was working it all by myself before you were born," Edward argued stubbornly.

Thomas knew what he was doing; he had done the same thing himself. He was trying to take his pain out on the earth, beat it down, and bury it. It hurt his heart to watch. He prayed his papa's strength would hold out until the pain ebbed.

Three months later, Thomas found his father lifeless on the porch. They buried him next to Blossom in the graveyard beside his first church. They were still grieving when Anna Bell gave birth to another son on May 24, 1881. Thomas stood beside his father's empty chair and shouted his thanks to the Almighty. The Lord returned to him what the devil had stolen. The boy was his hope for the future.

Chapter Two
William Edward Freeman
(born 1881)

Thomas named his only son William Edward
Freeman. Everything he did and every dollar he
made was for the legacy he would leave to his son.
He and Bell indulged William, but he was intent that the boy
would respect the virtue of hard work. The problem was, only
one generation from laboring in the fields, William proved
worthless as a tobacco farmer. The irony amused Thomas. His
only man-child had a back too weak to work the land.

In truth, it wasn't that William wasn't strong enough to
tackle the earth for a living. He just didn't want to be a farmer.
It was also his realization that if you owned enough land, you
didn't have to get your hands dirty.

"If you can't build up your body, then build up your
mind," Thomas announced when William turned 16. "For
that, you need more education than Grandma Jane can give
you."

Thomas had a decent amount of schooling, but he wanted
better for his son. He believed William could get the learning
he needed at the Richmond Colored Normal School. At the
end of the summer, Anna Bell packed his things, and Thomas
took him to Richmond to stay with his Aunt Maria. She and
Stanford had moved there ten years earlier when Stanford got a
good job working there in a tobacco factory.

"Remember why you're here," Thomas told William before he left to return to Ruthville. "The life you were born to will be waiting for you." None of that mattered to William. The blood of Grandma Blossom in him was overjoyed to be in the city.

William had never ridden on an electric streetcar or been in a building as tall as the Richmond Colored Normal School. It was three stories high and full of new experiences. Spending most of his day in classes learning Latin and Greek, arithmetic, business, and music, and keeping his hands clean was heaven to William. Whenever he was home during vacations working on the farm, he couldn't wait to get back to school.

William's vision for his life came into focus after one of his teachers gave him a copy of W.E.B. Dubois's book *The Conservation of Races*. After reading it, he found that he was much more interested in the growth of negro people than a bumper crop of tobacco.

***

William graduated from the Richmond Colored Normal School in 1900. He had been home for less than a month, but he already felt like a slave waiting for an opportunity to escape. The harvest season was just beginning, and pulling the bottom leaves off the tobacco plants in the oppressive heat was William's personal hell. Bent over for hours, his back ached, and his heart and head yearned to be back in a classroom, where he could expand his mind.

Thomas could sense his son's restlessness. He himself had felt that same urgency many times. Knowing how much William hated working in the fields, Thomas figured it was time to give him something else to keep him busy. At the end of the day, Thomas waited for his son at the edge of the field.

"You know, I'm proud of you, son," Thomas said, putting his hand on William's shoulder. "You did a good job in school. Now, I think the time has come for you to join me in the pulpit. Do you think you're ready to stand before the church and do your first sermon?"

William was taken aback. That was the last thing on his mind, but one thing he learned at school was how to think on his feet.

"There's a lot more I need to learn, Papa," he said pensively. "I was thinking that it might be helpful for me to study at the Union Theological Seminary in New York City. With the church growing like it is, I should be educated like these other preachers."

Thomas had a feeling there was more to William's request, but he didn't press it. "That's good thinking, son," he said in agreement.

William was young; he had time to find himself. Thomas knew that there are times when you don't go against the grain because there are always other routes to get to the same destination. Ultimately, William would stand in the pulpit beside him.

But William had other ideas. Once he was enrolled in seminary, he would figure out how to get into the School of Philanthropy at Columbia University.

***

There were no emotional goodbyes when William and Thomas left for the train station. Anna Bell didn't cry, but

Thomas recognized the look on her face as the same one he saw when he left for the war.

En route to the Main Street Station in Richmond, there wasn't much conversation between father and son as they rode in the wagon. In a sense, they were both going into unknown territory, and neither one of them knew how it would look on the other end.

"Maybe you'll run into your Aunt Eliza while you're there," Thomas chuckled, breaking the tension between them.

"I don't know. It's a big city," William answered.

"She probably wouldn't know who you are anyway," Thomas said, sighing. "You weren't born when she and your grandmama left."

"Papa, thanks for letting me go back to school," William said when they got to the railroad station. "I feel like there is something out there for me to learn."

"All right, son. Just make sure you bring all that knowledge back where it belongs."

William smiled. "I will."

Thomas helped William carry his trunk to the rear car of the train. "You got everything you need, the address to the house?" Thomas asked.

William nodded, yes, and turned to face him. "Goodbye, Papa," he said, stifling his excitement.

Watching his son board the steps to the railroad car for colored passengers, Thomas held his breath and beseeched the angel of the Lord to guide him in all his ways. "Bring him back a man, whole in his mind and body," he prayed. Then he stood transfixed long after the train was out of sight.

***

Four train rides later, William had no regrets about switching his farm overalls for the nifty tailored suits and bow ties he carried with him to New York City. "It was a culture shock at first, without fields as far as the eye could see, but the folks were just as busy. Tall buildings stretched high in the sky; and the streets were crammed full of carriages, bicycles, and streetcars.

Before William's arrival, Thomas had written letters and arranged for him to rent an apartment in Harlem from a Rev. Dr. Charles Satchell Morris, the associate pastor of the Abyssinian Baptist Church. William checked his pocket for the address and then hired a horse and carriage taxi to take him there.

Although, William was anxious to have a place of his own, for now, he would be sharing the apartment with another young man who was a second-year student at Columbia University. William was dragging his trunk up the front stairs when the door to the apartment building opened.

"I see you made it," a light-skinned young man said, reaching for one end of the trunk. "I'm Andrew, Andrew Simpkins." About a foot shorter than William, with straight hair that curled on the end, Andrew was dapperly dressed.

"Thanks! Good to meet you," William said, trailing him up the steps and inside. "This is my first trip to New York."

"So I hear," Andrew said. "The word is, your father is a big-time preacher in Virginia, and you're going to follow in his footsteps."

"I hope to help him do some big things for our people," William offered, wanting to downplay that notion. "That's why I'm here."

Andrew nodded in approval. "All right. Once you get settled, I'll show you around."

William was thrilled with the hot and cold running water, electricity, and water closets in the apartment. He quickly put away his things so he could start learning his way around town. The first place the two young men went was to the barbershop so William could get a big-city haircut. That evening, Andrew took William to Marshall's Hotel for dinner. William could not believe his eyes when he saw blacks and whites sitting together enjoying each other's company. For the rest of the week, each day held another eye-opening experience for him.

Walking into Abyssinian Baptist Church on Sunday morning was inspiring in many ways, too. It lifted William's soul to see so many black parishioners gathered together. Their voices moved him, and he was positive that he felt the Holy Spirit. When he closed his eyes to pray, he received a vision of the church he wanted to build for his father. Vividly, he saw Thomas standing behind the intricately carved podium. The strange thing was that William didn't see himself in the picture.

***

The rapture ended, and William was brought down to earth two days later on August 14, 1900. New York City was in the midst of a heat wave. It was as hot as hell is believed to be, and tempers flared. Outside a tavern in the Tenderloin, a black man killed a white plainclothes policeman he thought was accosting his white girlfriend. The next day, liquor flowed freely at the cop's wake, and a shot was fired, triggering a race riot. A violent mob of whites raged through the streets, viciously attacking every black person they saw, men and women. The vandalism and assaults lasted for two days.

A week later, the atmosphere was still edgy in the Tenderloin, but nothing could dampen William's excitement in the big city. He couldn't wait for his classes to begin. Sitting in class, sweating through his suit, he was back in heaven, relishing the profound discussions and the exchange of ideas with students from different backgrounds. He learned that theology encompassed a lot more study than just the Scriptures. The history reminded him of the stories his grandpapa had told him about his ancestors.

Equally as informative was William's education outside of the classroom. He was attending a lecture by W.E.B. DuBois when Andrew noticed an attractive young woman staring at them from across the room.

"Come with me," Andrew said, grabbing William by the elbow and leading him through the vestibule. "William Freeman, this is one of the daughters of Manhattan's finest families, Florence Farley."

Florence looked slightly uncomfortable as she nodded at William and said, "Good evening."

"Very glad to meet you," William said.

"Florence goes to Barnard College," Andrew added.

William did his best not to stare, but the way she held herself was as a work of art, perfect in every way. Some people probably thought she was white, but blacks recognize their own.

Florence avoided eye contact. Even though she felt an immediate attraction to William, she had yet to make the decision as to whether she would try to live the life of a white woman in constant fear of discovery or experience the prejudice and restrictions of a black woman. Taking up with a black man would limit that option.

"This is William's first term," Andrew said, smiling. "We have to show him what New York has to offer."

"We certainly do," Florence said, looking across the room as if she were preoccupied. Andrew took the hint and ushered William back to the other side of the room.

On their trek back to their apartment, Andrew answered all of William's questions about Florence. Her father was Shelton Farley, the premier undertaker for blacks in the city. He also owned quite a bit of real estate in San Juan Hill and was buying as much property as he could in Harlem. Her mother was from a prominent family in Washington, DC.

William couldn't stop thinking about her. Whenever he closed his eyes, he saw her face. She was regal, confident, carrying herself like a queen. He met her again at a private social function. Without other whites in the room, she talked freely with him.

"I had my doubts that you wanted to be associated with a man like me," William said.

"What kind of man are you?" Florence asked, being coy.

"A black man who looks black," he answered seriously.

"It would probably surprise you to learn that I probably know more about being unwanted than you do. As a man, more doors are open to you. And even though I attend Barnard, I'm excluded from most of the activities there and all the organizations. You judge me because I choose to fit in in some places without declaring I'm a negro."

"Then you admit it. Passing makes life easier, doesn't it?"

"No, it doesn't. It simply gives you a closer view to those who want to hold you down."

"I see your point," William said. "You gave me the cold shoulder, and I was disappointed. I misjudged you."

"Honestly, I've never met a man like you," she said, a bit intrigued. "There aren't many around here."

"You mean a man of my color?" he asked, unsure of what she was alluding to.

"No," she said, chuckling. "I mean a man who can admit when he's wrong."

William found Florence to be smart and thoughtful. She was the kind of woman he needed by his side to build the church and his legacy. She would be the mother to his children. He wrote to her, telling her of his interest in her becoming his wife. She responded with an invitation for him and Andrew to join her and her friends at a dinner party.

***

Over the next seven months, Florence introduced William to black society. They socialized in small groups of black elites, and William was fascinated and charmed by the liberty of life in the North. He walked where he wanted, enjoyed the vaudeville shows, and ate in fine restaurants. He went to nightclubs and tasted the finest brandy. He attended galas and the sedate church services of the Presbyterians. He learned what real money could buy, and he wanted more of it.

It had become clear to him that this was the life he wanted for himself—at least it was until he and Florence attended a particular literary gathering, a salon that was hosted at the home of T. Thomas Fortune.

William heard her voice before he saw her. Petite, full-bosomed, and the color of sweet caramel, she was reading a poem by Paul Laurence Dunbar called "An Invitation to Love."

A tremor ran through William's body as if the earth had shaken beneath him. She glowed in the flickers of the gaslights, and he hung on every word released from her lips.

. . . Come when my heart is full of grief
Or when my heart is merry;
Come with the falling of the leaf
Or with the reddening cherry.
Come when the year's first blossom blows,
Come when the summer gleams and glows,
Come with the winter's drifting snows,
And you are welcome, welcome.

She grinned at her audience, and the room filled with soft applause. She absorbed it as a bloom takes in the rain, and her smile reflected the sun. Then with a pat on his shoulder, Florence brought him out of his reverie.

"Come meet my sister," Florence said, placing her arm through his as they walked up to the woman. "Cora, this is William Freeman. He's here from Virginia. William, this is my younger sister, Cora."

William was confused. He had never been moved like this. Up had become down, light had become dark, and his dream had become a wild fantasy.

"Good to meet you," he stuttered, at a loss for words.

"I can see why Florence hasn't brought you to dinner yet," Cora said with a sly smile.

Florence skillfully changed the subject. "This evening, I thought we would be hearing about the goals of the National Afro-American Council to address the civil rights of negroes."

Cora ignored her comment. "Florence, I need to get to

know this new gentleman friend of yours. He must be quite special to have this much influence on you. You never cared about the plight of negroes before. I thought you were only interested in saving yourself."

"That just shows how little you know about what I think, dear sister. William is studying theology at Union Theological Seminary."

"Please don't tell me you're one of those religious fanatics who want to clean up the city," Cora said, half-joking.

"No, ma'am," William replied, unoffended. "I'm here to learn how to raise up our people."

Cora was impressed. "You must come to dinner, William Freeman. I'm sure our parents would love to meet you."

"Thank you for the invitation. It would be my pleasure," he said, having regained his composure.

"Good. Florence will let you know the day," Cora said, walking away.

No matter how he tried, William couldn't turn away from watching Cora for the rest of the evening. She seemed relaxed, unpretentious, and comfortable in her skin, the converse of Florence. From the rear of the parlor, he stole glances into the drawing room, where the women gathered. Occasionally, he observed Florence, but it was Cora who had him captivated. While Florence was the model, a mannequin, Cora was unabashedly alive. She was softer and more real. It was easy to see that perfection was not her goal, and interaction energized her. On her way out with her group of friends, Cora handed William the book of poetry she had read from.

Their paths crossed again and again. Each time they met and talked, William felt drawn to Cora. He spent many sleepless nights vacillating on what he should do. Should he choose the woman he admired or the one he desired? The night before the dinner with the family, he flipped over in the bed and winced from a pain he could not describe. What kind of cruel twist of fate was being exacted on him?

***

The Farleys lived in a brownstone townhouse in Upper Manhattan. William slowly climbed the stairs, unsure of the welcome he would receive on the other side of the door. He knocked, and an older black woman wearing an apron opened the door and ushered him into the parlor.

Florence, impeccably dressed as usual, smiled nervously and rose to her feet. "William, this is my mother and father, Mrs. Inez Farley and Mr. Shelton Farley."

William made a slight bow to Mrs. Farley, who refused to meet his gaze. Then he stepped toward Mr. Farley and extended his hand. Mr. Farley stood up, shook his hand, and gave him a once-over glance from head to toe.

At that moment, Cora walked in, singing her greeting. "Good evening, everyone! Have I missed anything?" she asked, grinning mischievously.

"You're late," Inez said, scolding her.

"Why don't we go into the dining room and eat this meal while it's hot," Mr. Farley said, helping his wife to her feet.

The older black woman put the food on the table and left the room. "Florence tells me you come from a long line of preachers," Mr. Farley said. "Would you do us the honor of blessing the meal?"

"Yes sir," William said, lowering his head. He closed his eyes and prayed, "Heavenly Father, bless the fruits of Thy hands in this wonderful meal placed before us. Bless the works that made it possible and the hands that prepared it. Bless it to nourish our bodies, and bless this home and the people gathered at this table, in the precious name of Jesus. Amen."

Inez watched him out of the side of her eyes with pursed lips. She was offended as much by his Southern accent as she was by his dark skin.

"Thank you for that blessing, William," Farley said, placing a napkin in his lap. "It is my understanding that you are from Virginia, up here studying theology."

William put his fork down, careful not to speak with a mouth full. "Yes, sir, I am, but I am also interested in bringing prosperity and civil rights to my people back home. It's important to me to be of service to them in more than one way."

Farley was unimpressed; he didn't care much for preachers. "I'm not an especially religious man myself," he said, propping his elbows on the table with folded hands. "The missus insists that I grace the doors of the church most Sundays, but it seems to me that the preacher takes his living from the folk. I prefer to make my own money and not feed off of the people."

William wasn't intimidated by his remark. He'd heard others state the same opinion.

"I prefer to speak from my own knowledge and experience, sir, but it seems to me that business in essence must feed off the people to survive. In our town, my father provides work for people so that they can earn money to feed themselves."

Getting defensive, Farley pushed further. "In my experience, they always want a donation from one man before they can help another man."

Florence tightened her grip on William's hand, signaling for him to hold his tongue; but he ignored her and spoke freely. "I'm sure you're familiar with the adage, 'Give a man a fish, and you feed him for one day. Teach a man to fish, and you feed him for a lifetime.' My father and I agree with that Chinese philosopher because our mission is the same. We want to empower our people, not just take from them to enrich ourselves. Land is power, as you well know. The difference is, we want to give them a living, not only collect rent."

Cora applauded slow and loudly. "Well said, William!"

"That may work in the South, but as you can see, there are no fields here in Manhattan," Inez said, coming to her husband's defense. "It's possible that your thinking won't fit in our world."

"There is only one world, and it belongs to our Lord," William told her graciously. "Only He can determine who fits."

Farley sniggered. "You are quite the fervent speaker, William. Remind me to speak to you about a proposition after dinner."

Florence changed the subject. She wanted to discuss the subway, the new train that was being built to run underground. After dinner, Farley took William aside for a private conversation.

"So, what are your intentions regarding my daughter?"

This wasn't a moment for indecision, but William was in a quandary. He was interested in Florence and Cora. He thought of Jacob sitting before Laban and asking for his second daughter to be his wife.

"Sir, I would like to marry your daughter," he answered, certain that he wanted one of them.

Farley lit his pipe and then spoke. "My daughters have not wanted for anything," he said. "I would have to be certain that you could provide for Florence. Prove that to me, and you have my blessing. You can begin doing that by accepting my job offer of preaching eulogies for those unfortunate migrants who have no church home in the city."

William was stunned by the offer, but he wasn't in a position to say no. And the extra money would help him accelerate his plan.

"It would be my pleasure to work with you," William replied, extending his hand in agreement.

Farley grinned wide and grabbed William's hand in a firm shake.

***

Farley wasn't the only one offering William a proposition. Cora had ideas of her own. On the following day, dressed fashionably in purple, with a matching hat, she was waiting outside the apartment for him when he got home from school.

"What are you doing here?" William asked, surprised to see her but no doubt pleased.

"I just figured, since you're a man of God, you should know where to find the sinners," she said, grinning up at him. "I'm here to show you the real New York."

"Give me a minute to change my jacket, and I'll follow wherever you lead."

William ran up the steps two at a time, anxious to be on his way before Andrew returned. He wasn't sure what this evening would hold for him, but he couldn't help but jump at the chance to spend time with Cora. He washed his face; brushed his hair; put on a fresh shirt, tie, and jacket; and headed out the door.

They rode on cable cars to the Tenderloin. They went into a club where there was plenty of music, dancing, and drinking. William wasn't shocked by it. Andrew had taken him to a few risqué places when he first arrived. More than anything else, he was intrigued with Cora. She was the ocean—free and fluid, unguarded and a tad menacing—the complete contrast of Florence, who was a rock—solid, dependable, and uncompromising.

Later in the evening, William tried to conceal his yawn. It had been a long day, but he wasn't ready for it to end.

"Are you tired of slumming?" Cora asked, teasing him.

"This isn't the place I would have chosen, but it doesn't matter to me, as long as you are enjoying yourself."

"Let's go someplace where we can get some decent food and talk," she said. "The Marshall is close by."

William got up, helped Cora to her feet, and they walked up to West 53rd. They ordered two chicken dinners, and Cora asked for two drinks. William would never drink liquor in front of Florence, but it seemed natural with Cora. They ate and drank until midnight, discussing their views on social activism, segregation, and the Jim Crow laws in the South.

"I should get you home," William said. "Your father is probably going to kill me."

"We don't have to leave," Cora said. "My father keeps a room here, and I have the key."

Instantly, William felt flushed, except it wasn't from the liquor. In his head, he knew he shouldn't go to the room with Cora, but every other part of him wanted to be alone with her. He followed her to the room and closed the door behind them. Cora wasn't shy about expressing her feelings or desires. That night she seduced William, and from then on, she was the sweet wine that kept him drunk whenever he was in her presence.

***

After working with Farley for six months, William had stood beside so many caskets that he had stopped looking at the bodies. He didn't know any of the deceased. It was only his passion for the lives of his people that made him a dynamic speaker. He preached to unfamiliar faces, doing his best to give them the comfort of God's word. For most of the eulogies of the poor, he used the same sermon. He preached it again for a black man who had been run over by a motor omnibus.

"Brothers and sisters, I stand here giving all the praise and honor to our Savior, Jesus Christ. To the family and friends of this dear departed soul, I want to express my sincere sympathy for the pain and grief that engulfs you today. Times such as this, we feel like Wednesday's child who is filled with woe. The burdens are great for our people, and it seems as if we can't find relief, that place of solace where we can remove the yoke that binds us. But I still shout hallelujah, Christian friends, for the trials of this faithful servant have come to an end. Matthew 5:12, 10 says, 'Rejoice and be glad, for your reward in heaven is great; for in the same way they persecuted the prophets who were before you. "Blessed are those who have been persecuted for the sake of righteousness, for theirs is the kingdom of heaven."' So, we thank God for His mercies. For while we shed our tears down here, the angels are dancing in jubilation. Sing with me saints of God."

When we all get to Heaven
What a day of rejoicing that will be
When we all see Jesus
We'll sing and shout the victory.

Farley's business increased with the charismatic young preacher. He had begun to see a long-term benefit of having William in the family. So, in mid-March, in the middle of Lent, Farley insisted that William join the family for church on Sunday. William politely accepted, but the thought of it had him completely unnerved. It would be the first time he would be with both women in one room since he had begun his secret liaisons with Cora.

***

"What's wrong with you, today?" Andrew asked William once they were finally out the door. "You been dragging your feet all morning. I would have thought you'd be in a rush to be baptized into the Farley family. Him inviting you to sit with him at 'Mother Zion' is the same thing as giving you his blessing."

"I'm not feeling so good," William said, rubbing his forehead and adjusting his hat.

William couldn't tell Andrew what was on his mind; he couldn't tell anybody. Dreading the day ahead of him, he had moved in slow motion from the moment he had awakened. Somehow, up until Farley asked him to church, he had been able to rationalize his relationship with Cora. He wasn't the first man torn between two women. He felt guilty for his indiscretion; but like any alcoholic or drug addict, he was hooked. Concealing it from Andrew had turned him into a liar as well as a cheat. In many letters to his father, he had written about the temptations of the city, but he never mentioned that he had surrendered to them.

When William and Andrew walked through the door of the Mother African Methodist Episcopal Zion Church on West 10th and Bleecker Street, William felt as if he had been stripped naked. Dressed in his smart suits strutting to the seminary, he thought himself different than the men who gambled, drank, and smoked in taverns, better than those who cursed, fought, and slept with prostitutes. But now, he stood in the doorway exposed and forced to confess he was the same as any other sinner.

"There they are, up near the front," Andrew said, pointing in the direction where Florence was subtly waving. "Go on, and take your place," he said, goading him. "I'll sit back here."

William took a deep breath. Then, as composed as he could, he walked up to the Farleys' pew. Florence scooted over to make room for him. William gave a polite nod to Mr. and Mrs. Farley, and Cora gave him a knowing smile. It was cool inside the church, but within minutes, he was hot with shame. As the service began, sweat dripped down his face and under his arms as he sat between Cora and Florence. Flushed with fever, William thought he might pass out. He got a reprieve during the hymns and musical selections when he could lose himself in the singing. When he bowed his head as the bishop prayed, William sincerely begged the Lord to forgive him for his trespasses.

William was just starting to feel better when the bishop mentioned his name in an introduction. William's stomach did cartwheels.

"Would you please come and give us a word this morning?" the bishop asked.

William's heart beat so loudly within his chest, he thought sure it could be heard. Reluctantly, he stood up and made his way to the pulpit.

"Good morning, saints of God. I won't give you all a sermon today. I'm sure the bishop has prepared a special message for you all. However, I would like to thank him and this wonderful congregation for welcoming me here today in this Lent season. This season has great meaning for Christian folks. It marks the 40 days that Jesus was led into the desert to fast and pray. During His journey into the wilderness, the devil tempted Jesus three times. I'm so thankful that Jesus resisted the temptation of the devil that day, because if He hadn't, none of us would be here today. Because of His unwavering faithfulness, completing His Father's plan, and taking the weight of our sins on His back, those who believe in Him can be redeemed and have life everlasting. That is the good news I share with you today, brothers and sisters."

There were a few stately amens said when William finished. He made a slight respectful bow to the bishop, shaking his hand as he returned to his seat. He thanked God for his mercy when the service ended.

Farley was pleased. William had passed his test. He could see a bright future for him in New York. Florence was proud of the way he looked in the pulpit and how he handled himself. As far as Inez was concerned, there was nothing he could do to please her, short of shedding his skin like a lizard. Cora, however, was filled with questions after seeing him speak. She realized he wasn't who she thought he was.

"Will you join us for supper?" Farley asked after the service concluded.

"I would love to, thank you, but I have exams to study for," William said, bowing out.

"I'm disappointed," Florence said, frowning.

Cora eyed him closely. "So am I," she added.

"That's too bad," Inez said facetiously, finally pleased about something he said.

"Another time, please," William said, looking to the rear of the church. "I'd better catch up with Andrew and head home."

William rushed out, anxious to put as much distance between him and the Farley family as soon as he could. He found Andrew talking with some acquaintances.

Andrew was surprised to see him walk out alone. "I thought you might be having supper with the family," he joked.

"Like I told you, I don't feel so good," William said, motioning for him to come along. "Besides, I've got a lot of studying to do."

"I don't blame you," Andrew laughed. "They might want to know about you keeping Florence out on all those late nights."

"You've got it all wrong," William said, and for once, it was the truth.

***

By the end of the week, William had recovered from the shock and had justified his passion for Cora. She lay next to him in the hotel later that week.

"Have you decided which life you want?" she asked, gently rubbing his chest.

"I don't have a choice, Cora. My life was chosen for me," he said, thinking of his father, Thomas.

"Does that mean that you won't stay in New York after you finish your studies?"

"I can't. I have an obligation to my family. Would you come back to Virginia with me?"

Cora laid back on the bed and exhaled. "I could never leave New York. Without the air of this city, I couldn't breathe."

"What if I asked you to be my wife? Would that make a difference?"

"You haven't asked me. We meet in secret, in the dark. Florence is on your arm in the light of day."

William paused. She was right. He was guilty. "Meeting you was something I never expected. I didn't know how to make it right. Tell me what you want me to do."

Cora sat up beside him and looked him in the eye. "I'm not the woman you need, Will. I'm a butterfly, flighty and unfaithful. Florence is the virgin queen bee. She's stable, respectable, and what you need in a wife and a mother. You will always be in my heart and I in yours, but she is the woman for you. I prayed that it would be me that you chose, but the prayers of the unrighteous aren't granted, are they?"

William wanted her to be wrong, but he knew better. He pulled her down close to him and dug his face into the crook of her neck, deeply inhaling her scent to imbed it in his memory.

***

In the spring of 1902, William finished his seminary degree and proposed marriage to Florence. He thanked the Lord when she said yes, knowing he didn't deserve her hand in marriage.

"I promise to be a husband worthy of having you as his wife," he told her on bended knee.

"I don't expect anything less," she said with a straight face. "I've waited for you to ask me for a long time. I was starting to get worried."

"Going to school and working for your father was more demanding than I thought it would be," he explained. "Hopefully, we can get married before the fall term."

"My mother and I can plan things in a month. Write your family, and see when they can come."

William didn't tell his family about the wedding. Instead, he made excuses for their absence to the Farleys, feeling that his family's presence would cause conflict and confrontation.

Inez put together a beautiful wedding. Florence was dressed in white silk and satin, and William in white tie and tails. They made a handsome couple. Few people noticed the awkward look on William's face when Cora stood beside her sister. The reception was a catered affair, and Farley announced the gift of an apartment in Manhattan and a month-long honeymoon to Washington, DC. On the following day, William and Florence caught the train to spend the month with Florence's relatives, namely Inez's mother.

William learned quickly why his mother-in-law had no tolerance for him. Her family members were black, but they appeared to be white. Attending gatherings of this elite group, he was introduced to some of the most prominent black people in the country. From their attitudes, it was obvious that they thought they stood several rungs higher on the social ladder than he did. Most of them discreetly expressed sympathy to Florence for falling in love with a man of darker complexion.

William, who was well-read and possessed impeccable manners, ignored the snubs, adapted well, and enjoyed hobnobbing with those people W.E.B. DuBois called the "talented tenth."

***

Meanwhile, Thomas was back in Charles City County praying for the Lord to bring William back home. Anna Bell was ailing with lupus. Some days felt as if they would be her last, and it had been over three years since she had laid eyes on her son, and she wanted to see him. Thomas had faith that the Lord would answer his petition in due time; but to speed up the process, he wrote a letter.

Dear William,

The years of youth are fewer and more precious than all the others. For that reason, I gave you my blessing to explore and experience the world outside of Charles City and to educate yourself before you were required to accept the reins of your responsibilities. Though we are free, time is still our relentless taskmaster, dictating when, where, and why we must act. Your beloved mama has taken ill. It breaks my heart to see the healthy, vibrant woman I love weaken and ache in her body. Caring for her and tending to the flock of our church has become an increasingly heavy load to balance on my shoulders. Your sisters do their best to help, but they have their own families to look after. As a family, we need you, and our church needs you.

Our people are suffering under the evil laws of Jim Crow. I need your strong broad shoulders to share this weight with me. Come home as soon as you can. The mere sight of you will uplift your mama's spirits.

Your loving Papa

When he received the letter, William was torn. He knew the day would come, even though he had put it off longer than he had expected.

"I got a letter from my father while we were gone," he told Florence as she unpacked. I've got to go back to Charles City."

"How long are you going to be there?" she asked calmly, assuming that she wouldn't be going with him.

"I don't know, but eventually it will be permanent. I've got obligations there that you may not understand, but they are real."

Florence stopped unpacking and put her hand on her hip. "There's one thing you have got to understand, William, and that is, I'm not about to spend my life out in some fields on some farm."

"That's not the life I'm offering you," William said, moving close and taking his wife's hands in his. "I'm going to build you a beautiful home in Richmond, I promise."

She shook her head doubtfully. "You're asking a lot of me. I wish I didn't love you so much."

"We'll be happy wherever we are," he said with a tender kiss.

***

Even after transferring twice, William rocked with the motion of the third train, wondering how he was going to find a way for the two separate roads in his life to merge together. When he got to Richmond, he still didn't have a clue. Blacks were boycotting streetcars after the law to segregate races was passed. Still, he couldn't deny that it felt good to be home again, away from the complications of his life in New York. He took long strides when the house was in his sight, resisting the impulse to run like an eager young boy.

"It's good to lay eyes on you again, son!" Thomas exclaimed when William walked through the door. "You've been gone a long time," he said, embracing him and patting his back.

William put his bags down on the floor. "It's good to be home, Papa. Where's Mama?" he asked, feeling uncomfortable with his father inspecting him from head to foot. So much had happened that he hadn't shared with them.

"She's back there lying down. Go on, and say hello."

William slowly walked back to the bedroom, afraid of what he might see. "Hello, Mama," he said, pushing the door wider. He wanted to cry when he saw her. She was thinner, and her face looked so worn and tired. "How are you feeling?"

Anna Bell struggled to sit up, but her face brightened. "Come here, boy!" she said, stretching out her arms. "I've missed you around here! I thought I was gonna have to go up there and find you!"

"I would have come sooner if I'd known. You should have told me you were sick."

"I didn't want to bother you none. This was your time to get your schooling. You look so good, son. Did you meet any nice pretty girls up there in New York?"

"Yeah, Mama, but I'm worried about you. What does the doctor say?"

"They got me taking pills, but seeing you has done me the most good," she said, smiling. "I'm so glad you're home. Are you hungry? I can make you something to eat."

"You rest right now," he said, rubbing the swollen knuckles on her hand. "I already had supper. I been on my own; I know how to cook. Tomorrow, I'm gonna make something special for you."

"All right, son," she said, leaning back in the bed.

William gave her a kiss and went back out to the parlor where Thomas sat in his chair, smoking his pipe. William sat down on the sofa across from him.

"I can see in your face that you're a man now. I'm proud of you, William."

"Yes, I'm my own man now," William said, reserved.

"That's good, because it's time for you to come home and take your place in the church," Thomas told him, wasting no time with small talk.

"I know I went to seminary to prepare me to do that, Papa, but lately I've been thinking that it's not for me," William told him. "I love Jesus, I praise God, but I'm not sure I want to be a preacher. I think I can serve the people in a better way. Preaching is your calling; I don't believe it's mine."

"It's a calling on all the men who have the same blood that flows through your veins. It not a choice. We were designated by God."

"That's the same thing as making a slave out of me. That's behind us now. I'm sorry, Papa. My life is not your life. I'm free to do what I want."

That got Thomas riled up. He leaned forward toward William. "I don't know what you think you learned up there in New York, but it's my life that gave you the life you have," he said through gritted teeth. "How do you think you went up there to go to school? Those bills were paid with the sweat off my back and the offering from those who hunger and thirst for

God's word. First, you tell me you don't want to work the land, and now you say you don't want to lead God's people. What exactly do you want to do with your life?"

"I want to make money, as much of it as I can," William said, standing up to him. "You should know, money is freedom."

"I refuse to worship money; my treasure is my freedom!" Thomas snapped back.

"That's because you have money. Would you trade it for a life without any? Get your Bible, and show me in there where it says being poor is the answer to hate."

"You're an ungrateful child if I've ever seen one!" Thomas shouted. "This land will be your land. It's for you to pass down to your family. It's your shelter from all the storms out there. It will feed you and keep clothes on your back."

"You're right about that. I intend to buy more land. Land is leverage; land is power."

Thomas settled back in his chair. "God has all the power you need."

There was silence between them for a minute. Then William said, "I have a wife. Her name is Florence. I have to build a home for her and provide for a family soon."

Thomas tapped his foot to calm his nerves. This was more than he was prepared to deal with.

"God provides, son," he said, more composed. "Your life is here, not up there in New York."

"We'll talk about it tomorrow," William said, dragging his feet to his old bedroom.

***

William stared out the window for most of the night. The bridge he was trying to build was still so far from either shore. He had to be there for his father, but he also had to be his own man. He wanted to be free from the influence of Florence's parents, but he wanted the woman he loved by his side. "Speak to me, Lord," he whispered, staring at the sky. Just as the sun peaked through the darkness, the answer became clear. Richmond was the place for him to plant new seeds. He dressed quickly.

"Where are you going? You haven't eaten a bite," Thomas asked, puzzled when William appeared dressed in a good suit and was headed out the door.

"I've got some business to tend to in Richmond," he said, rushing out the door before his father could ask any more questions.

William had heard about Maggie Lena Walker, the black businesswoman who started *The St. Luke Herald* newspaper and then chartered the St. Luke Penny Savings Bank in Richmond. She was the first woman to serve as a bank president. It was a huge accomplishment for a woman whose mother was a former slave and a cook for a Union spy. Mrs. Walker was just the person he needed to get to know. He hooked the horse to the wagon and rode to the bank in Richmond.

Mrs. Walker met with William and he explained what he wanted to do. He learned that she needed investors to buy stock in the bank. That day, William invested the bulk of the money he earned working with Farley in the bank. Next, he would need to convince his father to do the same. He rode back to Ruthville, confident he had found the path to bring his two lives together.

***

"Papa, the money you have saved with the Knights of Gideon is just sitting there. Fraternal societies don't have the organization that the St. Luke Penny Savings Bank has. We can use that money to buy stocks that make more money. We can buy more land, plant more, and sell more. Then I can build you the finest church in Richmond.

"Are you ready to take your place in that church?" Thomas asked, getting straight to the point.

"I'll stand beside you, but I'm not the man to take your place."

"It's not my place, William! It's the place God has designated for you and your sons that will come after you."

"If that's what God has for me, He'll make that known to me," William said, not wanting to argue with him. "Right now, what I feel is that He wants me to build this church for you."

"What I do know, is that you have a commitment to do the Lord's work, and that's not preaching for some shyster undertaker."

"Papa, there's a poem written by Paul Laurence Dunbar that spoke to me. It's called 'A Creed and Not a Creed.' Part of it says:

I am no priest of crooks nor creeds,
For human wants and human needs
Are more to me than prophets' deeds;
And human tears and human cares
Affect me more than human prayers.
Take up your arms, come out with me,
Let Heav'n alone; humanity

Needs more and Heaven less from thee.
With pity for mankind look 'round;
Help them to rise—and Heaven is found.

"All right, son, that sounds good enough, but what does it mean? What are you saying to me?"

"What I'm saying is that I don't think my calling is to preach the word to my people. I think my calling is to help lift up my people. It's not enough for us to own a few businesses here in Ruthville and in Jackson Ward. We have to become independent of the white man in the North, South, East, and West. To do that, we need to own more of this country."

"Seems you are quite the preacher! Bring that message to the people. If they are convinced, then I'll go along with it."

***

On Sunday morning, William stood at the front of the church, with Thomas sitting behind him. Anna Bell didn't feel well enough to come; but his sisters, Althea and Susanna, and their families were there for extra support. He knew how important this message would be in bringing his ambitions into existence.

"Good morning, Christian neighbors and friends. I have missed seeing you all while I was away in New York. Leaving Charles City County was a scary thing for me, but it helped me to grow and to see things from a different point of view. It helped me discover what I feel is our destiny. Jeremiah 29:11 says, 'For I know the plans I have for you, declares the LORD, 'plans to prosper you and not to harm you, plans to give you hope and a future.' Brothers and sisters, we can't be afraid to move into our future, we have to move boldly. The Israelites were freed from Pharaoh, but they wandered for 40 years before they moved to the place they were meant to be. We have been freed here in Charles County City for 40 years. It's time to move into the place God has for us. He has another plan for us, more opportunity for us, a place where this church can flourish. The vision I was given for the church: The place is in Richmond. Are you all willing to take that journey with me?"

The people shouted hallelujah. They were filled with the Holy Ghost and inspired for the future. They liked William's vision. It was one they couldn't have even imagined.

William kept using his gift of persuasion. He convinced Florence that Richmond was a modern city with electric streetcars and that he would build her a beautiful home on Leigh Street in Jackson Ward, the black Wall Street. He assured her that they would join the elite citizens of Richmond. He convinced the board at the Penny Savings to let him borrow money with the land in Charles City County as collateral. He bought land for their future church and his home in Richmond.

Still, things were getting tougher in Richmond with more Jim Crow laws being passed. Thomas rocked back and forth on the porch and shook his head in amazement when William came home with the property deeds.

"Seems you know more than I do, son. You've got the land you wanted. I didn't think they would sell that prime ground."

William grunted. "I had to pay twice the price than any white man would have offered, $10 an acre, that's the only way I could buy. They think they beat me; but in a few years, it will be worth a lot more, and it will be their greed that made it possible."

"Well, I suppose there's nothing I can tell you about money."

"I'm only following your lead, Papa," William said. "You and grandpapa are the ones who taught me how valuable land is and how important it is to get your financial freedom."

"There were some other things I tried to teach you, too," Thomas said.

William gazed at the deeds in his hands and said, "Give me some time, Papa."

***

Before William could build the church for his father, he had to build the house he promised his wife. He had gone back to New York to get Florence, but she insisted on living with her parents until the house was finished. For two years, William went back and forth between New York and Virginia, preaching for Farley and helping his father with his mother and the church. He invested profits from the farm into more stocks with the bank.

Then the day came when Thomas's back refused to bend. William traveled back to Charles City County, rented out the bulk of the land, and hired workers to work the rest, except for 40 acres that his father refused to relinquish. William was about to return to New York the next morning, but his mother died in her sleep.

It wasn't completely unexpected when Anna Bell succumbed to her illness, but it was a crushing blow just the same. William felt as if he were being ripped in two. He wanted to please his wife in New York, but his family needed him at home. He cried out the words of David, "Hear my cry, O God; Attend to my prayer. From the end of the earth I will cry to You, When my heart is overwhelmed; Lead me to the rock that is higher than I," Psalm 61:1-2.

After Anna Bell was buried in the family plot, William went to Richmond to find a house for him and Florence. He found a large and stately home at 711 Leigh Street, which he completely refurbished. It was finished in early 1907. Florence approved and finally moved to Richmond; and before the year was out, she gave birth to a son, William Junior.

Although Florence was fond of Papa Thomas, she rarely came to the farm. She made friends with the well-to-do blacks in the city. It wasn't New York or Washington, but she found a level of contentment in her women's clubs and summer vacations at Harper's Ferry. Three years later, they had a daughter, Pearl. William was blessed. Everything he put his hand to prospered.

In the summer of 1912, Thompson Boulevard Church of God in Christ was completed, consecrated, and dedicated. William stood proudly beside his father at the door of the church as the congregation assembled in front of him.

Thomas delivered the words of dedication: "Having been prospered by the good hand of our God, who enabled us by His grace and power to complete this house of worship to be used to the glory of God, we stand before these doors and His holy presence to dedicate this building to Him. To the glory of God our Father, from whom comes every good and perfect gift; to the honor of Jesus Christ, our Lord and Savior, Redeemer and King; to the praise of the Holy Spirit, our source of light and life."

***

Five years passed, and with each one, William became more prosperous. He was an educated man with a degree, money in his pocket, sporting clothes, and a horseless carriage that most white men in Charles City County could only dream about. Most of his time was spent in Richmond, where his success was tolerated; in Ruthville, it was unpalatable. Thomas, who preferred to live at the family house in Charles City County, took every opportunity to caution his son.

"You can have everything you want, son, but you can't dangle it in their faces like meat over a hungry dog," Thomas warned. "That's just baiting them to come after you."

"I ain't never been nobody's slave, and I'm not going to act like one!" William said brashly, leaning against the porch post.

"Don't get too big for your britches! You have no idea what was done so you can stand here in your tailored suit. And make no mistake, it was done by someone kept as a slave, somebody who did whatever they had to do to survive."

"I'm sorry for saying that, Papa, I don't mean any disrespect," William said, taking the edge out of his voice. "It's just that I've worked hard for everything I got."

"That don't make no difference to these po' whites around here who don't have an ounce of what you have. They can't stand to see you have it."

"If they stay out of my way, I'll stay out of theirs."

"Lord, help us!" Thomas said, rocking his chair faster. "Well, anyway, it looks like all y'all that wanna fight are gonna get the chance. The way things is looking with them Germans sinking all those American ships, we probably gon' get into that war overseas."

William grunted. "You don't have to worry about me fighting no white man's war."

"My worry is about the fight we gonna have here," Thomas muttered.

***

One month later, on April 6, 1917, the United States declared war against Germany and entered World War I. William watched as many young black men enlisted. With increased demand, he hired more help on the farm to plant more tobacco and wheat and doubled his harvests. With increased profits, he was able to pay off his loan at the bank.

William was elated and wanted to celebrate his accomplishments. He asked Florence, who loved any opportunity to dress and entertain, to plan a special dinner at their house. Though Florence had hoped to have several guests, William wanted to share this meal with just his father. So Florence had their housekeeper, Jean, prepare tomato soup, broiled steak with parsley butter, baked potatoes, asparagus, wheat bread with butter, and Lady Baltimore cake for dessert. She insisted that W. J., who was now ten years old, dress in his knickers and suitcoat; and Pearl, who was seven, wear one of her nice party dresses.

Pearl watched for her grandpapa through the front window and met him at the door before he could knock. "Come on in, Grandpa!" she said, pulling him by the hand into the parlor, where William was reading *The Richmond Planet*.

"Let's go on into the dining room," William said, standing up. "We've been waiting for you."

Florence was putting flowers on the table when they walked in. "Good evening, Papa Thomas," she said, giving him a hug and a kiss. "You know Pearl wants you to sit next to her."

"That's exactly where I want to be," Thomas said, smiling

at his granddaughter as he sat down. Jean brought the platters of food and placed them on the table. "Everything looks and smells delicious!"

Thomas blessed the food. He shook his head as Jean prepared plates for W. J. and Pearl.

"Y'all gon' spoil these children with Jean waiting on them hand and foot. Being too easy on them makes them weak."

"My children aren't spoiled," Florence said, offended. "They're blessed."

"You weren't hard on me, Papa, and I turned out all right," William said. "You let me use my brain. You know, brawn ain't the only way to make it in this world."

"Hard work ain't never hurt nobody. It's about time for me to teach W. J. how to plant. That's why I asked you to reserve those 40 acres near the house."

"You don't have to worry about that, Papa Thomas," Florence said. "Not all black folks need to know how to farm. We're like everybody else. We begin in different stations and travel different paths. Thankfully, some of us are born miles ahead."

"One thing I've learned in my life is that nothing is guaranteed or promised to you. Take for instance, after emancipation, we could vote, and there were negro politicians representing us in the Congress. Then Jim Crow came along and snatched them rights back. These children got to be ready to fend for themselves. White men don't never rest when it comes to persecuting black folks. They gonna need strong hands to hold on to everything we've gained."

"You're gonna scare the children with all that talk!" Florence said, wanting to change the conversation to a more pleasant subject. "If things get too bad around here, we can always go back to New York."

"I'm not scared, Mama," W. J. said, jumping into the discussion.

"Hush, boy!" William told him playfully.

"Don't forget about all that devilment they did last summer to start that riot in St. Louis and the one in Philadelphia this year," Thomas reminded them.

"This is supposed to be a happy occasion," Florence insisted. "Now, can we please talk about where we are going on our summer vacation?"

"Yay!" Pearl squealed, and Thomas acquiesced.

***

When the distant war ended, a new war began for blacks in the South with the resurgence of the Ku Klux Klan. At the same time, immigrant quotas were put in place by Congress. Factories in the North and out West needed laborers. Blacks wanting to escape the terror of the KKK and the backbreaking work on farms began the Great Migration. For the next few years, it was even harder for William to keep good help on his farms. For those blacks who stayed below the Mason-Dixon Line, the KKK raged hell with violence and intimidation.

One night in the spring of 1924, William was leaving a meeting between local members of the National Negro Business League in Charles City, when he heard footsteps and rumblings on the other side of some bushes, near the spot where his automobile was parked.

"Get thee behind me, Satan!" William roared, sensing evil intent.

A white man came out of the shadows. He spit on the ground, most of it landing on William's freshly shined shoes. William didn't recognize him.

"Who do you think you are, nigga?" another white man shouted.

"I know who I am," William replied without blinking. He felt for the pistol he carried in his suitcoat pocket.

"You think you smart, don't you?" the first man said, sneering. "You don't know your place. We might have to teach you a lesson."

"I don't think there's much I can learn from you," William said, staring down at him.

Another man came and stood beside the first. "Some of you done gone up North and forgotten how things go 'round here."

William closed his eyes and began to pray loudly. One by one, the men walked away grumbling. They knew they needed to get away before the noise drew attention to them.

William didn't mention the incident to anybody until a few days later. Early Sunday morning, the pounding on the door woke up William and his family. When William opened the door, he found Thomas standing there with two men holding shotguns. The men owned land in the area.

"What's going on?" William asked, opening the door, disconcerted, and Florence coming behind him just as alarmed.

"I woke up to a cross burning in the front yard of the house!" Thomas said.

William shook his head in disgust. "When I was leaving a meeting in Charles City, four of them were hiding in the bushes, waiting for me. I figured they'd be back, but I didn't know when."

Florence's usually cool façade broke like shattered glass as she began to cry.

"Come on in, Papa," William said.

"No, meet us over at the church," Thomas said, turning to leave with the men.

As soon as the door was closed, Florence grabbed William's robe. "Please, William, we need to leave here right away!" she begged.

"I'm not going to let any man run me off my land! It belongs to me! We have to stand up for ourselves, or they'll never stop hounding us."

"They're not going to let us have one moment of peace in this city, and I don't want to live like that. Can't you see that the cross burning is only the beginning."

William paced across the parlor floor. "We have what we have because somebody stood up and fought against this evil treachery. We have to be an example for the people."

"What about our children? Don't you want them to be safe?"

"Of course, I do, Flo, but I don't want them to fear these cowards."

"This is not the life you promised me," she said, crying.

"I'm sorry for that," William said, dropping down into his chair. "I've done the best I know how."

***

Thomas and the men of the church organized a watch group to keep an eye on the house and the church. They were on alert for the whole summer, but nothing else happened.

Since it seemed as if the situation had calmed down, the group relaxed. Florence had regained her composure and was back to entertaining their friends with a Victrola phonograph William had bought for her.

One fall evening, Florence was preparing to host a dinner party. William drove to his father's house to pick up his children. Pearl heard William drive up, and she ran to the window. W. J. put down his Bible and got up to take a look. William smiled and waved at Pearl, but she didn't smile back. W. J. got to the window just as the men shrouded in white robes came out of nowhere behind William. The children heard the blasts of gunshots and saw their father fall.

Thomas, asleep on the sofa, was startled by the gun blasts. He jumped off the sofa, grabbed his rifle, and charged out the door; but the attackers were gone—and so was William.

Chapter Three

William Edward Freeman Jr.

William Edward Freeman Jr., affectionately known as W. J., was born in Richmond, Virginia, in 1907. His father, William Sr., was a college-educated man and owned land, and that was the very reason he was dragged away and lynched just before harvest when W. J. was 17 years old. His sister, Pearl, three years younger, was there staring through the window beside him when it happened. The murderers shrouded in white sheets were so hateful of Will Sr.'s success and pride that they couldn't stand to see him walk with his head held up high in front of them. They shot him in the back before he got to the edge of the front yard, but that wasn't enough to make them feel superior. They tortured his body and hung him from a huge white willow tree a mile away from their property.

Neither W. J. nor Pearl would ever be the same after that. Something clicked in W. J.'s brain that affected his heart, shutting off the soft, gentle side of his psyche. Something clicked in Pearl's brain as well. She retreated from the world we exist in and created her own, a world with friends and creatures only she could see and talk to. Florence, their mama, who wasn't there when it happened, was heartbroken. Her first instinct was to back her bags and head back to her family in New York.

Thomas, W. J.'s grandfather, sat on the front porch. Florence sat beside him. W. J. stood just inside the door, eavesdropping while they talked.

"I've got to get away from here, Papa Thomas," Florence said, her face covered in tears. "There's enough money in the bank for me and the children to go to a place where we don't have to relive this nightmare over and over. There's nothing left here for me or the kids except for more pain and misery."

Thomas's head hung low, and he shook it in dismay. "That's not true, Florence. This is their home, and ain't nobody gonna run them out of it. William worked hard for them to have this land, and he would want them to stay here."

"There's nothing you can say to make me stay here. This place is dead! Will should have never come back here."

"You're wrong, my dear. This place is life. Look out at all the green. Green is the color of life."

Florence stared at Thomas as if he were crazy. "Can't you see my children damn near lost their minds seeing their daddy killed out there? I can't ask them to walk that path every day! What kind of life is that showing them?"

Thomas leaned close to Florence. "You can't hide life from them now. They've already seen how ugly it can be. If you want to get away for a while, take Pearl, but leave W. J. here with me. This is his land, and his father died for it. My papa and his papa worked and died on this land to grow tobacco. I bought it to build a temple for the Lord, to honor Him for his faithfulness. With Will gone, W. J. is gonna have to take over the church after I'm gone."

Florence looked up to the sky. "Who's to say they won't come after W. J. next?"

"They can come if they want to. I'm gonna hire me an army. Anybody trespass over my property line in the light of day or under the cloak of night is gonna meet their maker at the end of a rifle. I guarantee they'll never be heard of again."

"I don't want him to live like that, scared of the devil trying to come after him day and night."

"God's word says we don't have to live in fear. And when I get through training W. J., believe me, he won't fear any of them."

"W. J. is old enough to decide for himself, but I'm taking Pearl with me as soon as Will is buried."

"If that's how you feel, I have to respect that," Thomas said, opening his hands in surrender. "Call W. J. out here so we can see what he wants to do."

"W. J., come on out here," Florence shouted sternly, suspecting he was just on the other side of the door listening.

"Yes, ma'am," he said, stepping out onto the porch.

"This ain't no place for civilized people," she told him. "Right after your father's wake, I'm leaving this godforsaken town, and I won't be back. I'm taking your sister, and I want you to come with me, too. But I've told your grandpapa that you're old enough to decide for yourself."

"What do you want to do, son?" Thomas asked.

W. J. looked out into the field and thought hard. What life did he have away from this town? He wanted to look after his mama and Pearl as his father had asked him, but he knew from birth that he had other responsibilities. He knew the men in his family had preached the gospel for generations, even before they were brought to America as slaves. He revered the word of the Lord, and being designated and chosen by God wasn't something he could turn his back on.

The only other thing W. J. felt strongly about was the land. He had been drawn to the soil from the time he was a baby toddling around in the fields. He loved the grit and the smell of the rich soil. He never stopped being amazed at how a tiny seed could grow thousands of times its size into huge plants. Thomas had taught him how to prepare the dirt for seed beds, plant the seedlings, weed the ground, pluck the worms, kill the pests, and gather the harvest.

Furthermore, W. J. saw how it made the difference between his well-to-do family and other negroes who groveled at the feet of white men for meager wages. No one in Charles City County was shocked or surprised when William Sr. was murdered. Whites and Blacks had been whispering for years that he'd gotten too big for his britches, especially the poor white sharecroppers without their own pots to piss in. They couldn't stand seeing a nigger have more than they did, and they would be damned if they didn't do something about it.

"I'm gonna stay here with Grandpa, Mama," W. J. said, still looking out over the field. "I'm not going to let them run me away from here. They're gonna have to drag me away, too."

Florence shook her head and walked into the house. She knew she wasn't going to change his mind any more than she had changed Will Sr.'s. If only he would have listened to her, they would have left this remnant of slavery years ago, and he would still be alive.

Thomas took a deep breath, sat back in his chair, and starting rocking. "Your mama and Pearl will be all right, W. J. She'll probably come back after a while; she just needs a break from the craziness. This is where you belong."

***

William was laid out in a pine box in the parlor. W. J. sat next to Florence as she rocked from side to side as if she were seated in a small boat on a rocky sea. Pearl sat on the other side, rubbing her hands over an imaginary pet seated in her lap. The house was filled with mourners, and the smell of food from a seemingly endless parade of covered dishes wafted through the room. Some people spoke in whispers as they ate, while other mourners sat behind the grieving family, humming a sad song.

Thomas, standing a half foot above the tallest man in the house, commanded the room as he did in the pulpit every Sunday morning. That may have been another reason why his son had been reluctant to take his place at the helm of the church and instead was satisfied to preach midweek and at revivals. For William, it had been more important to grow the wealth of the family. Even though blacks in Virginia had pretty much lost their privilege to vote, William's schooling had taught him that wealth was power, the great equalizer. In the end, however, he was wrong. No matter how much money he earned, the law wasn't on his side. Most likely, the poorest white men in the county had taken William's life and would never be punished.

They may have taken William's life, but they couldn't take his land: 900 acres, 400 Thomas had bought, and 500 that William had added to it. W. J. eased out of his seat and quietly walked out the front door. He kept walking until he reached the edge of the field. He had only been there a short while before Thomas walked up beside him.

"Your papa is dead now, W. J., and I don't know how long I'll be here," Thomas said, putting his arm around his grandson's shoulder. "A black male child in this country has to be a man from birth. These white folks may call you a boy, but the truth is a black man don't have time to be a boy. If you don't know it by now, you're like a beast in the jungle being hunted. You have to learn how to fight to survive."

"They're the ones who need to learn how to survive," W. J. railed. "'Let a cry be heard from their houses as warriors come suddenly upon them, for they have dug a pit to capture me and have hidden snares for my feet. But you, LORD, know all their plots to kill me. Do not forgive their crimes or blot out their sins from your sight. Let them be overthrown before you; deal with them in the time of your anger,' Jeremiah 18:22-23. I want to be the instrument that God uses to do His will."

"You don't need to worry about what the Lord is going to do to punish his people, son. You got enough on your hands," Thomas said. "You're going to have to take your place at the head of the church. You're going to have to be a worthy leader. For most, that might be too hard; but for a man designated by God, it's harder because you have to be obedient to the word before you can preach it."

W. J. turned toward Thomas. "I want to be like you, Grandpa."

"Not me, son. No, you have to be like Jesus. You have to educate yourself, you've got to sow seeds into your field, and you have to tend to your flock."

W. J. stared back out at the horizon. He didn't care about getting any more education. He could read, write, and cipher numbers as well as anybody else. He had never been without money, so he didn't care about the business of farming; he preferred the physical part, the laboring in the field. It reminded him of the Book of Genesis, where God created the earth. It was the power of making something out of nothing with your own hands. It was an awesome feeling, the satisfaction with oneself at the fruits of one's own labor.

"I'm ready. I'm ready to do God's work."

Thomas squeezed his arm tighter around his grandson's shoulders and nodded. "Not yet, son, but you will be."

The next day, Thomas preached a powerful eulogy for his son from Job 5:6-11, 18-19: "For hardship does not spring from the soil, nor does trouble sprout from the ground. Yet man is born to trouble as surely as sparks fly upward. 'But if I were you, I would appeal to God; I would lay my cause before him. . . . The lowly he sets on high, and those who mourn are lifted to safety. . . . For he wounds, but he also binds up; he injures, but his hands also heal. From six calamities he will rescue you; in seven no harm will touch you.' So, while my heart is broken today, I praise Him and honor Him.

"We all know it isn't easy to praise through pain and strife. We are discouraged because the battle never seems to end. We are tired because we have been fighting for so long. We are weak because we have suffered so much. When my dear wife passed away, I thought that grief would be the worse that I could sustain in this life, but today my sorrow is immeasurable. I asked God to lift me up as he lifted David and Psalm 23 filled my being, 'Yea, though I walk through the valley of the shadow of death, I will fear no evil, for thou art with me; thy rod and thy staff they comfort me. Thou preparest a table before me in the presence of mine enemies; thou anointest my head with oil; my cup overflows.'

"Brothers and sisters in Christ, we will get through this battle, God will give us the victory. We must remain as steadfast and immovable as a massive rock. On days like today, when we feel broken down, remember the words of the hymn writer, 'On Christ, the solid Rock, I stand; all other ground is sinking sand, all other ground is sinking sand.' Sing, choir," Thomas said, stepping down from the pulpit and taking his seat.

W. J. sat stiff and tight as a drum. He balled his fists and clenched his teeth, his anger refusing to give way to his grief. Florence listened with dry eyes; she had cried all her tears, and her bags were already packed. Pearl talked quietly to her imaginary friend.

***

On the following Sunday, Thomas instructed W. J. to take his father's place in the seat next to him in the pulpit. W. J. sat there for the next three years. During that time, Thomas nurtured and taught him as carefully as he did when he showed his grandson how to put down a crop of his highest quality leaves.

On the morning of W. J.'s twentieth birthday, Thomas said, "It's time, son. You handle the Lord's business, and I'll handle these fields."

"I'm ready, Grandpa," W. J. said.

Three years should have been enough time for W. J.'s soul to heal, for him to hunger for joy again, but that didn't happen. Instead, the bitterness lingered. A young, privileged man should have been prepared to preach the goodness of the Lord. He should have been optimistic, not jaded. But W. J. wasn't joyful or hopeful for the future. On his first Sunday in the pulpit, he stood boldly before the congregation and vehemently preached the wages of sin, fire and brimstone, hell and damnation. The angry words spoken in the Bible on the vengeance of the Lord became his passion; and he, like no other, could put the fear of God in the belly of the strongest nonbeliever.

As grim as W. J. appeared when he preached the Book of Revelation, his status as a pastor and a landowner drew people to him. It paved the way for him to court and marry the prettiest girl in town. If you asked W. J., he'd tell you that that's when his troubles started.

***

A week after his twenty-first birthday, W. J. sat on the front porch catching the breeze while listening to the radio through the open parlor window before he prepared his sermon. He stared across the yard at his brand-new forest green 1927 Gardner sedan. Grandpa Thomas had bought it to lift his spirits, but it hadn't helped much. He was lonely. He missed his mama, and he missed his sister. Maybe Pearl wasn't so crazy after all to create a friend who never left her side. He relaxed his head against the back of the chair and closed his eyes.

Dozing in and out, W. J. hadn't been paying attention to the announcer when he introduced the new record by Juanita "Arizona" Dranes, a blind singer from Texas. The music from the piano energized him. He began tapping his foot, and then she started singing, *I Shall Wear a Crown*. Unable to keep his seat he jumped up and started clapping and did the holy dance. The music was powerful, more powerful than the best quartet in Charles City County. It was the beat, the urgency in the melody on the piano. If he could have that sound in his church on Sunday, he was sure he could rouse the spirit of even the most fervent sinner.

Later, W. J. told Thomas about it. "Grandpa, this morning I heard this record of a woman playing piano and singing gospel on the radio. It touched something inside me. I want us to get a piano for the church."

"We don't need no piano to carry a tune in our church," Thomas said, dismissing the idea. "We got the best a cappella singers in Virginia standing in our choir."

"That's been all right in the past, but it won't be that way in the future. Things are changing fast. People are going to go where they can hear music played. What good will it be for us to build a new church if we don't have people to fill it. This music will bring folks from miles around. I know it will."

Thomas felt W. J.'s enthusiasm and smiled to himself. The boy was finally coming back from the grave they buried Will Sr. in. That was certainly worth the price of a piano.

"All right, son," he said happily. "We'll send an order for one straight away."

They ordered a baby grand piano from the Baldwin Piano Company in Cincinnati. Excitement filled the church when it was delivered. There was only one critical detail that W. J. had forgotten: Who was going to play it?

"I've heard there's a girl living over there in Jackson Ward who can play the devil out of a piano," one of the deacons told him.

"Can you arrange for me to meet her?" W. J. asked eagerly, anxious to hear the sounds in his head fill the sanctuary.

The deacon nodded. "I'll see what I can do, Pastor."

***

Violet was born and raised on the other side of Jackson Ward, otherwise known as the "Harlem of the South" because of the big-time entertainers. entertainers who performed there. It was also known as "The Black Wall Street of America" because of the 100 black businesses located there.

Violet's daddy, Sammy Tillman, was a trumpet player at Tat Turner's Place. Her mother, Opal, was a clerk at Miss Maggie's bank. They lived in a small clapboard house on unpaved St. James Street, not far from the state capitol. They fared pretty well making a few extra dollars taking in musicians as lodgers.

Although she had never had a lesson, Violet was a musical prodigy. She could play any tune after hearing it once, and she composed songs that could only have been sent from heaven. People who heard her play said she had the "gift."

Superstar performers such as Duke Ellington, Louis "Satchmo" Armstrong, and Bill "Bojangles" Robinson came to jam with local musicians and entertainers on Second Street, popularly known as "The Deuce." Even though Violet was only 17, her father had been taking her to the club to play for years, and she could hold her own with the best of them. She earned her own money playing for the theater, gospel performers, and the funeral home from time to time.

At the deacon's invitation, Violet came to the church hoping to make some extra money. Her dream was to follow in the footsteps of Mary Lou Williams by going to New York, playing stride piano with a great band, and making records.

W. J. heard her playing before he saw her. The melody floated out of the church windows as he came up the walk, and he slowed his pace to listen. The notes spoke to him as the beat changed to rapid urgency, slowed in contemplation, and then quickened again. He felt the intensity, the depth of feeling. He didn't need to hear any more. It was settled in his mind. This woman would be the church's pianist.

W. J. walked through the door and stopped in his tracks. The silhouette of Violet's back seated on the piano bench as she played was as mesmerizing as the music. Suddenly, W. J. was aware of the joys life has to offer. He had missed out on the lightheartedness of a young man without responsibilities and the ease and flexibility that comes with it. He had become rigid, focusing on the rules and not the laughter. But in that moment, he had his first glimpse of the bliss he had overlooked when he saw Violet at the piano.

When Violet sensed another presence in the room, she stopped playing and turned around. W. J.'s heart skipped and then it began to race. He thought she looked like a beautiful angel, too marvelous to be real.

"Pastor, this is Violet Tillman," Deacon Charles said, jumping up from his seat on the front bench. Violet stood up, smoothed her dress, and extended her hand toward W. J. "Violet, this is Pastor William Freeman. He's the assistant pastor here."

"It's nice to meet you, Pastor," she said, nodding politely.

W. J. took Violet's hand. "I heard you playing as I came in. You're very talented. I'm sure you been told that before."

"Thank you. Yes, I have," Violet said, surprised to see that he was so young and good-looking. She had heard a little about him from her mother, who told her that he came from a family of preachers who had land and a nice pile of money in the bank.

"I don't know if Deacon Charles told you, but we're looking for a pianist to play on Sundays, the morning and the evening services. From what I've already heard, I think you are exactly who we have been looking for. I can offer you a generous salary of $25 per week."

"I would like that very much," Violet said, containing her smile. She was pleased with the pay but surprised at how easily she had gotten the job.

"You may have to rehearse with the choir on Saturday afternoons. They haven't been accompanied before," W. J. said.

"Definitely, Pastor Freeman, I'm sure I can follow them."

"We have a midweek service on Wednesday and two services on Sunday."

"I look forward to it," Violet said, thinking about how it would fit in her schedule. She was raised Baptist, but her family wasn't particularly religious. Sunday was more of a family rest day than a day of worship in the Tillman household.

"Deacon Charles has some other duties to handle, so I can drive you home," W. J. said. He gave the deacon a quick glance to signal that the deacon was no longer needed.

"Oh, yes!" Deacon Charles said, catching on. "She lives on St. James Street."

"Thank you, Pastor Freeman, that would be fine," Violet said.

Violet's smile grew even bigger when she saw the shiny new car outside the church. W. J. opened the car door for her without taking his eyes off of her. He liked the way she talked and the way she moved. It reminded him of a swan, graceful but strong. He hurried to the driver's side and got into the car.

"I hope we can get to know each other better, Miss Violet, aside from you playing the piano for the church," he said before he started driving. "I would like to call on you, if that isn't disagreeable to you."

"I think that would be fine, Pastor Freeman," Violet said, avoiding his gaze.

"Why don't you call me, W. J. My family does, and I hope one day I might be able to call you family as well."

"You don't like to waste time with small talk, do you?" Violet said, chuckling.

W. J. answered her earnestly. "It's not my strong suit. I make up my mind fairly quickly, and then there's not much that can be done to change it."

"I think I would like to get to know you better," she said, glancing at him. "You're different, an interesting puzzle that I'd like to figure out."

W. J. started the car, his heart lightened. "I am at your service, ma'am, but you'll find there is no mystery to me. I'm an open book."

"I know you're a preacher, so I guess that means you don't smoke, drink, gamble, or dance. So what do preachers do for fun?"

W. J. laughed. "We have our share of fun. I like going to the picture show, playing baseball, and driving my car. What do you like to do for fun?"

"Mostly, I like listening to music on the radio, records, and in the night club where my father works."

W. J. paused for a moment. He had never been in a club, but he knew the multitude of sins that were committed in those places. They were no place for an upstanding young lady, especially for the one who would be his future wife.

"If you ask me, the most beautiful music in the world is the music that praises almighty God. That is the joyful noise that He instructed His people to play. I hope you understand that playing for our church, you will have a reputation to uphold. It would be unseemly for you to be seen in a nightclub while playing for our church."

Violet's brow furrowed. "I hadn't thought about that, but I can see what you mean," she said, growing quiet.

Violet's silence worried W. J. He turned to look at her. "I hope that doesn't cause you to have second thoughts about accepting the position. We have over 2,500 members in our church, and I'm sure they would certainly get a blessing from your musical talent."

Violet thought about it for a second. It wouldn't be a big problem for her. Besides, she reasoned to herself, she only wanted to work at the church long enough to get the money she needed to head off to New York.

"No, you haven't changed my mind. I look forward to playing for your church members."

When W. J. pulled up to the Tillmans' house, he got out of the car to open her door. "If you need me to pick you up, call the church, and I'll be here."

"Thank you again, W. J. That is very kind of you."

"Truly, it is my pleasure, Violet."

***

W. J. was true to his word. He picked up Violet every Wednesday and Sunday for church, and he invited her to have supper with him after Sunday morning service. Her parents gave him their blessing and were in favor of the friendship. It removed their worries about her taking up with a slick, no-good hood or dandy in one of the joints on The Deuce.

Violet didn't know much about the life that W. J. led. She was raised to believe in God and love Jesus, but her family never went to church or encouraged her to go. To her, church was an artistic expression, creative and fluid. The words of the preacher were prose; the lyrics sung by the choir were poetry. She brought some of that openness out in W. J. as he courted her.

For the first time that W. J. could remember since before his papa was murdered, he was giddy. The tough exterior around his heart cracked, and his heart was filled with love. Everything was Violet.

For Violet's part, she loved the attention she received when she rode down the street in W. J.'s fine car, and how he shot her a quick wink before every pitch he threw at the church baseball games. She loved how the members of the church treated her with respect.

The truth was they watched each other. Violet was a great performer, and she admired a great performance in another. That's what she saw when she looked at W. J. He entertained and enthralled a faithful crowd at least twice a week. People outside Richmond bought recordings of his sermons. In the pulpit and on the baseball field, W. J. put on a show worthy of a standing ovation, and most days, he got one. When Violet was at the piano, W. J. couldn't take his eyes off her. He wondered where the depth of feeling that she put into the music came from. It was pure magic to him.

W. J. and Violet were sitting together on a blanket, eating fried chicken after a game, when he approached the subject that had been on his mind from the first time he saw her.

"I haven't hidden my intentions toward you, Violet; I want you to be my wife. The Bible says that when a man finds a wife, he finds a good thing and obtains favor from the Lord. If you marry me, I promise you that I will love you more than any man could love a woman. There would be nothing you would want for, and it would make me the happiest man on God's green earth."

W. J.'s intentions toward Violet were no surprise. She cared for W. J., but marrying him was a different thing all together. Violet paused to gather her thoughts before she spoke.

"Every girl in Virginia would consider herself lucky to be your wife, W. J. I'm overwhelmed that you would want me. I wouldn't hesitate to say yes, except for the dreams we dream at night are different dreams."

"What do you mean?" he said, fearing the worst.

"I'm not sure we want the same things."

"I want whatever you want, Violet. All I want to do is make you happy."

"What if the happiness of one of us makes the other miserable? What if I can't be the wife you want me to be?"

"You're the only wife I want. I would be miserable without you."

"You don't understand. I want to go to New York and play my music one day."

"I know that your music is very important to you. I'm not asking you to give that up."

"Don't you think that our lives are so different?" she asked, thinking about him growing up with money on a farm, while she grew up poor in the city.

"It's love that brings people together," he said, reaching for her hand. "I don't think you're all that different from me."

"There are things that give us satisfaction that another person can't give us," Violet said, thinking about the thrill she got jamming with the jazz and blues musicians on The Deuce. She felt relaxed and comfortable and in her element.

It was only in that atmosphere that she breathed the air she needed to survive. In the church, with everyone watching with judgment in their eyes, she felt tense, ill at ease, as if she were suffocating.

"I will do everything I can to give you all the things you need. I'll provide for you, protect you, and take you to New York if you want me to. All I want is for you to love me back."

Violet hadn't met any other guy who came close to W. J. He was handsome and strong, and he and his family were respected by all of Richmond. There was only one thing holding her back. She liked her freedom, and she suspected that he wanted to put her in a cage where he could keep a close eye on her. She wasn't sure that he would let her fly high to see how far she could go. Something was telling her that he couldn't wait to clip her wings and keep her tied down with a bunch of babies.

"Give me a little more time to think about it," she said with a smile.

***

W. J. refused to take maybe for an answer. For over a year, he did everything he could think of to show Violet how devoted he was to her. But loving him was not the problem; she'd developed strong feelings for him. But could she give up the life she always wanted for the life of a woman married to a preacher? That was like asking her to choose between a beach sunrise at the edge of the sea or dusk deep in a wooded forest.

In the end, it was her mother's influence that convinced her to say yes to W. J.'s proposal—that and the Stock Market Crash of 1929.

"Don't be a fool, Violet. There's nothing on The Deuce or in New York but hard times. Folks around here don't know where their next meal is coming from. When you're drowning, you can't choose the hand that reaches out to save you. Your daddy isn't making a dime, and I'll be lucky if I keep my job at the bank."

"I don't think I can live the life he wants me to, Mama. I love Jesus, but I don't want to spend most of my days sitting in church and my nights bored to death on a farm."

"Child, you're gonna have to take a chance on some man sooner or later, unless you want to be by yourself for the rest of your life. There's nothing wrong with a God-fearing man. That's a blessing. I thank Jesus every day that you don't have to live the life I've lived. W. J. loves you. Anybody can see that. He's offering you security when there isn't much of that to go around. Marrying him is not the worst thing that could happen to you."

"If I marry him, I know I won't get my chance to play in New York."

"Hush up 'bout that New York talk! There ain't no guarantees on that anyway. How many of these musicians you know are earning a living? Give that man a chance to make you happy."

So, on a cold January day, W. J. and Violet were married. Knowing her parents were struggling financially, W. J. ordered a fancy white gown for her to wear for their wedding.

"There was never a more beautiful bride!" Opal said, tearing up as she touched up her daughter's hair. "I'm so proud of you, Violet."

Violet smiled, despite her last-minute doubts. It made her feel good to see her mother so happy. She had done so much to provide for her, and now maybe she wouldn't have to work so hard. Opal took Violet's hand and led her up the stairs, where Sammy was waiting in the vestibule. He took his daughter's hand, and Opal walked to the front pew.

"You look like an angel, baby," Sammy said. "You got a handsome groom waiting up there for you."

The music started to play. Tears welled up in Violet's eyes, and her lips trembled. Sammy could see Violet was nervous. He hugged her close and gave her one last word of advice: "Live for today because tomorrow may not come. Don't worry about the future; it's in God's hands." Then he walked her down the aisle toward her waiting groom.

Violet surrendered all her worries once she stood at the altar next to W. J. All her friends had told her she was lucky to get W. J. She wiped her eyes, pledged her love to him, and vowed to be a good wife.

***

Violet felt like a queen in a palace when she moved into the Freeman house. There was an electric stove and a telephone. Things were tighter because blacks didn't have much to put in the offering plate, but even the most poverty-stricken smoker in the country had to have cigarettes. Even though farm prices were depressed, too, the farm kept food on the table and clothes on their backs, necessities that had somehow become luxuries.

Grandpa Thomas's back problems flared up again, but he refused to let them keep him out of the field. Six days a week, albeit slower and slower, he headed out at daybreak. Every evening, he barely made it to his place on the front porch, and he had to sit there for an hour before he recovered enough to make it inside the house.

"You gettin' too old to be out in the fields every day. It's time to slow down," W. J. would tell him in the evening, trying to convince him to rest.

"If I can't go out there and work, there ain't much reason to be in this world."

"That's not true, Grandpa. The church needs you, and I need you."

"Well, I need to work," Thomas said stubbornly. "Things are tough around here. I'll take my rest when times get better."

It got to the point where Thomas walked the fields more than he worked. One evening, W. J. looked for him on the porch, but he wasn't there. He walked the field yard by yard, looking for his grandpa. He found him lying on a cushion of tobacco leaves.

W. J. was more disappointed than sad. He had long suspected that his grandpa wouldn't be around much longer. He preached the eulogy with words from the Book of Job: "The LORD gave, and the LORD has taken away; blessed be the name of the LORD." Grandpa Thomas was gone, but a new life was coming into their lives.

***

With a smile on his face, W. J. worked the land and started new seedlings for the tobacco crop. He was thrilled that he would soon have a child to provide for. He considered it his good fortune that Violet had gotten pregnant on their wedding night. After fall harvest, when the leaves were almost cured, in October 1930, Violet gave birth to a son they named Philip. Before he learned to walk, Violet was pregnant again. In March 1932, she gave birth to a second son they named Franklin.

W. J. was proud of his sons, but he was strict with them from day one. He forced Violet to let them cry when they woke in the night. When they learned to walk, he wouldn't let her carry them. He was determined to raise them to be strong men.

W. J. also insisted that they eat all the food on their plates. When Philip was two years old, he pushed his plate on the floor to avoid eating his butter beans. In a flash, W. J. pulled him out of his high chair and spanked him.

"I don't see any reason to spank him just because he doesn't like the beans," Violet said, confused and upset, rocking Franklin in her arms.

"I don't care if he likes the beans or not. He can't behave that way," W. J. said.

"He's only a baby, W. J. He has time to learn."

"This is the time to learn," he said, putting Philip back in his chair. "'Those who spare the rod of discipline hate their children. Those who love their children care enough to discipline them,' Proverbs 13:24. 'It takes hard work and pain to grow a good crop.' It will take the same to raise our boys to be good men."

Violet didn't agree with W. J.'s beliefs on how to raise their children. She thought he was too hard on the boys. After all, they were only babies. It bewildered her that he could be so gentle and loving with her and then be so callous with their children. When Philip was four and Franklin was almost three, W. J. started teaching them how to work in the fields. Together, they planted a small vegetable garden, while their father preached the merits of hard work.

To balance out W. J.'s strictness, Violet loved to spoil her boys with sweet treats like Tootsie Roll pops and Mary Jane candy. She entertained them playing old ragtime tunes on the piano, playing jazz and bebop for them on the phonograph, and letting them dance on the floor and be silly. She even got them a puppy that she let run through the house with them when W. J. wasn't home.

***

In January 1936, just as Richmond was feeling a reprieve from the Depression, a cold wave spread across the country; the Chesapeake Bay froze; and the rivers were ice-bound, with temperatures dipping below 15 degrees. Record amounts of snowfall covered the city. People froze to death in their homes; while some died from inside fires they burned trying to keep warm. Quite a few families had to stay inside the church for shelter; others just came for food.

Violet wanted her parents to stay at the Freeman house until winter was over, but W. J. objected. He heard that her daddy was running numbers, and he wasn't about to let anybody doing the work of the devil lay their head under his roof. With the weather being so harsh, it wasn't until spring that Violet could take the children out to visit her mother.

That's when she found out that Opal was sick with tuberculosis. Nurses were scarce, and black doctors were rare. Blacks had to visit spiritualist mediums, or they went without medical care and relied on old-time health remedies instead of medicines.

"I've got to go and stay with my mama for a while. She's sick," Violet told W. J. when they got home. "She don't have anyone to care for her except me."

"You can go, but I don't want my boys going over there," W. J. replied matter-of-factly.

Frowning in confusion, Violet asked him, "How can you

expect me to leave them? They're too little to be without their mama!"

"They'll be fine, Vi. I can take care of my sons," W. J. said, picking up the newspaper. "Go on and care for your mama."

W. J.'s attitude irritated Violet. She wondered if he was bitter because his own mama had left town, taking his sister with her. It didn't matter. She was too tired to make a fuss.

"Hopefully, she'll be better in a few weeks," she said. "Then you can bring the boys to visit."

"I won't have my boys wallowing in trash over there. They'll be here when you get back."

That insult hit Violet hard. She looked at W. J. in disbelief. This wasn't the man she married. He had always been firm, but now he was as hard as a rock. How could he stand up there and preach the goodness of God, His mercy and forgiveness, when he had none to offer himself?

Starting the next morning, Violet walked a mile to where she could catch the trolley to her mother's house. When Opal had good days, Violet went home after dinner. On her bad days, Violet stayed the night. Her father had the blues; he couldn't get a steady gig, and the numbers game was getting dangerous. Whatever money he was able to scrounge up, he drank half of it. Violet pilfered what she could to keep them going, but W. J. kept an eye on every cent.

***

When the cold weather broke, Opal started to feel better, but nature can be so cruel. They had barely breathed a sigh of relief from the frigid temperatures when the heat wave rolled in. It was seething hot. In June, Richmond had record highs of 100 degrees; in July, temperatures approached 110 degrees.

Land that was once covered in ice was now dry and dusty from the heat. Crops were scorched by the lack of water and moisture in the ground. Harvests were ruined. People wondered what manner of hell it was that had come to torture them. They argued over which was worse, freezing or burning. The elements proved to be too much for Opal. She gave up the fight on a sizzling day in August shortly after noon.

Opal's was the voice that soothed the restlessness in Violet's spirit; the voice of reason that encouraged her to think about what was best for the boys; and the voice that told her to be patient, for time would change things. With that voice now silent, Violet's yearnings grew greater. She wanted more; she wanted her dream.

Under the guise of seeing about her father after her mother died, Violet's trips back to Jackson Ward were about something else. Violet would sneak back to The Deuce to see the younguns tapping and shuffling their feet on the street corner for a nickel, hoping to be the next Bo Jangles. Secretly, she had started playing in nightclubs again.

Violet was discreet at first. She told herself that she only wanted to listen to and feel the vibe that was so alive it transformed everyone in the room to a place of ecstasy, moving like the Holy Spirit did throughout the sanctuary at church. Toes tapped, arms flailed, and shouts rang out.

But Violet couldn't keep her seat, and one of the musicians recognized her. He waved her to the front and introduced her to the audience. She took a seat on the piano bench, laid her hands on the keys, and poured herself into the music. She lifted the entire room, playing with abandon. She was a woman who had found herself again, a woman who had been bound but was now free. The impossible was possible again.

Violet came back again the following Friday and played until her emotions were spent and her fingers were numb. Fate had given her a pass on her previous interludes from the rules of conduct becoming a first lady, but black Richmond wasn't big enough to keep such a secret. One of the deacons, who was tipping out on his wife, saw her and carried the word back to W. J. When Violet went home Saturday afternoon, buoyed from her moment in the sun, the news had already been delivered.

"Philip, Franklin, come and give your mama a hug," Violet yelled across the garden, where they were working, waving them over to her. They stared back at her with the eyes of animals who were helplessly caught in a trap. Immediately, she knew something was out of sorts. W. J. was always too hard on them. She hurried up the porch stairs and threw open the screen door.

"W. J., what's wrong with the boys?" she asked, surprised to find him sitting in the parlor with a strap in one hand and the Bible in the other.

"There's nothing wrong with the boys. There's something wrong with you!" he answered, furious, speaking through gritted teeth.

"What are you talking about?"

"I made you my wife! I have given you all that I have, and you disgrace me."

Violet looked at him dumbfounded. "You're not making any sense!"

"You're the one not making any sense," he said, standing to his feet. "I took you away from the gutter and all that sinful trash and put you on a pedestal before God, but that low-life demon is still in you. Why would you lie to me, leave the home

I've made for you, to degrade yourself and this family with those sinners on Second Street?"

"I haven't done anything like that!" she cried. "I've only gone to play my music. You knew that was part of me when I met you."

"The Lord put me in authority over you when I married you. I've prayed for you to be released from doing the devil's bidding, but you continue to stray."

"You're talking crazy, W. J.!" she said, wondering if he'd lost his mind. "You're here growing tobacco for folks to smoke cigars and pipes, and you say that's a sin. How can you say that the music I play is a sin? You listen and you feel it in your heart and soul. What is so wrong with that?"

"Proverbs 12:4 says, 'An excellent wife is the crown of her husband, but she who brings shame is like rottenness in his bones.' Why do you behave like this? Why do you force me to discipline you like an unruly child?"

"If you lay a hand on me, I promise you I will take my boys and leave here, and you will never see us again! The only evil in this house is inside of you. You hide in that book with all the laws about what somebody can't do in this world, and it has made you mean. All your preaching is draining all the life out of me and our boys."

"You will never take my boys from me, Violet, and that is as good as the gospel here in my hand. Because I love you with all my heart and God tells me to be merciful, I won't punish you. I'll forgive you."

That day was the pivotal point for W. J. and Violet. The trust between them was destroyed. He feared what she was doing outside of his presence, and she feared what he would do while she was in his presence. The love between them turned into pretense. He pretended for those outside their home that everything was perfect between them; she pretended for those inside their home that everything was fine and dandy. She played her part too well, so well that she found herself pregnant again.

***

In the spring, Violet gave birth to another son they named William Edward Freeman III. Violet was content to name him after his father because she knew he would be the last one. In appreciation, W. J. hired a maid to help with the cooking, cleaning, and washing. For her sons' sakes, Violet tried to be the wife and first lady of the church that everyone expected her to be. For sitting dutifully at the piano on Sunday mornings and afternoons, her reward was a car of her own. For two years, she managed to focus on what was best for everyone except herself.

In the summer of 1941, W. J. was invited to speak at a large revival in Norfolk. Violet feigned illness, the possibility that she was pregnant again. W. J. was pleased with the possibility and took the three-day trip without her. He took Philip and Franklin with him but left William home with Violet and the housekeeper.

That night, while W. J. stood in the chapel preaching, Violet was already on The Deuce. Money was flowing on the street again, and her father was playing in a band in one of the nightclubs. She sat there all night, relishing the moment and the music.

The next night, Violet bought tickets to Count Basie and Billie Holiday's show at the Hippodrome Theater. She heard the tears behind the music, and they fell heavy on her heart. She couldn't stop herself from crying over her own sadness. She had the blues like nobody's business. Sitting there among strangers, there was no need to pretend. She met up with her father at the nightclub after the show to have a drink.

"I'm glad to see you, baby!" Sammy said, rubbing her head. "I've missed you."

She reached for his hand and squeezed it. "I've missed you too, Daddy."

"Things are finally picking up, baby girl. The time is right for me to take that ride to New York. With your mama gone, you with your family, there's nothing to keep me here."

"I wish I could go with you," she said, her voice full of longing.

"No, I don't think that's a good idea. You've got those great sons to raise."

Violet sighed. "Sometimes I think about packing up and running off with them."

"Taking kids away from their daddy is no good. I know how you feel, but you have to hold on. Things will get better."

"How? When? I don't know how much longer I can take it. I feel like I'm a prisoner out there on the farm."

"I blame myself," Sammy said, shaking his head. "I spoiled you. Life isn't easy. You've got a pillow to lay on; most folks are sleeping on a bed of rocks."

"I'd trade places in a minute."

"You're breaking my heart," he said, feeling the depth of her anguish. "I wish there was something I could do."

"So do I, Daddy."

***

Violet's housekeeper was a jealous woman; but because she valued her job, she hid it well. But when she found out that Violet had faked her illness to avoid going to Norfolk with

W. J., the housekeeper's jealousy drove her to betray Violet. She called W. J. and told him what Violet had done, that she had left Little Will with her and had been gone for two days.

When W. J. got home late Saturday night, Violet had already gone to bed. He didn't come in quietly, though. He ranted as he stormed into the house. Philip and Franklin trembled in fear and crept in behind him.

"Get Will and go to your room!" he roared at his sons. "Close the door, and don't come out until I call for you."

W. J. made a mad dash to the bedroom and jumped on the bed. Violently jarred out of her sleep, Violet screamed and tried to jump out of the bed, but she couldn't. W. J. was kneeling on top of her as if he were about to pray on her chest. She stared stupefied up at him, and he glared down at her. Frightened and horrified, she was still lovely in his eyes. But now he despised her beauty because he believed that he had been taken in by it, and he was convinced she used the power of her beauty to tempt others over in Jackson Ward, which to him was nothing but a modern-day Sodom and Gomorrah.

Violet could feel all the weight of W. J.'s body pressing against her lungs, and she could barely breathe. She was in a fog of disbelief as he punched her face over and over. She screamed in terror when he grabbed her around the throat. She scratched at his hands to pull them away, tugging at them while she looked into his eyes. She didn't recognize him; fury had changed his appearance.

In a last-ditch effort, Violet gathered all her strength to shift her weight and throw off W. J.'s balance on her chest. It gave her a chance to wriggle out from under him and she could feel the cloth ripping as he pulled on her nightgown while she struggled to get away from him. It slipped out of his grip and she fell to the floor. When he jumped up, she curled into a ball to shield herself from his wrath.

"Why, you Jezebel! Why would you betray me?" W. J. bellowed as he took off his belt.

"I haven't done anything wrong!" Violet screamed with her head bowed between her knees.

W. J. struck Violet across her back. She tried to shield the back of her head with her hands and waited for the next strike but it didn't come. She snuck a glimpse from under her arm and saw Philip holding the end of the belt and W. J. gawking at him as if he were in shock.

W. J. spun around and shouted. "Didn't I tell you to stay in your room!"

"You can't hit Mama!" Philip screamed, tears running down his face.

W. J. dropped the belt, fell down to his knees, and called out, "Lord, the devil seeks to kill and destroy the righteous! Deliver us in the name of Jesus!" Then he began to cry. "It's my duty as the head of this family to protect it from all danger, to lead you all in the right path. I don't want to be harsh, but you all leave me no choice. The way of the Lord is not easy."

Violet crawled across the floor to where Philip was standing. She eased his fingers from the belt and took his hand. Once they were out of the bedroom, she rushed down the hall, where Franklin was crouched in a corner holding William's hand. They spent the night there in the corner, scared to close their eyes.

W. J. left early the next morning. He didn't speak to his family. When they heard the door close behind him, they relaxed their grip around one another.

"I want you boys to get yourselves cleaned up for church while I get breakfast ready," she said, rising to her feet.

Violet bathed her bruised body. She combed her hair, put on a housedress and slippers, and ambled into the kitchen. She made the boys their favorite breakfast, pancakes with molasses and sausage. She set the table and filled three cups with milk. They came to the table holding hands. Violet helped William into his high chair, Philip and Franklin sat at the table, and then she took her seat.

"All right, boys, let's join hands and say grace before we eat," Violet said, trying her best to smile. "Heavenly Father, I ask that you bless this meal before us today. I ask that you bless my sons, watch over them, and be a cover above them. Bless them to love and care for one another. I pray they will always know how much I love them, even when I'm not with them. Amen."

Violet sat watching the three boys eat, wishing that that moment could last a lifetime. Her sons amazed her. Never during the years when she was growing up did she think she would have three beautiful boys. She also never thought that her greatest joy would have caused her to shed so many tears.

"You're not eating, Mama," Franklin said.

"I ate earlier," she said, lying. Her stomach was tied in so many knots that she couldn't possibly hold down a meal. She sat there with a weak smile on her face as she watched her sons eat.

***

Meanwhile at the church, W. J. had the piano removed from the sanctuary. He didn't want Violet or anyone else to play it. He wanted to kill the music. As far as he was concerned, it was a bad influence on those who heard it. Grudgingly, he admitted to himself that whenever she played, the notes moved his congregation more than the preached word did, and that was unacceptable.

W. J. could have saved himself the trouble. Violet had no intentions of playing that morning. She walked in with her eyes barely visible. A small tilt of her hat covered half of her face. All during the service, W. J. kept glancing over at her, trying to gauge her mood, but her face remained blank. There was nothing there to read, and it made him angry. Why was she so defiant? Why couldn't she just repent of her sins so they could be happy again?

W. J. stood to preach. Gripping both sides of the lectern, he began.

"Brothers and sisters, today's lesson comes from the Book of Daniel, where the people of Israel had drifted away from God again. Beginning in verse four, Daniel says, 'I prayed to the LORD my God and made confession, saying "O LORD, the greatest and awesome God, who keeps covenant and steadfast love with those who love him and keep his commandments, we have sinned and done wrong and acted wickedly and rebelled, turning aside from your commandments and rules."'

"Time and time again, the people of Israel sinned against God; but, thankfully, there was at least one righteous man who went to God on their behalf. This God-fearing man asked for mercy upon them, even before they ceased from sinning. That was a blessing, saints. God never leaves us alone. There is always a shepherd present to bring back that lone sheep that has gone astray."

There were nods of agreement sprinkled throughout the sanctuary as W. J. preached, along with the reliable amens that peppered the service.

There was nothing unusual going on, nothing out of the ordinary, not even when Violet took Little Will by the hand and walked out of the sanctuary. They had done that many times before. It was a little strange when Little Will walked back into the sanctuary by himself ten minutes later. W. J. noticed his son walking in alone, but he was in the throes of his message and couldn't analyze what was happening. Something about it was bothersome, but he had to close his sermon.

After the service, no one could find Violet. W. J. picked up his youngest son in his arms and asked him, "Where is your mama, son?"

"She drove away, Papa."

***

Violet knew she couldn't stay with W. J. He was suffocating her. She was like a flower that needed the sun and air to breathe. For her, it had become a choice between life and death. Not a physical death, but in every other way. She chose life. She prayed that the hell brought on the boys from the arguments between her and W. J. would be over and that peace would come into the home in her absence.

The boys cried and pleaded with their father to go look for Violet and bring her back. The older boys, Philip and Franklin, begged him to let them find her and bring her back.

He replied, "'She gives no thought to the way of life; her paths are crooked, but she knows it not. Now then, my sons, listen to me; do not turn aside from what I say. Keep a path far from her, do not go near the door of her house!' Proverbs 5:6-7."

***

William watched his older brothers toil long hours in the tobacco fields, shivering in the cold, preparing seedbeds and sowing them, pulling weeds and killing bugs in the spring, and laboring and sweating in the heat during the summer harvest. W. J. would work alongside them, quoting Scripture passages like Ephesians 4:27-28: "Neither give place to the devil. Let him that stole steal no more: but rather let him labour, working with his hands the thing which is good, that he may have to give to him that needeth."

There was no such thing as free time. When the boys weren't in the field or at school, they were in church, where W. J. groomed them on their obligation "to serve the God of your fathers" and warned them never to let themselves be tempted by a pretty woman. "Don't lust for their beauty. Don't let their coyness seduce you. For a prostitute will bring a man to poverty, and an adulteress may cost him his very life, Proverbs 6:25-26." He taught them the ways of the Lord and the wages of sin. He wailed on and on about the evil tricks and enticements of the devil whenever he had their ear and preached the same message to the entire congregation on Sundays and at midweek services.

"The devil is amongst us, church. He never lets us alone, whispering in our ears, enticing us with pretty things, pretty women, pretty cars, and pretty clothes. He knows our weaknesses, church. He tempts us with our desires: smoking, drinking, and gambling. The wages of sin are death. God sacrificed his son for us to have eternal life. Make your choice, brothers and sisters. Will you choose the fire in the pits of hell or the streets paved with gold in heaven? Repent of your sins, depart from your wicked ways, obey God's commandments, and follow Christ Jesus."

"There he goes again," William heard Philip whisper to Franklin. "Always talking about somebody's wicked ways, and he's worse than the devil himself."

Franklin nodded. "If he wasn't so evil, Mama wouldn't have left us. He made her life the hell he's talking about. Now he's up there all self-righteous."

William sat between them listening. He didn't remember that much about his mother, only that she was as beautiful as an angel and her voice was as soothing as a warm buttermilk biscuit.

"He's a hypocrite, and my days sitting here listening to him and breaking my back over tobacco are coming to an end," Philip said. "I'm leaving in two months, and he can't stop me."

"Are you going to find Mama?" Franklin asked.

"No, not yet. Me and a couple of my buddies are going to join the Marines. I can make a few bucks, and then I'll find her."

"I want to go with you," Franklin said, uneasy about being left behind.

"You're not old enough," Philip told him. "Plus, somebody's got to look out for William."

The boys talked among themselves until W. J. made an announcement.

"Church, you all know that the mother of my sons was ensnared in a web of sin, committing adultery, playing the devil's music, and was lost to the world. Children need a mother and a father, and a man needs a helpmate. I'm happy to announce that Sister Eleanor has consented to be my wife and a mother to my sons. We ask all your blessings on our union."

Murmurs went through the congregation, and the three boys were dumbstruck. Miss Eleanor wasn't just plain; she was plain ugly and over 40 years old. As pastor and owner of a nice piece of land, W. J. could have had any woman he wanted in the church, single or married.

"I bet she'll help him contain his sinful desires all right," Philip sniggled to his brothers.

Deacon Wilson came to the rescue. "Praise the Lord, church!" he shouted.

Applause and a few hesitant amens filled the room.

Chapter Four

William Edward Freeman III

illiam III was the youngest son of William Edward Freeman Jr. His oldest brother, Philip, was eight years older; his second-oldest brother, Franklin, was six years older. Conceived in the midst of bitterness between his parents, William had never known what it was like to grow up with happiness in the house.

William's mother, Violet, was a pretty woman at first glance; but when you looked closely, there was a shadow of sadness on her face. As far back as he could remember, she was always nervous and talked to him and his brothers in whispers. His father, W. J., was a hard man by any definition. He seldom smiled or laughed before Violet ran off; and after she did, he never laughed or smiled again.

W. J. woke his sons every morning, standing in the door wearing overalls and spouting Romans 12:11: "Not slothful in business; fervent in spirit; serving the Lord." He was determined to keep William and his brothers in line in order to minimize the wayward blood of their mother, which he knew was running through their veins. He rode the boys hard, holding them in a tight grip like a cowboy trying to ride a wild bull. But his efforts only egged them to run off the first chance they got.

Philip was the first to go. He joined the Marines when he was 17. William could never forget how furious W. J. was when he found out. It wasn't so much that he didn't want Philip to go into the service; it was that after all of W. J.'s hard work raising his sons, Philip had the nerve to defy him. So W. J. took his anger out on Franklin and William, determined to correct the mistake he had made with Philip. He chastised them continually, saying, "A fool despises his father's instruction, but whoever heeds correction is prudent, Proverbs 15:5."

Two years later, after Franklin finished high school, he left to join Philip in the Marines. His parting words to William were, "Be strong, little brother. Your chance will come." This time, W. J. blamed the errant behavior of his sons solely on the influence of their rebellious mother. William sat across from Miss Eleanor, while his father ranted at the head of the table.

"I showed your mama a better life; but like the rest of them rats on the other side of Jackson Ward, she was more comfortable wallowing in the gutter!" he fumed, as he stabbed the roast on his plate, violently shredding it into small pieces. "I trusted her to raise my sons in the right way, but she was a bad example. I pray you weren't poisoned by the serpent, son."

"William's a good boy," Miss Eleanor said to calm W. J.

"You don't have to worry about me leaving," William told his father, attempting to placate his temper. "Besides, Philip and Franklin will be back sooner or later."

"Who knows when that'll be!" W. J. roared. "They going to war over there in Korea."

William dropped his fork, and it clanged loudly against his plate. He couldn't eat another bite. It suddenly occurred to him that he might not see his brothers again. He knew men didn't always come home from wars.

"I don't feel so good," he said, getting up from the table.

"Where are your manners, boy? Miss Eleanor worked in the kitchen all day to prepare this meal."

William didn't answer, keeping his eyes on the floor.

"Leave him be," Miss Eleanor said, touching his arm. "He can finish later."

W. J. grunted and went about finishing his supper.

***

Philip and Franklin wrote letters to William at least twice a month, and he answered them back as soon as he received them. Philip had become a fighter pilot and flew combat missions over enemy lines. He always had great stories to tell in his letters.

With letters from his brothers coming in regularly, William had begun to relax, and he became confident that Philip and Franklin would return home safely after all. But his confidence was premature. Early one morning, the Freemans received news that Philip had been killed in a plane crash.

Philip's death cracked W. J.'s hard shell. His whole demeanor changed. He spoke slower in hushed tones, and he rarely quoted Scriptures at home any more. William was frightened to see his father so broken. He would have rather taken a beating than to see the proud W. J. subdued. To rouse his father's usual tough demeanor, William slacked off at school and didn't do his chores, but he still couldn't get a rise out of his father. Then he tried studying harder at school and working harder in the fields to please him, but W. J. remained disconsolate.

One day, William came home from school and saw his father sitting on the front porch, weeping. W. J. held a letter in his hand, and Eleanor stood behind his father, looking up to the heavens. Something was horribly wrong, and William feared the worst.

"Franklin is dead," W. J. said, crumpling the official-looking letter in his hand.

William's eyes filled with tears. Not Franklin, too! "What happened, Papa?"

W. J. shook his head. "It doesn't matter how. All that matters is that it is. Philip and Franklin were born 17 months apart, and they died 17 months apart."

William dropped his books and sat next to the wet spot on the wood that his father's eyes were fixed upon. He bit his lips to hold them together. There were no words that could express what he felt. He had lost more than half his family, his mother and two brothers. Despite his dreams of a happy reunion, William now realized that his family could never be whole again.

The three of them stayed there on the porch like that for a long time. Long enough for the wet spot of tears to soak into the wood and disappear.

Then W. J. stood up. "It's all on your shoulders, son," he said to William. "You're the only one left. We come from a long line of men of God, and we've been designated by Him to protect and profess His word. Philip was the oldest, and it was his place; but then it was passed to Franklin, now both of them have gone to glory When the time comes, you have to stand in my place."

When he was done talking, W. J. walked into the house. Miss Eleanor followed without saying a word. William kept sitting; he wasn't sure if he could stand or walk. He felt hollow inside, like the empty shell of a peanut thrown aside, having nothing left to offer. His father's words had turned his sorrow into fear. All his life, he had watched his father vehemently preach above the congregation with a Bible in his hand, putting the fear of God in the hearts of every member. He never imagined himself up there. He could see Philip up there, and even Franklin, but never himself.

Unsure of anything at that moment, William accepted his birthright and responsibility to preach God's word. His greater reason was as a soldier doing his duty in honor of his fellow fallen soldiers. Those fallen soldiers were his older brothers, Philip and Franklin.

***

Seven years later, William was out working in the tobacco field with the hired hands. He was especially tired, having forced himself to stay awake after another nightmare. The bad dreams started after Philip and Franklin were killed in the war. Never told how they died, he imagined them being killed over and over, either shot face to face, drowned on a downed ship, or blown to bits by a missile.

When William saw his father standing in the distance, he knew something was going on because W. J. rarely came out to the fields anymore. Losing his sons not only softened W. J.'s outward demeanor, but inwardly, he couldn't muster the spirit or energy to work the land. William dropped the hoe he was using to dig up weeds and ran over to where his father was waiting.

"It's time for you to come out of the fields, son," W. J. said. "You ain't making much difference out here anyway."

William trailed him as he turned and walked away, wondering what brought on his latest revelation. There was no telling what was on his papa's mind.

"You're not strong like your brothers, so at least you need to be smart," W. J. said, talking all the while he was walking. "I reckon it's time for you to go to college."

William didn't respond right away.

"You hear me, Will?" W. J. asked, stopping to look at his son.

"Yes, sir," William said, following him up the back porch and into the house.

William resisted the impulse to jump in the air and cheer. He acted as if it was a punishment that he was obligated to endure. He remembered the last words Franklin had told him before he left for the war: "Be strong, little brother. Your time will come." William wanted to scream up to the heavens, "Franklin, you were right!" because his time had surely come.

***

When William arrived in Hampton, Virginia, he wanted to fall on his knees and thank God for his wonderful blessing. For the first time in his life, he had gotten away from his father's long reach, and being at Hampton Institute was a taste of freedom he had only dreamed about. Finally, he could be himself, or at least have a chance to discover who he was. He'd spent his whole childhood trying to live up to the formidable statures of his brothers and father without ever feeling comparable.

During his freshman year at Hampton, William thrived like a seedling transplanted away from its established tree. Free from the large swath of shade cast by W. J., William soaked up the sunshine, matured, and flourished.

William had never played sports in high school, but during his sophomore year, he tried out for the football team; and thanks to his natural born and field-tempered abilities, he made it. The camaraderie he had with his teammates was entirely different than the male relationships he'd experienced with his family. At home, they were divided by fear and disappointment. On campus, they were united by friendship and their desire to win.

William stopped having nightmares. Then during the spring semester of his junior year, a recurring dream that he had from time to time came true. It happened on a Saturday afternoon when he and a couple of fellows went to a concert at Bethel Christian Church to see the Blind Boys of Alabama.

She was the prettiest girl he had ever seen. Instantly, he knew he had to make her his wife just to snatch his soul back from the devil's gnarly hands, for every thought he'd had from the moment he saw her was coated in sin. He watched her walk to the front row close behind a woman wearing a huge hat bedecked with flowers. The woman sat down and the girl took a seat in the chair next to her. His church upbringing told him from the way the woman strutted in and the position of her seat, she was the preacher's wife, and the pretty girl was probably his daughter.

The show started with the group being led in, each man holding on to the shoulder of the one in front of him. Despite the uplifting performance, William couldn't name one song he'd heard during the whole concert to save his life because all his attention had been focused on the pretty girl in the front row. William's only thought was how he could work his way through the crowd and meet her.

After the concert, the guys got a chance to mingle with a group of girls from another college, while William searched for the pretty girl who caught his eye. When he got a glimpse of her, he noticed she never strayed more than a few feet from her mother. When his friends were ready to leave, they pulled him away before he got a chance to meet the unknown beauty. William didn't put up too much of a fuss; he already knew he'd be there for church on Sunday morning.

***

Dressed in his best suit, William walked into the sanctuary of Bethel Christian Church and sat through the service like a deaf man. He never heard a word the pastor said. All he could think about was what he was going to say to the girl of his dreams. He knew enough that he couldn't just walk up to her. Growing up under W. J. taught him a lot about body language, and from what he could tell, the first lady was the absolute gatekeeper to what he wanted.

William approached the pastor's wife after the service was over. "Hello, ma'am," he said, extending his hand to her. "I was seated a few rows behind you, and I just had to tell you how lovely your hat is."

"Why, thank you!" she said, smiling. "I hope it wasn't blocking your view."

"Oh no, ma'am, not at all! The colors reminded me of the flower garden my mother kept at home."

"That's so nice," the pastor's wife said, eyeing him curiously. "I haven't seen you here before. Is this your first time visiting with us?"

"Yes, ma'am. I'm a student over at Hampton. I'm looking for a church home while I'm studying here at school," he answered, pretending not to notice the girl beside her.

"Well, I'm Sister Sarah Davis, the pastor's wife. It's commendable that you conduct yourself properly and remember to worship the Lord on His day. Where are you from?"

"I'm from Richmond, ma'am."

"What church do you attend there?"

"My father's church, Church of God in Christ on Thompson Boulevard."

Her face lit up. "I'm familiar with him, Reverend William Freeman Jr. I once attended a revival where he spoke. What's your name, young man?"

"I'm William Freeman III."

"Well, welcome to Bethel, William. This is my daughter, Goldie," she said, nodding toward the pretty girl. "We're having supper downstairs. She can show you where it is."

"Thank you, ma'am. I'd appreciate that," he said, pleased that his plan had worked perfectly.

Sister Davis's attention turned toward another sister who was wearing an equally impressive hat. "Excuse me," she said, sashaying away, "I need to chat with Sister Beatrice."

"You're not slick," Goldie said once her mother was out of earshot.

"What are you talking about?" William asked, pretending to be confused.

"I saw you at the concert. You stared at me the whole time."

"How could I help myself? You were the prettiest girl in the room."

"You're loose with the flattering words, aren't you?"

"My intentions are honorable, I promise you, Miss Goldie," he said, smiling down at her.

Goldie didn't smile back, but it wasn't because she wasn't interested. She'd heard of William's church, too. It was big compared to Bethel. Seeing him in his fine suit and driving his own car, she figured he was a spoiled preacher's kid used to getting everything he wanted. She couldn't have been further from the truth.

***

William came to church faithfully, and he joined the local chapter of the NAACP where Sarah Davis was active. By the end of the semester, he was eating Sunday dinner at the Davis house. In 1956, Sarah invited him to attend the annual state convention of the NAACP at Mt. Olivet Baptist Church. That was the first time he heard Martin Luther King Jr. speak. The meeting opened his eyes and his mind to the world outside of the farm in Charles City County, the church in Richmond, and the Hampton football field.

From that day, William saw a new purpose for his life: to fight against the injustices just as his brothers did when they joined the Marines and went to war. The only thing he wanted more was Goldie. He planned to ask her to marry him before he went home for the summer. The best alternative would be if he could find a job in Hampton and stay there until the fall semester, skipping sweating at the farm over the summer. Goldie's kisses were the one thing he didn't think he could do without.

W. J. sensed that something was going on with William. His son's visits back home were getting fewer and farther in between, and he had started talking about protests and boycotts. Whatever William was up to, W. J. had decided that he would surely put a stop to it. He had let the boy get out there to grow up some, but William had gone far enough. Now it was time to reel him back in. But William wasn't about to be yanked back home that easily. He called his father to set the groundwork for his plan.

"Papa, before I come home for the summer, I would like you to come to Hampton and have dinner at the pastor's house. He and his family and the members of the church here have been really nice to me, and there's somebody special that I would like you to meet."

W. J.'s curiosity got the best of him. "All right, son. I can't say I haven't been wondering about the folks you've been keeping company with."

"Can you come this Thursday evening?"

"I'll be there."

"Miss Eleanor is welcome to come, too."

"That's good, son, but she has other things to tend to."

William hung up knowing he should have said more about his intentions. W. J. had always discouraged him and his brothers from being corrupted by wayward women. Then again, he hadn't done that, so what reason would he have to complain? After all, Goldie was a God-fearing woman raised in the church.

***

On Thursday evening, William climbed Pastor Davis's porch steps with W. J. on his heels. He took off his hat, but before he knocked on the door, he closed his eyes and began to pray silently. *Lord, please be a guide on my father's lips today. In the name of Jesus.*

The door flew open, and Sister Sarah stood there smiling widely, wearing a purple and black dress with large light blue flowers it.

"Come on in, gentlemen!" Sarah said, opening the door with one arm while she held the other open in a welcome. Pastor Davis stood behind her in the foyer. William stepped in, and W. J. followed with squinted eyes.

"Welcome to our home, Pastor Freeman. We've been anxious to meet you," Pastor Davis said, extending his hand. "You have a wonderful son. I'm sure you're very proud of him."

"Yes, I am. Thank you," W. J. said. "And, please, call me W. J."

"Certainly," Pastor Davis said. "Call me John."

Sarah clapped her hands together. "The food is hot and ready. Come, let's sit down."

She led the men down the narrow hallway and then left into the dining room. She told them all where to sit, with both pastors at the ends of the table, and then fussed over the centerpiece. At that moment, Goldie walked into the dining room looking as pretty as a picture. She wore a crisp white dress with bright yellow daisies scattered down the front. William moved toward her and took her hand.

"This is my daughter, Goldie," Sarah said, beaming with pride. "Goldie, this is William's father, Pastor W. J. Freeman."

"It's nice to meet you, sir," Goldie said with a polite nod.

Sarah clapped her hands together again. "Everybody, sit down. Goldie and I will put the food on the table."

After Sarah and Goldie left the dining room, it became awkwardly quiet for the two men who talked for a living. The only sound was the faint ticking of the grandfather clock in the hallway. The silence made William nervous, and his right leg began to jump. He tapped his fingers on the table, wishing he would have spoken to his father in private. But he had put it off again and again, and now it was too late. He wasn't sure what W. J.'s reaction was going to be, but he figured it would be better if the women weren't there to see it. There was no time to break it to him gently, so he blurted it out.

"Papa, I want to marry Goldie. Pastor Davis and Miss Sarah have given me their blessings and permission to ask her to be my wife."

W. J. frowned and shifted in his chair. He took his time responding to William's news.

"You have a responsibility, son, to take your place as head of the church. It's an awesome task for which you have not adequately been prepared. It would be premature for you to be taking on the extra responsibility of a wife."

"I'm not a child. I can decide when I want to get married. Goldie is the one I want. 'An excellent wife, who can find? She is far more precious than jewels,' Proverbs 31:10," William said, mocking his father's old habit of quoting Scriptures.

"What do you know about heading a household, boy? You're still eating from my table," W. J. argued. "That means you do what I tell you to do when I tell you to do it. 'Children, obey your parents in everything, for this is pleasing to the Lord," Colossians 3:20."

"This isn't your decision to make, Papa," William said, refusing to take orders from him.

Pastor Davis could see that William's father was about to lose his religion, so he chimed in before W. J. could respond. "I understand your hesitancy, W. J. William should have discussed this with you before now, but this is a conversation for you two to have in private. I must ask that you respect my home and my family and have this meal in peace."

The door from the kitchen opened, and Sarah and Goldie walked in loaded down with steaming bowls and platters.

"Here it is, piping hot and ready to eat!" Sarah said.

They put the dishes in the center of the table and took their seats, Sarah on the corner next to John, and Goldie next to William.

"As our guest, would you bless the food?" Sarah asked, smiling at W. J.

W. J. bowed his head and began to pray. "'Bless the LORD, O my soul, and all that is within me, bless His holy name.' Bless, O Lord, this food we are about to eat; bless the hearts and the hands that have prepared it. We thank You for this time of fellowship, and Father we thank you for the priest's anointing for 'He is able to deal gently with those who are ignorant and misguided, since he himself is beset by weakness,' Hebrews 5:2. Amen."

"Amen," Sarah said, looking at her husband and then casting a wary eye at W. J.

"You've outdone yourself again!" John said. After taking a slice of ham from a platter, he passed it to William.

"We don't eat the pig. He's a filthy animal," W. J. said rudely, turning up his lip.

"Pardon us, W. J. My wife wasn't aware of your restrictions. Please help yourself to some of the hen and some dressing," John said. "You know, Mark 7:15 says, 'You are not defiled by what you eat; you are defiled by what you say and do.'"

W. J. grumbled under his breath and begrudgingly put the food on his plate.

"It seems as if we have offended you, W. J.," Sarah said. "Things may have gotten off on the wrong foot. William has made his intentions known as far as Goldie is concerned, so maybe we should clear the air and get along as family."

W. J. set his fork aside and said, "Well, ma'am, this is the first I've heard of these intentions, and I'll admit it has caught me by surprise. William may have gotten a little ahead of himself."

"I'm not a child, Pop. I know what I want," William insisted.

"Unfortunately, life is not always about what you want. There are many things that have to be considered before you take on a wife. You don't even have a place of your own to live. I think you need to slow down and think this thing through."

Goldie kept her eyes on her plate without saying a word. There was no need. William wanted her, and she wanted him; nothing was going to change that. They were going to be married sooner or later, one way or another. And after today, she was positive she wasn't about to live in a house with or near his father.

John, always the peacemaker, smiled. "I can't argue with anything you've said, W. J. It makes sense. These young people are in love, and we are here to help them in any way that we can. William has shown me that he is a good man, and I can see that he comes from a good family. Why don't we finish our meal? I'm sure things will work themselves out."

Sarah breathed a sigh of relief, deciding not to give W. J. a piece of her mind. "You're right, John. After all, Rome wasn't built in a day."

After that, there wasn't much conversation during the meal. No one knew how to salvage what was left of the congenial ambiance. W. J. started eating like he had a bus to catch, and the rest of them at the table followed suit, as if they were the ones who had to get him to the bus station on time.

"That was a delicious meal, Sister Sarah. Thank you and Brother John for the warm generosity and hospitality that you've shown my son and me today." W. J. stood up and gave William a look that told him it was time to go. "I'm sorry to say that I must rush off this evening. I have a meeting in the morning, so I'll be driving back to Richmond tonight."

John stood up. "I wish you could stay longer. We didn't get much of a chance to talk."

"Another time," W. J. said, reaching for his hat.

"I'm sure we will," Sarah said, keeping her seat.

William leaned over to Goldie. "I'll see you tomorrow," he whispered.

***

This wasn't the way William wanted the evening to end. He wanted his father's blessing.

"Pop, I brought you here to meet my future wife and her family, and you embarrassed me," William said as soon as they were in the car.

W. J. started the car and looked over at his son. "I'm not the one who embarrassed you; you did that all by yourself."

William stared back at the Davises' house. "After the way you acted, they may not even want Goldie to marry me."

W. J. laughed. "Good, then they'll be doing you a favor."

"What are you talking about?" William asked, indignant. "I love her and want to be with her. Why would you want to mess that up for me?"

"She's no good for you, son. I know her kind."

"How can you say that? You don't even know her!"

"She's too pretty. A pretty woman is nothing but heartache and trouble, just like your mama was. This Davis girl is not the kind of woman you need to stand by you in the walk you're going on."

"Well, she's the only one I want."

"Pray about it, Will, and you'll get over it. It's nothing but the devil trying to tempt you."

"You're right, Pop. It's the devil, but he's not on my back, he's on yours."

W. J. brought the car to a sudden stop. "Boy, you must have forgotten who you're talking to! You better watch your mouth, or I'll forget you're my son! I see she done already got you half crazy, thinking you a man and disrespecting your father. One thing you need to know is there's a whole lot more to being a man than finding a woman who'll let you lay down with her."

"Goldie and I haven't done anything wrong. It doesn't matter what you say. I am a grown man, and you can't stop me from marrying who I want! Maybe it'll be best if I don't come home. I think I'm gonna stay here for a while."

"No, William. Now listen to me," W. J. urged, trying to get

his son back on his side. "I know about those kinds of folks. They can't wait to get their hooks in you and have you doing their bidding."

"Isn't that what you want, too?" William hollered.

W. J. knew he had said too much. Most of his fury had exploded out of jealousy. He resented another man, especially another preacher, insinuating himself into their lives and trying to commandeer William. W. J. had already lost two sons; and if he pushed too hard, he would lose another one, the only one left to fulfill his legacy. What he needed to do was to put some time and distance between William and Goldie.

"All right, William. I'm done with it," W. J. said when he stopped at a traffic light. "Give yourself a year. Enroll in seminary after you graduate. When the year is up, if you want to marry that girl, go ahead. I won't stand in your way. And while you're over there judging me, remember this: I only wanted to save you from making the same mistakes I did."

"You don't have to worry about that, Pop," William said, still too mad to look his father in the eyes. "I won't."

W. J. chuckled to himself over the sweet ignorance of youth and pressed his foot on the accelerator.

***

The time and the distance between William and Goldie while he attended Virginia Union Theological Seminary wasn't enough to separate them. Halfway through his second year, William told Goldie to set a wedding date. Within a month, Sarah was busy planning the wedding she had always wanted.

William and Goldie's wedding was a big to-do in Richmond, the marriage of the children of two well-known preachers. W. J. officiated, and John gave his daughter away. Among the 300 guests in attendance were all the big shots and society folks. Standing with her handsome groom, Goldie looked like a princess out of a fairytale. Everything- the flowers, the decorations at the church, the reception venue, the food, and the music- was top of the line. It was a happy day for Thompson Boulevard Church of God in Christ and Bethel Christian. The newlyweds were showered with expensive gifts and money, enough money for William to get the place of their own that he'd promised Goldie.

W. J. watched all the festivities with skepticism. He saw the marriage as William trying to pull away from him, and he needed to tighten his grip. Now it was him wanting his own home; next, he would want his own church. W. J.'s thoughts stirred him to make an announcement.

"Ladies and gentlemen, I'm delighted that you all could share this wonderful occasion with our families today. My son has made me a very proud man. It's been my privilege to watch him grow and mature into the man he is today. The years passed so quickly. I remember so well the day I was standing right where he is today.

"I've been a farmer, and I know that you can't leave old fruit on the tree or it won't produce new fruit. William and his beautiful new wife will be going to Mexico for their honeymoon. When they return, William will be installed as the senior pastor of Thompson Boulevard COGIC. I've had my day in the sun, and now it's time to make way for new fruit."

The crowd grew quiet, stunned into silence, until W. J. began to clap. More of the guests joined in, and the crescendo of applause became a standing ovation. William's tightly balled fists dug his short nails into his palms. Once again, W. J. had thrown him off his feet; it wasn't physical this time, but it was just as effective. Rising from his chair beside his bride, William searched for words as the guests anxiously waited for his reaction.

"This is much more than I expected today. To have the woman I love agree to spend the rest of her life with me was enough, but to hear my father say that he trusts me to lead the church beside him makes this an even greater day for me. I humbly accept this honor with the same enthusiasm and joy that I have in taking Goldie as my wife."

William raised a glass of champagne to his wife, and the room erupted in applause. Sarah signaled to the band to play before W. J. could steal any more attention from the happy couple.

***

William had been with other girls before he met Goldie, even though technically he was as much a virgin as she was when they got married. On the wedding night, when they finally got to make it into the end zone, he thought he had died and gone to heaven. For the first months of their marriage, he couldn't seem to get enough of heaven. He spent most nights making love to her, and most of his days were spent preparing for peaceful protests with students at Virginia Union University. He shouldn't have been surprised when Goldie told him she was pregnant five months later, but he was. On the next Saturday afternoon when he went to the church to work on his sermon, he shared the news with his father.

William walked into W. J.'s office and stood in front of his desk.

"Goldie's going to have a baby, Pop," he said soberly, as if he were making a confession.

W. J. replayed the words in his head before he sprung out of his chair.

"That's wonderful news, son! Congratulations!" he said, hugging William and slapping his back. "I'm so happy for you!"

"I'm happy too, but the timing isn't the greatest. The movement is picking up steam, and I don't want to have to worry about Goldie and a baby."

"Family comes first, Will. You have big responsibilities: this church, your wife, and now a baby. You can't put any of that in jeopardy. You know these white folks around here are crazy."

"Times are changing, and white folks have to change with them, whether they like it or not. They can't have our money without paying us our respect."

W. J. didn't approve of William's efforts in the movement because he wasn't totally against segregation. As far as he was concerned, he didn't want to have anything to do with a white man unless it was strictly business. They could have all their stores and restaurants as long as they left the black ones alone in peace.

"You can't prove anything by forcing them to let you in their schools, stores, or restaurants. If you want to prove something, show them you don't need to go to their schools, shop in their stores, or eat their nasty food. You win when you get your own."

"We want to do that, but how can we if we don't get an equal shot at it? That's what the Brown court decision said, separate ain't equal."

"There are many wars out here to fight, son. We all have our battles. Yours is to fight for the Lord, to praise His holy name, to see that His word is exalted. Don't get sidetracked trying to fight other men's battles."

"The church is front and center in the Civil Rights Movement. It's about helping our people who are still being oppressed in this country almost 100 years after Lincoln freed the slaves. The Bible says that God is our refuge. If the people can't come to the church for help, then the church is not fulfilling its purpose."

"Oh, my Jesus!" W. J. said, throwing his head back and pounding his desk. "Don't preach that to me! I've seen the evils of this country. White folks don't give a damn about killing. They took my father and your brothers. We're here to be a solace and a protector, not to put our people in harm's way."

"God has always delivered his people, Pop!" William said, his voice filled with passion. "It has always been a man of God who led them. God chose Moses to deliver His people out of Egypt and Joshua to lead them into the Promised Land. Now He's calling the current men of God to lead the fight to free the people from the taskmaster of our present day, what we know as Jim Crow."

"You need to understand that God's chosen leaders are not all assigned the same duties. Some are called to fight, others to feed. You, me, my father, his father before him, and scores of generations have a permanent anointing to minister as high priests. We are His servants designated to proclaim His Word."

"The men of God can't hide in the church. Jesus said, 'I am sending you out as lambs amidst wolves.' We have to go outside of the church to do His will, despite danger or fear."

"William, you have a baby on the way, and the future of this church is on your shoulders. You can't afford to put your life on the line. There always has to be someone to pick up the pieces, and that person is you."

"I have to do what God tells me to do," William said, turning to leave the office.

"Yes, you do, son. I won't argue against that. Just make sure you're not hearing only what you want to hear."

***

A month later, before her belly had a chance to round out, Goldie had a miscarriage. William took it as a sign that he should be more involved in the movement. He went to more meetings under the guise of attending lectures. There were many conversations and informal debates among the students on which philosophy best suited their aims in demanding their equal rights, Malcolm X's or Martin Luther King Jr.'s. It was no secret that even though W. J. was reluctant to get involved either way, he agreed with every word that Malcolm X spoke. That may have been the reason William was more receptive to Martin's point of view.

The energy and urgency of youth had William convinced that he could make some kind of difference. Logically, he still hadn't made peace with his brothers dying without a reason or effecting some change. He didn't want that to happen to him. So, when he heard Martin Luther King, Jr. was coming to speak at Virginia Union University he planned to be there.

William didn't tell Goldie where he was going because he didn't want her to worry. She was supportive of the movement, but she wasn't the type who wanted to rock the boat. She wasn't alone in her thinking. Most church people didn't want to bring negative attention to themselves. None of them wanted to be the next target for their churches or homes burning or being bombed. Those with the most to lose were less likely to take the risk.

Inside the lecture hall, William listened intently as Martin Luther King Jr. explained the morality of nonviolence and how it exposes the morality, or lack thereof, of the oppressor and how the violent are confused by nonviolence and don't know how to handle it. For those reasons, it was the most appropriate defense to fight segregation. King emphasized that we shouldn't lower ourselves and stoop to the level of violence and hatred. He told the group to love their enemies through *agape* love, the love of God that moves in the human heart. Even though it was a cold evening in January, the depth of his faith and commitment touched the students at VUU, and the fire within their hearts and minds was stoked.

The next day, the group began training for a nonviolent protest at downtown department stores. On February 22, 1960, over 30 students headed to Thalhimer's Department Store in the center of downtown Richmond. They walked into the main floor lunch counters and demanded to be served. They were denied service and asked to leave. The students kept their seats. Minutes later, police came into the store with dogs, threatening the students with arrest if they didn't leave. The students refused, were arrested, taken to jail, and charged with trespassing.

This would be the first mass arrest of the Civil Rights Movement. William was there as a member of the NAACP when they arrived with the funds to pay the bail for the students. He stood outside the jail at the front of the blocks-long line of black people on the street in support of the students. Ignoring the police on horses, those with German shepherds, and those with sticks and guns, the crowd waved and cheered the students as they emerged from the jail. William grasped hands and patted backs in solidarity, but he had the feeling that he should have done more, that he should have been sitting at that counter with them.

***

William became more active in the movement, joining other young black clergy members in the Southern Christian Leadership Council (SCLC). He wanted to become like them, movers and shakers who traveled to wherever the hotspots of protests might pop up in the country to right the wrongs of injustice. He could see the movement was significant, relevant to the future of the equality of black people in the country, and he wanted to play an important role in that progress. That accomplishment would be a reason to hold his head high and be proud about, something his father couldn't give him.

At the same time, W. J. needed to control his son, and that was the reason he hadn't totally relinquished the church to him. What he told William was that he wanted him to have the time and flexibility to finish his theological studies. He proposed that the two of them alternate preaching on Sundays and share the other responsibilities and needs of their congregation. This plan worked to W. J.'s advantage. Whenever William wanted to participate in a protest or a direct-action campaign, W. J. knew he could always shift some duty or meeting to cloud up William's schedule.

Goldie had no complaints with the arrangement. She smoothly made the adjustment to pastor's wife, sliding into the role of first lady like a comfortable pair of shoes—stylish ones at that. W. J.'s second wife, Eleanor, had never been at ease with that privileged perch. She preferred to be lost in the center of the sanctuary than to sit prominently on the third pew on the left. Goldie never sat anywhere else. Being trained at her mother's hip, she enjoyed the exalted status that came with her position.

Then another big opportunity came for William to put his principles into action. It came after the Supreme Court ruled on the Boynton *v.* Virginia case. The Student Non-Violent Coordinating Committee (SNCC) was already considering a follow-up campaign to test the ruling. William brought it up to Goldie first while she was watching the story on the news.

"We can't let it stop there," William said, scooting to the edge of the sofa.

"What do you mean?" Goldie asked, focused on the television screen.

"That ruling means nothing if things stay the same," he answered, fired-up. "Even before that brother was arrested at the Trailways terminal for trying to eat in the white section of the restaurant, the law forbid any interstate bus, train, or motor vehicle to unjustly discriminate. But he was still arrested, fined, and found guilty of trespassing. The Interstate Commerce Act is useless unless it is enforced. It has to pass the test everywhere, North and South."

"So what test is that?" Goldie asked, not really interested.

"We're talking about a group of us riding a bus out of here, going down through the Carolinas to Georgia, then Alabama and Mississippi, and stopping in New Orleans."

"Why don't y'all boycott riding the buses like they did in Montgomery? That worked."

"That took over a year, and why should we have to get off the bus to exercise our rights? Besides, the law against interstate discrimination is already in place. We just have to change the minds and hearts in the South and get them to accept the inevitable."

"That's sounds dangerous to me, Will. White folks down there don't care nothing about killing a negro. They do it to pass the time."

"That's exactly why we have to do it. They have to abide by the laws just like we do. It's 1961. This craziness has got to end!"

"That's what black folks say. Those others, they're singing another tune. Remember when they told the white folks here in Virginia they had to desegregate schools? You know what happened? They took the white kids out of the schools. When they tried to integrate the library, they closed it. When they reopened it, they had taken the chairs out. There are no limits to what they will do to see things stay like they are."

"All that means is that we have to be twice as determined to see that change is gonna come."

***

W. J. didn't argue or try to talk William out of participating in the Freedom Rides. He sat on his porch, listening quietly without questions or criticism. But with each sentence, his chest rose higher and higher as if he were out of breath. William noticed it, paused, and then kept talking. W. J. threw his head back to open his air passage, but it didn't help. William figured this was another of his father's ploys to keep him from being involved in the movement, so he turned and looked across the yard. Then William heard the thud. When he turned around, he saw his father sprawled on the porch.

The doctors said it was adult-onset asthma and that W. J.'s condition could be controlled with an inhaler. For W. J.'s part, he used his condition to further control William.

"Your first responsibility is to be a good shepherd and to guard your flock from the wolves," W. J. said, clutching his inhaler and looking pitiful. "If I can't be there, you have to stand in the gap."

"I agree, Pop. That means I can't always stay where it's safe. There are times the shepherd has to go out and fight the wolves. 'The good shepherd gives his life for the sheep,' John 10:11."

"I won't argue against the word," W. J. told him. But somehow, maybe simply by coincidence, he would always become ill and have to take to his bed whenever William thought about going more than 50 miles from Richmond.

William, feeling powerless, had to watch the drama of the Freedom Riders unfold on the television from his living room sofa. Beside him, Goldie breathed a sigh of relief. A few miles away, W. J. smiled and breathed a sigh of satisfaction.

***

For the next 18 months, black people in Richmond boycotted stores with picket lines and conducted more sit-ins. The Civil Rights Movement was gaining momentum all through the South. On June 5, William got a call saying that over 200 protestors had stormed into Danville City Hall, demanding that blacks get more city jobs and services. A judge had indicted three leaders of the protest under the grounds of the John Brown Statute, alleging that they had incited violence against whites; their bail was set at $5,000 each. The leaders of the Danville Christian Progressive Association were sending out a call for assistance.

William had driven to Danville several times in the last two years with the NAACP, but the blacks there wanted faster results than filing court cases could bring. He had just been there a couple of months back in March when Martin Luther King had been there to speak. William had formed friendships in Danville with Rev. Thurman Echols and Rev. Wyatt Tee Walker. Their group planned a series of nonviolent protests that had begun early in May. He wanted to be there to assist, but he was hesitant to risk upsetting his family.

Four days later, on Sunday morning, William was still debating whether he should go down to Danville and get involved. Protests had been going on there for almost a week, but he didn't want to upset his father or Goldie. W. J. was pretending he could hardly breathe most of the time, and Goldie was pregnant again. To be on the safe side, the doctor had placed her on bed rest for the first trimester. The message William had prepared the night before was more for himself than anyone else.

William stood and slowly approached the podium. His eyes scanned the congregation from left to right and from the front pew to the back pew. The black faces of his congregation filling the sanctuary spanned several generations. He saw those whose hair had turned grey and whose skin was loose and wrinkled. He saw those who were tired from working long hours and raising families, those young and bursting with restless energy, and the innocent babies unaware of the world's struggles.

"Brothers and sisters, our people have traveled along an awesome journey. We have gone through many things and had more than our share of suffering, yet our trials are not over. We are continually persecuted. We have a ways to go to get to our true destination.

"In Luke, Chapter 6, Jesus stood before his disciples and a crowd of people wanting to be healed. Looking at his disciples, he said, 'Blessed are you who are poor, for yours is the kingdom of God, blessed are you who hunger now, for you will be satisfied. Blessed are you who weep now, for you will laugh. Blessed are you when people hate you, when they exclude you and insult you and reject your name as evil, because of the Son of Man.' That is good news, Christian friends. We have a Savior, an ever-present help in times of trouble. So whatever battles are ahead of us, all we have to do is remember, 'The LORD is my rock, my fortress and my deliverer; the God of my strength, in Him I will trust, my shield and the horn of my salvation, my stronghold and my refuge, my Savior, You save me from violence,' 2 Samuel 22:2-3." William took his seat as the people sang and worshiped.

On Monday morning, William was in his office at the church when he received another call telling him that more protestors had been arrested and that a prayer vigil was planned for that evening. That was all he needed to hear to make up his mind. Danville was only 140 miles south of Richmond; he could drive there in less than three hours, be there for the prayer vigil, and drive back before midnight. He picked up the phone and called his home number.

"Hello," Goldie answered, sounding upbeat.

"Hi, sweetie. I wanted to call and let you know that there is a prayer vigil in Danville this evening. I'm going to ride down there, but I'll be back tonight."

Goldie hesitated, wary of William going out of town for the movement. "Are you sure about this? From what I hear on the news, things are getting bad there."

"You don't have to worry; I'll be back tonight."

"All right, Will, be careful," she said, hanging up the phone.

***

William parked outside of the Bibleway Church on Grant Street where a large group had gathered to march down to the court house. They all lined up with Rev. Campbell's wife, leading, men, women, teenagers and adults, shoulder to shoulder, in a dozen rows that stretched across the street from sidewalk to sidewalk. They began at a steady pace, chanting as they marched.

When the group got to Main Street, the area around the jail was congested with cars and crowds of people. Next door at city hall, peaceful demonstrators lined the steps. The group marched around the jail once while singing a hymn. They were about to circle the building again when squad cars pulled up and blocked their way. In an instant, state troopers and local police surrounded the marchers.

Rev. McGhee stood in the alley between the jail and city hall and began to pray. Suddenly, a voice hollered out, "Let 'em have it!" Firetrucks pulled up in front. Then there was the sound of water rushing as it shot toward them. William and most of the protestors moved forward into the alley with the others to protect themselves; but at the rear end of the alley, more police cars blocked them in. They were trapped. That's when all hell broke loose. Police and garbage collectors, who had been freshly deputized, began to attack, swinging billy clubs against the heads of anybody with black skin—male and female, child and adult.

None of the training sessions and role-playing about how to react to violence had prepared William for the abject hatred and disdain he saw that day. He felt and heard the crack of the club when it crashed against his skull. Instinctively, he grabbed his head with both hands. Then he felt another blow across his back and elbow. He dropped his arms to fend off those blows when another nightstick made contact. His knees turned to jelly, and he fell hard against the concrete. He couldn't block the blows, so he closed his mind and visualized his brothers, Philip and Franklin, kneeling beside him to block the pain.

William laid in the alley, watching the melee above him, seeing a man fall near him, and then another a few feet away. Parked cars held others on their feet. People covered in blood were being handcuffed and dragged away by troopers. Mist filled the air before he felt the full pressure of the water when the fire hose was turned on him. Through the gusts of water, he saw some of the men take off their shirts and raise their arms in defiance. Unable to get up, the high-pressure hoses pushed him alongside the sidewalk like a piece of trash to be washed away.

***

Newspaper headlines called the savage attack on the demonstrators in Danville "Bloody Monday." William was one of 47 who were badly injured and taken to the hospital. He was still unconscious the next day when Martin Luther King came to the city as a show of support for those who had been brutalized. He woke up on June 12, the same day that Medgar Evers was shot and killed.

William heard the familiar stern voice above him. "Wake up, son," W. J., said urgently.

William peered through the slit in one eye and saw W. J. staring down at him. His swollen lip, which was stuck to his teeth, kept him from speaking.

W. J. leaned closer to his face. "You're in the hospital, son. You were beaten pretty bad. You got a cracked skull, fractured rib, broken arm, and Lord only knows how many bumps and bruises. If it wasn't for God's grace, you'd be lying in the morgue."

Scenes from the attack at the protest vigil rushed back into his head, and he winced from the pain that radiated from every part of his body.

"You've been unconscious for two days. When I first got the call, I thought it was a mistake. I didn't even know you were down here. They wouldn't tell me if you were alive or dead. I called Goldie, and she insisted that I bring her with me. When she saw you looking like this, she passed out. They got her here in another hospital room."

"Is she okay?" William asked, grunting through his throat without moving his mouth.

W. J. nodded. "Eleanor's with her. She's all right."

"The baby?" William strained to ask, his eyes pleading for reassurance.

W. J. responded in a hushed tirade. "That girl is weak, Will! I told you she wasn't the one for you, but you didn't listen. How many times have I warned you not to get involved in these protests? But you ignored me on that, too. Now you know there's always a price to pay for disobedience."

William wanted to cry from the tongue-lashing, cry like he did when he was a boy and W. J. whipped him with a belt. That's exactly how he felt, as if he were taking another beating for disobeying his father. The only difference was, now he was a man, and he refused to shed a tear and give W. J. the satisfaction of being right. Instead, he turned his face to the wall and willed himself into unconsciousness.

***

It took about six weeks for William to physically recover. Mentally, he would never be the same. Something was broken inside of him that couldn't be put together again. Possibly, it was the tiny chips on the edges of his faith that would forever be lost. Danville was their Jericho. They had marched around the city, and they had prayed, chanted, and sang with the courage of their convictions, but the walls didn't come down. He and so many others were beaten down. He had trusted God to protect him and his fellow demonstrators, prayed that no harm would come to them; but they were damaged, and his family was damaged. He couldn't understand why God had abandoned them.

Sitting at the side of the pulpit, he gazed over at Goldie as he listened to W. J. preaching. Even with the sadness behind her eyes, she was still the prettiest girl in the sanctuary.

"God is not on our timetable; we're on his," W. J. stated firmly. "The Bible tells us to 'wait upon the Lord.'"

Goldie smiled at William when he caught her eye. That simple gesture gave him hope; it soothed him. After all, they were young, and she was stronger than W. J. believed she was. They had only been married for four years. Why were they pressuring themselves to have a child so quickly anyway?

"Yes, fellow saints of God," W. J. said, turning to William and then to the choir. "God had to teach the children of Israel patience and faithfulness. They had short attention spans. Once they had their freedom, they would forsake the Lord time and time again, breaking His commandments and worshiping other gods. The Lord who had delivered them from slavery wasn't enough for them. They wanted a king. First Samuel 8:19-20 says, 'You will shed bitter tears because of this king you are demanding but the Lord will not help you.' But the people refused to listen to Samuel's warning. 'Even so we still want a king,' they said, 'For we want to be like nations around us. He will govern us and lead us to battle.'

"Saints, that was the very mistake that kept them fighting war after war for years to come. Foolishly, they didn't want to put their faith wholly in the Lord; they wanted a man, merely flesh and blood, to rule over them and to guide them. Let's not make that same mistake, saints, as the answer to our struggles. These are desperate times. I know that we as a people are being persecuted from all sides, with trials on every hand, and the burden of injustice is breaking our backs. But remember that old hymn that says, 'On Christ the solid rock I stand, all other ground is sinking sand. My hope is built on nothing less than Jesus' blood and righteousness. I dare not trust the sweetest frame but wholly lean on Jesus' name.'"

"Amen," William said, standing beside his father.

Shouts of praise filled the room, the organist began to play, and the congregation rose to its feet.

***

Much to W. J.'s satisfaction, William refocused his attention on the church and the needs of the congregation. He had even missed several NAACP meetings. On August 28, 1963, a parade of buses rolled out of Richmond headed up to Washington, DC, for the March on Washington where Martin Luther King Jr. was scheduled to speak. But William dutifully accepted that his place was at the midweek service. His mind was stayed on Jesus.

Then an unspeakable tragedy happened on the 15th of September. William was sitting in the pulpit, waiting to preach, when Deacon Wilson stumbled up the altar and handed him a folded piece of paper. William read the note, but instead of passing it to W. J. seated next to him, he crushed the paper into a tight wad in his palm and squeezed it, wishing it would disappear.

William got up and stepped to the podium. "Brothers and sisters, I have just received dreadful news from Alabama. The 16th Street Baptist Church in Birmingham was bombed this morning, and four innocent young girls were murdered."

A guttural cry went up from one of the mothers. "Have mercy, Jesus!" another cried out.

"The devil is busy, brothers and sisters!" William said, his voice full of emotion. "'God is our refuge and strength, a very present help in trouble. Therefore, we will not fear, though the earth be removed, and though the mountains be carried into the midst of the sea. Though the waters thereof roar and be troubled, though the mountains shake with the swelling thereof. . . . God is in the midst of her, she shall not be moved. . . . The Lord of hosts is with us, the God of Jacob is our refuge,' Psalm 46.

"The evils of Jim Crow, prejudice, and discrimination continue to rise against us. The Bible tells us that Satan is strong, and jealously guards his possessions. It also tells us that Jesus is stronger. We as Christians have the power to bind up the strong man in Jesus' name and claim the victory. It hasn't been easy, and I'm sure that's not going to change; but we have to be faithful.

"This circumstance reminds me of Paul on his journey across the sea to go into the great city of Macedonia. It was a vision in the night that beckoned him to go there and to save that city, to bring them the gospel. Macedonia was the place between the East and the West, Europe and Asia. It was his mission to unite the factions of the civilized nations in one, in Christ. He wasn't welcomed there, church. The word says, 'When we arrived in Macedonia there was no rest for us; outside, trouble was on every hand and around us; within us, our hearts were full of dread and fear.' We all recognize those feeling, brothers and sisters. We feel that way today. We've been hurt, cut to the bone. And even in the depths of our despair, we can't give up the fight. God will give us the victory."

"Amen!" someone shouted as the organist began to play. The church hummed and moaned together as they grieved over the horrors of the day.

***

"That was a horrible thing that happened," W. J. said to William in his office after the service. "We have to understand that God's ways are not our ways. We have to be patient."

"I can't see how you can say that, Pop. From the time your own daddy was killed, you've kept two loaded rifles, one behind the front door and one under your bed; but you say be patient and leave it in the hands of the Lord."

"The difference is I'm not looking for a fight. If a white man comes into my home, I will defend my home; if they come into the church, I will defend the church. I will defend them both with my life. Do I want to sit at the table with them? No. Do I want to mix in with people who are so filled with hate that they murder without remorse? No, I don't."

"You can't just take care of your own. That's not what the Bible teaches. You have to care about all the people. You can't expect me to sit in the comforts of my home while others, even teenagers, fight the fight I should be in."

"That's the same things your brothers thought, and it got them killed. That wasn't their fight to be in either, and it didn't change anything."

"You want me to hide behind my brothers. I can't do that; it's not right."

"You're the only one I have left, Will. The responsibility for the church and preaching God's word is on your shoulders; and when you have a son, the responsibility will rest on his. Focus your time and energy on starting your family."

William took off his robe, put on his jacket, and hurried to find Goldie. He needed to get home, where he could think without his father in his ear. The question that echoed in his mind throughout the rest of the day and through the night was, How can a man of God sit back and watch the people suffer and not act? Wasn't most of the work of Christ done outside of the church walls? God wanted more for His people.

William returned to the NAACP meetings and participated in voter registration drives, anything that would further the movement, except none of his efforts seemed to calm the restlessness that was growing inside of him. He wanted to be on the frontlines, to feel the power he felt marching to the jail in Danville. Watching King, Abernathy, and Adam Clayton Powell on television and not being able to contribute or mobilize his own congregation made him feel more helpless than he did when he was facedown on the ground taking a beating.

***

William's helplessness grew as the months passed, and then a year, and then another year. What did it mean to be a man if he wasn't free to make his own decisions about what he wanted to do? W. J.'s reliance on him felt more like control; he was a puppet on a string. He could teach and preach, but W. J. kept the finances of the church off limits from him. On top of that, as hard as William tried, Goldie hadn't gotten pregnant again, and his father was always on his back about it.

"It's in God's hands," Goldie kept telling William. "He'll bless us when He sees fit. Where is your faith?"

William thought about faith and its purpose. He knew it required complete trust and belief in God, whom he had not seen. Then Malcolm X was assassinated, seemingly by his own people. That's when his thoughts were flooded with questions, not about the existence of God, because he had complete trust and belief in Him; his questions were about God's will. What was God's plan, and what did He want from him? From what William could see, the strong men God chose to use were taken down, while other strong men were not chosen to be used.

William's faith was being tested, his faith in his own abilities and his purpose. His questions caused him to turn on himself, questioning his significance, questioning his manhood, and questioning his worthiness. All the questions filled him with doubt and insecurity, things he hadn't felt since he was a boy. Playing football, he was a winner; now when it really counted, he was a loser. In his spirit, he thought he should be a conqueror. He couldn't go into the jungle and slay a beastly animal or go into war and defeat the enemy. Nevertheless, he had something he needed to prove.

William didn't intentionally set out to do wrong; the temptation had always been there, only now he was caught in a weakened state. For years, he had ignored the innuendos and the invitations that might have led to compromising situations. But now something inside him clicked, a switch flipped. Whether it was turned on or off didn't matter; things had changed. In his mind, it didn't have anything to do with Goldie. He loved her and wouldn't intentionally do anything that would hurt her.

All the same, it was becoming close to impossible to ignore Mamie Carson sitting on the fifth pew to the left of Goldie. She always wore bright colors-yellow, lilac, pink, and light blue-against her cocoa-brown skin that reminded him of wild flowers begging to be picked. She gave him a certain inexplicable energy when she shouted amen and when she fanned herself so fast, as if she were burning up. He thought he could feel the heat from her up in the pulpit.

"The Lord will supply our needs if we put our trust in Him," William said with raised arms. "Manna rained down for the Hebrew people for 40 years while they were in the wilderness. God will not allow his people to go hungry. Thank you, Father, for feeding your people!"

"Praise Him," Deacon Wilson shouted.

Tambourines rattled, and hands clapped as the Spirit moved through the sanctuary. The aisles filled with those who were moved to run and those who were moved to dance. Mamie stood up and began to jump and flung her arms up with joy. William did his best not to look in her direction, but her cries of "Thank you" rang loudly in his ears.

"The children of Israel were full of complaints!" William yelled, bringing the congregation to a fever pitch. "Whatever God did for them it was never enough, they always wanted more. His grace is sufficient, saints. I just want to say thank you, Lord!"

The organist played, and the floor of the church rocked with the uproar as emotions were released into the air. William waved his arms high in the air. In his robe, he looked like a huge black bird ready to take flight. Then he sat down, drained, leaning his head in his hand.

W. J. finished the service, gave the benediction, and William followed him out. Together, they stood at the sanctuary door, shaking hands and chatting with members. Mamie patiently waited her turn.

"Your message touched me today, Pastor," she said, wrapping her arms around him. "I need you to pray for me. My husband is in the service, the army. I'm afraid he's going to be sent to Vietnam. I miss him so much."

"Certainly, Sister Mamie, you will be in my prayers," he said, pulling away from her embrace.

"Thank you, Pastor, but I need a special blessing. Can I speak with you privately?"

"Of course, sister, come to my office on Wednesday before Bible study."

"I'm about to go out of my mind with worry. I was hoping I could talk with you sooner."

"My schedule is clear tomorrow. What time do you want to come by?"

"I don't want to give the wrong impression to anyone here at church," she said in a hushed tone. "This is something I want to keep private. It might be better if you could come by my apartment after I get home from work. I could cook dinner for you."

Proverbs 3:5 rang in William's ears: "For the lips of an adulteress drip honey and smoother than oil is her speech." Mamie had never attempted to hide her intentions toward him, and he knew exactly what she was inviting him for. Still, her request wouldn't deter him from offering her the prayer that she obviously needed.

"That won't be necessary; I'll stop by around 7:00."

"Here's my address," she said, shaking his hand and leaving a small piece of paper in it.

W. J. watched William and Mamie out of the corner of his eye. He had seen the scenario many times and had experienced it for himself. His son was being tested. He wasn't sure whether William would resist temptation or fall short, but he hoped that this trial would shake up his marriage. He never thought Goldie was the right woman for his son; and after five years of marriage, she still hadn't given him a grandson.

***

Mamie had done everything she could do in a room full of people to entice William, but he remained steadfast and faithful, turning a blind eye to temptation. His predicament had been tolerable, flattering even, but it was becoming difficult to ignore. Mamie wasn't the only one who had set her sights on him. There seemed to be an unspoken competition going on for his affections among several women in the congregation. They tracked him like a hungry pack of wolves sensing weakness or vulnerability in their prey.

Growing weary from the monotony of his life, William was beginning to waver. It was the news of Bloody Sunday in Selma, another high-profile march where he had had to sit on the sidelines and watch. He hated that feeling. He didn't even care if they busted his head again; he wanted to be in on the action. It didn't matter whether he was on the losing side or the winning side; he just needed to be in the game. He needed the adrenaline-pumping thrill of a contest.

But the youthful exuberance that once pumped hope through William's veins and convinced him that progress and change were just around the corner was fading with each passing year. His work in the Civil Rights Movement had been limited to fights through the courts; and even though the NAACP in Virginia had filed more lawsuits than any state in the country, the resistance was strong. He felt stuck. He'd pushed and pushed, and he couldn't get anything to move. The case Loving *v.* Virginia had been appealed over a month ago, and there was no sign of a decision coming any time soon.

Everything seemed to add to William's frustrations: little things, like his tire being flat, and big things, like W. J. hounding him about Goldie not getting pregnant. The mountain of frustrations inside him seemed to reach higher and higher every day. They grew so high that the day came when he couldn't get over them. It was March 9, 1965, two days after the march. He got word that Martin Luther King was going to lead the second march from Selma to Montgomery the next day. He wanted to be there, but he couldn't. He was hemmed in by his responsibilities.

William sat across from Goldie at the dinner table, staring into his plate as he pushed two peas through gravy around in a circle with his knife.

"Is something wrong?" Goldie asked, noticing him picking at his food.

"No, I just have some things on my mind."

"Things like Selma?"

"I guess so."

"The work you're doing here in Richmond is just as important as what's going on down South, Will. What you do makes a difference. Helping to change laws is important."

William dropped his fork and got up. "I've got to go," he said, agitated.

"Wait a minute, and I'll ride with you," Goldie said, getting up.

"I'm not going to the church this evening. I have a meeting to go to."

Goldie was used to him making excuses about not coming home for dinner or leaving right after. She assumed he was involved in some protest or an SCLC meeting.

"All right, maybe it will help you feel better," she sighed, picking up his plate and staring at the uneaten food.

"Who knows? It might," he said, putting on his suit coat.

***

Sitting in his parked car, William looked at the wrinkled piece of paper with Mamie's address on it. More than two weeks had passed since she'd slipped it into his hand and invited him to come and pray for her. He hadn't gone. The logical side of his brain told him it was too dangerous of a prospect. Now he was a half block away from her apartment. The curious and imaginative side of his brain had been more convincing. He opened the car door and stepped out onto the dark, hot asphalt. He had to do something, even if it was wrong.

"I didn't expect to see you today," Mamie said, pleasantly surprised when she opened the door. "I thought you were coming over weeks ago. I cooked dinner and everything. You're quite a bit late, but I think I can warm up something."

"I've already eaten," William said, walking past her into the living room.

Mamie came up behind him, slid his jacket off his shoulders, and whispered in his ear. "I'm going to make you forget all about that 'holy' wife of yours."

He turned around in a huff and faced her. "This has nothing to do with my wife!"

"Then why are you here?" she asked, smiling seductively.

William knew he was wrong. He had regrets for what he was about to do, but he wanted to be there.

"I'll leave if that's what you want," he said, looking her in the eyes. "You're the one who invited me to come here and pray for you."

She ran her finger over his lips. "Yes, Pastor, I confess I am a sinner, and I need prayer."

"It's William. Call me by my name," his said, staring down at her.

"Can I get you something to drink, William?" she asked. "I have beer or liquor."

"A glass of water is fine."

Mamie switched out of the room, and William stood there gazing around the room. It was filled with knick-knacks crammed together on the coffee and end tables. Frames of old family pictures hung on the wall. It was quaint and comforting. Not one thing in the room represented Mamie's personality. Her place was nothing like he had imagined.

"Is this your apartment?" he asked when she came back in the room carrying two glasses of clear liquid.

"It is now. My grandmother raised my mama and uncle here and then me. But she moved back down South—Florida— —a few years ago. She can't take the cold anymore."

"You haven't changed anything since she left?"

"Only the bedroom," she said, handing him a glass. "Would you like to see it?"

William turned up his glass and took a big gulp and almost choked. "This isn't water!" he said, holding back a cough.

"I'm sorry. I must have gotten our glasses mixed up," Mamie said grinning. She took it from his hand and gave him the other one.

William had drunk beer from time to time with his buddies back at Hampton, but he had never drunk hard liquor. W. J. had preached to Philip, Franklin, and him many times about the priests and prophets stumbling in judgment from strong drink and they should leave it alone. He felt the power in the drink as it allowed him to separate himself into two men. There was the upstanding man who refrained from sin and debauchery, and there was the other man who followed Mamie into her bedroom.

Mamie drained her glass of clear liquor, then she put an album on the record player. The song that began to play was B. B. King's "Confessin' the Blues." She sang with the record, "I'd rather love you man than anyone else in town...don't you want a woman like me," while she did a sensuous dance for him as she slowly took off her clothes. "If you take me to your heart I'll be there for the rest of my days." She moved like a sidewinder snake with her arms, hips, and legs twisting and turning in opposite directions as she sang. William was spellbound. This woman was so carefree and uninhibited, everything he wanted to be. Before she could finish her song, he grabbed her by the waist and jerked her down on the bed.

William wrestled with Mamie, physically and figuratively. She thrilled him in ways he had never experienced before. He wanted to pull himself away from her and away from the sin, but the pleasure was too great, and he was too weak. He got a reprieve when the effects of the alcohol lulled her to sleep. He eased himself off the bed and gathered his clothes that had been strewn on the floor along with Mamie's. He wanted to take a shower, but he didn't want the noise of the water to wake her. He dressed quietly and tiptoed out of the bedroom, with his shoes in his hands. He put them on at the door before he let himself out.

William caught a glimpse of himself in the rearview mirror as he was driving away. His conscience confronted him, and he was remorseful. Mamie was the delicious dessert he regretted partaking soon after the last bite. He promised himself that he wouldn't succumb to her temptation again, that he would have the strength and self-control to deny his sinful desires.

***

The light in the front window let William know Goldie was still awake. He had hoped she would be asleep. He didn't want to add lying to the list of sins he had already committed that night. He knew she would ask him about the meeting, who was there and what they discussed, and he wasn't prepared to deal with the barrage of questions.

Once he came through the front door, William moved through the darkness of the house, dropping his keys on the end table in the living room. The noise rang loud in the silence. He started moving faster, like a man running in the rain trying not to get soaked.

He stuck his head in the doorway of their bedroom. "Hey, sweetie, I'm going to take a quick shower to get the smell of cigarettes off."

"How was the meeting?" she shouted after him.

The gentleness in her voice made him feel ashamed.

"I'll be there in a minute," he said, closing the bathroom door.

William dropped his clothes on the floor for the second time that evening, and his thoughts raced back to Mamie's bedroom. He shook his head to clear it and turned on the shower. The water was uncomfortably hot, but he stood there and took his punishment, scrubbing himself vigorously with the bar of soap and washcloth. He had to remove any trace of where he had been and what he had done.

He dried himself in the cloud of steam that filled the bathroom, thankful that the mirror was covered in mist and he wouldn't have to look himself in the face. He wished he could take the fog of steam around him into the bedroom to hide in, feeling self-conscious about Goldie being able to see through him. He wrapped a towel around his waist, took a deep breath to steel himself, and headed into the bedroom.

"Thank you, Lord," he murmured when he saw the bedroom light was off. The sliver of light from the moon provided an outline to the furniture in the room. He found a pair of pajama bottoms in the dresser drawer, put them on, and slid into bed.

"So what did you talk about in the meeting?" Goldie asked, propping herself up on her elbow.

William didn't turn to face her. "All the focus is on the march in Selma. A lot of my fellow clergy are going to be there. I want to be there, too. How can I be a leader for my congregation or for the people of Richmond if my feet are tied together? I have to be free to lead. I need to be able to make my own decisions."

Goldie knew where this conversation was going; she had heard it all before. She leaned back against her pillow and listened to William vent his frustrations.

"The church will be yours one day, and you won't have your father dictating your every move. You just have to be patient," she said, trying to soothe him.

"That's all I hear: 'Be patient, be patient, be patient,' and I'm tired of hearing it! I've been patient, and nothing has happened. If you want something to change, you have to change it for yourself."

"That's not in the book, Will," Goldie said, propping back up again. "The Bible says, 'They that wait upon the LORD shall renew their strength; they shall mount up with wings as eagles; they shall run and not be weary; and they shall walk, and not faint,' Isaiah 40:31. You're not the only one who has to wait. I have to wait; we all have to wait."

"You're right, Goldie," he said, finally turning to face her and giving her a quick kiss on the lips. "I'm wrong, and I'll have to pray about it."

"We can pray together," she offered.

"Don't worry about me, pumpkin. Go on to sleep," William said, patting her arm.

Goldie rolled over on her side, and William lay next to her, trying his best to keep his head filled with pure thoughts instead of the devilish ones that kept creeping in.

***

Guilt crashed down on William when he stepped into the church vestibule the next day. He barely made it to his office before he fell to his knees. He kicked the door closed with one foot and cried out, "Father, forgive me! I've sinned against You, and I've sinned against my wife. I'm a filthy rag unworthy to wipe Your feet. Pick me up, Lord, for I have stumbled. Set my feet back on solid ground, so I can walk closer to thee, Father."

William was still praying and asking for forgiveness when the door swung open.

"What are you doing wallowing in the floor and whining?" W. J. asked, standing over him.

"What difference does it make to you?" William asked, rising to his feet. "Can't a man pray in peace and privacy around here anymore?"

"Sounds more like a man screaming to get Satan off his back to me."

William moved behind his desk. "What do you want? I've got work to do."

"I know what you're going through, son. I've been through it. Every man of God has been through it. It's temptation. It rides your back like a bronco buster. The harder you try to fight it and break free, the tighter it holds on. You have to put your blinders on so you won't be distracted. You have to focus on what's ahead of you."

"Is that what you did about Mama?" William asked with contempt.

"Don't talk about things you don't know, son. You only sound ignorant. What I do know is that you're playing with fire from the depths of hell, and it will consume you and everything around you."

"I'm not a child; I'm a grown man. I know how to take care of myself."

"Uh huh, I'm sure you do. That's why you were lying in the floor hollering for help."

"I didn't call for you, Pop," William said, raising his voice. "You don't want to help me; you only want to control me. I'm not one of your animals you keep locked in a pen. The time is coming when I've got to be on my own. Too many cooks in one kitchen spoil the food. This church might not be big enough for both of us."

W. J. was a lot of things, but he wasn't a fool. His years on the battlefield had made him a master general. It was time to retreat.

"Pardon me, son," he said, softening his tone. "I didn't walk in here to make you angry. I don't want to control you. I love you, and I want the best for you. Maybe I've made some mistakes doing that. So when you pray, pray for me, too."

William nodded and W. J. walked out.

***

After his foot slip with Mamie, William prayed and fasted for the next two days, rededicating himself to the church and to his marriage. On Sunday, Mother's Day, he approached the podium to preach.

"Church, this morning, I want to talk about the most significant mother in the Bible for all Christians. That mother was Mary, the mother of our Savior, Jesus Christ. Except Jesus wasn't her only child. The Bible tells us she had four other sons-James, Joseph, Judas, Simon-and more than one sister. She had to raise at least seven children and, at some point, as a widow. With six younger children, she wasn't able to follow Jesus when it was His time to begin His ministry. Her faith had to be strong to let Him go.

"Imagine all the emotions Mary felt during the years that He traveled and preached. Hearing of His goodness to others, hearing of the miracles He performed, then hearing He was out of His mind, and that He was filled with demons. She heard of Him being praised and worshiped, and then she heard of Him being ridiculed and scorned by others. All the while, she had to stay at home while she heard of others who faithfully followed

Him, and too also hear of those plotting to take His life. That's the life of a parent, brothers and sisters, feeling so proud of your child yet humbled by the responsibility God has bestowed upon you.

"The Bible tells us that Jesus' brothers had no faith in Him, leaving Mary to hold together a divided home. She was no doubt pulled in opposite directions by the people she loved. Nevertheless, her faith never faltered, even when it seemed that Jesus' mission was greater than His loyalty to her. Brothers and sisters, my mother left me at an early age, and I missed that nurturing and unconditional love that only a mother can give.

"There are times when you have to sit back and allow your children to find their own way. You have to give them the independence to become all that God has intended them to be. That doesn't mean that you have to turn your back on your children, but there are things you can't shield them from. Whenever Jesus needed Mary, she was there, supporting him in His mission. She was there when He took His first breath, and she was there when He took his last." William stamped his foot three times and shouted, "So today we thank God for the blessings of mothers."

The congregation rose to its feet, clapping and shouting amen. Some danced, and some stood with raised arms, thanking Jesus. Goldie sat in her spot on the third pew, dabbing her eyes with a tissue. Ushers were busy fanning those who had gotten "happy." The Holy Ghost had filled the sanctuary and was moving from heart to heart. William joined in the praise at the side of the pulpit just in front of W. J.

No one paid much attention to Mamie, who had danced and shouted her way down to the front of the altar. They were all caught up in the Spirit. William had been ignoring her phone calls, and she didn't like it. She moved close enough to William to touch him. She twirled and twirled in a circle, flailing until one of her arms got tangled up in his robe. That caught William's attention, but W. J. had been watching her the whole time.

William pulled his robe away from Mamie's clutch and moved back into the pulpit to speak. "Brothers and sisters, we serve a mighty God and a merciful God, and while we are in awe of His greatness, we are more thankful for His mercies. We are all sinners and fall short of His glory. This morning, I'm so thankful that God sent His only Son, Jesus, to be birthed by His mother, Mary. So if we confess our sins, He will be faithful and just, and we will be forgiven, purified from all unrighteousness and have everlasting life. Hallelujah!"

W. J. could see that his son was under attack by this harlot dressed in white, and his useless wife wasn't any help to him. Mamie glared up at the pulpit with eyes hot enough to start a fire in any man. She was being obvious, and that was dangerous. W. J. didn't care much about William's marriage, but he knew this hussy could bring down his church. He'd seen her kind before; they never rest until they get what they want. W. J. didn't want to do it, but he had to get William out of harm's way.

After the service was over, he stayed at the church and made several phone calls.

*****

William was surprised to see W. J. standing outside his screen door when he came to see who was knocking. He could count the times his father had come to his house on one hand, even though they'd lost count of the number of times he and Goldie had invited him. He checked his watch to see how late it was.

"Is anything wrong?" William asked, worried.

"No, there's nothing wrong. I wanted to come over here and tell you that you have my blessing to have time off from the church to be part of the movement. Personally, I don't want to spend my days fighting to be in the company of a white man, but I don't want to stand in your way if it means that much to you. God has work for his servants in and outside of the church."

William was amazed. This was just what he needed. It was obvious during the Mother's Day church service that Mamie wasn't going to give him room to breathe unless it was inside her apartment bedroom. If she kept on pushing on him in public, Goldie was bound to find out. Getting out on the road for a while would allow the overheated situation to cool down.

***

A week later, William stood near the front of the demonstration that would march from Selma to Montgomery. With his arms clasped elbow to elbow with the marchers on either side of him, he felt useful and alive again. He could see Martin and Coretta King just a few steps ahead of him. That was where he wanted to be, on the front line of the movement making a difference.

Those five days and 50 miles of marching were the most thrilling of William's life. They all camped out in the yards of people supporting the march, and celebrities who participated entertained them at night. He got to hear Lena Horne and Harry Belafonte sing. He almost didn't want it to end when they made it to steps of the capitol in Montgomery. He was proud to stand there in the crowd when Martin Luther King spoke about the honorable moment in American history, where the clergy and laymen of every race and different faiths had come to Selma to support the march for the fight for the equal rights of negroes.

The march was successful but was more symbolic at that point. It was the threats, beatings, and demoralization of the previous marches that had made the real difference. President Lyndon Johnson had accepted that the Civil Rights Movement was not about to be turned around, and he signed the Voting Rights Act of 1965 before the summer was over.

The Watts Riot broke out a few weeks later over the brutal police arrest a of black man, his brother, and his mother. The riot lasted five days, and 35 people were killed. William and other members of the SCLC waited at home while Martin Luther King, Bayard Rustin, and Bernard Lee went out to Los Angeles to assess the situation. Word came back that the devastation was massive, and the living conditions of blacks there were less than deplorable. Discussions within the SCLC determined that the circumstances had escalated way past the point where the people were open to a peaceful resolution. Local blacks weren't interested in a nonviolence campaign; their manifesto was "Burn, Baby, Burn."

A rift developed in the SCLC when King, greatly affected by what he saw in Los Angeles, wanted to switch the focus onto urban issues and racial inequality for blacks living in large Northern cities. Most members objected to the change in direction, fearing it would alienate Southern white liberals who were offering much needed financial support. King opted to take the risk of tackling the neglected problems of urban blacks in the North.

William was walking on air when he was selected to join King on a People to People tour of five major cities: Chicago, Cleveland, Philadelphia, New York, and Washington, DC. The tour was to determine the location for the campaign that would bring urban poverty to the forefront.

***

"Hey, pumpkin, put on your best dress!" William hollered, bursting through the door like a cannonball. "I'm taking you out to dinner. We have to celebrate!"

"What are you talking about?" Goldie asked, rushing from the kitchen and drying her hands on her apron.

"You won't believe it; I'm going with Dr. King on a trip across the country to decide on a Northern location for his next campaign. Then we're going to set up shop to take the movement into that city."

The contagious excitement faded from her face. "That sounds like something that could take months, or even longer."

"It doesn't matter how long it takes. We're committed to changing things for poor blacks in this country, change that will last forever."

"Is this something we're going to do together, Will, or is this just another opportunity for you to leave me and the rest of your responsibilities?"

"Baby, this is about the movement. It's time to make some progress in the North; the South isn't the only place where blacks are having it hard. Things are hard for us all over the country. Inner-city ghettos are as close to hell as you can get. The SCLC wants to find out if nonviolent direct-action protests can bring about change there, too. I wouldn't mind you coming with me, but it's not a vacation. This is bigger than you and me."

"In that case, I don't think I have anything to celebrate," Goldie said, walking back to the kitchen. "As you said, it's not about me."

"Come on, pumpkin, don't be like this," he said, following her. "I'm not leaving you. Once things get settled, you can come and visit sometimes. I'll call you every day, I promise. It's just like a soldier going off to Vietnam; only it's a different fight."

"You have a choice in this, Will, and you're not choosing me."

"How can I be a man of God and live my life as a disciple of Christ if I don't go out and help His people? We have to make sacrifices to do to His work sometimes. I have to go where I can do something good and worthwhile, and I need you to support me in this."

"Why are you bothering to convince me? You had your mind made up before you got here. Go on and do whatever you want. Just know, I won't be here waiting for you to call me. I'm going back to Hampton. My daddy is sick, and my mama needs my support more than you do."

"I don't want things to be like this between us," William said, anxiously. "You're my wife, and I love you. I need you to understand what this means."

"Pray for my understanding," Goldie said, turning back to the sink to wash the dishes. "I'll pray for yours, too."

William walked back out of the house and sat on the porch steps. He knew he was hurting Goldie, but what she didn't know is that he would probably hurt her more if he stayed. Mamie was constantly calling him at church and making up reasons to come and see him. Once, she even took off her clothes in his office and begged him to touch her. She was a sexy, passionate woman, and he was finding it harder and harder to say no. W. J. had seen her coming or going on more than one occasion, and some of the church members were beginning to notice. William had gone to her house a week ago just to keep her from coming to the church.

William thought that him being on the road would give Mamie a chance to cool down and give him time to figure out how to get out of the mess he had helped create. He didn't want to lose Goldie. He loved her, and she was a good wife and first lady of the church. When he looked at her, he saw all that was good in the world. She was the calm at the end of a chaotic day, his place of peace. He should have been satisfied, but he wasn't. He craved the same adrenalin rush that comes from excitement or danger, the same rush or stimulation others get from hunting, fighting, drinking, taking drugs, and gambling. He got it from women, not from a good woman like Goldie but from one like Mamie.

***

Midway through the summer, Martin Luther King Jr. had decided that Chicago, one of the most racially segregated places in the nation, would be the ideal city for the Northern campaign focusing on urban poverty. Chicago may not have had segregation by law, but the limited opportunities for blacks to gain adequate employment and affordable housing through redlining, steering, intimidation, and other discriminatory real estate practices created de facto segregation. Whites lived in the suburbs, and blacks lived in city slums.

The SCLC planned to address the problems that kept blacks contained in poor ghettos: skyrocketing rent and home prices, unemployment, crime, drugs, and youth street gangs. King told them that if they could break the system of inequality in Chicago, it could be broken in any other place across the country.

Many of the SCLC clergy moved their families to Chicago to participate in the campaign for fair and open housing, but William didn't think he could ask Goldie to live in a slum. He had already asked her for too much. Besides, he had promised her father that he would take care of her in the way she had been raised.

William joined James Bevel, who was directing an inner-city outreach ministry at the West Side Christian Parish. Working in an alliance with the CCCO and the AFSC, they formed the Chicago Freedom Movement. They went block by block trying to organize tenants in a program called Union to End Slums. Coordination was sluggish as the group lacked resources—mainly people and money—and significant progress was slow, too. Six months into the program, morale was low without any concessions from the city in opening better housing.

A large freedom rally was scheduled at Soldier Field, where King would speak for the first time since the SCLC had come to the city. He hoped to add fuel to fire up the campaign. More than 35,000 people came; and entertainers, including Stevie Wonder and Mahalia Jackson, performed. William stood on the podium, listening to King's speech. He was in awe of King and his masterful skills as an orator. As William looked around at the crowd of people, he could see that they, too, were moved by every word.

The campaign gained momentum from the demonstrations and the inspired marches into all-white neighborhoods and outside of real estate offices on the northwest and southwest sides of Chicago. The people were fired up, and with the heat of the summer added to the mix, tempers exploded. In July, racially charged riots broke out on the West Side. A few weeks later, during another march through Marquette Park, another all-white neighborhood, demonstrators were viciously attacked by hostile whites throwing bricks and bottles. Even Dr. King, who was leading the march, was hit by a rock. That blow stunned him into a new reality about the hate and hostility in the North.

Toward the end of the summer, after various negotiations, a summit agreement was announced by Mayor Richard Daley. The Chicago Housing Authority had promised to build public housing in all-white areas, and the Mortgage Bankers Association agreed to make mortgages available without regard to race. But after it was all said and done, all the agreements and promises didn't amount to much. William was disillusioned. This was the only time that he had been able to participate in a movement campaign from the start to the finish, and as far as he could see, there was no victory. Nothing had changed for the people he had worked to organize.

The months whisked by after the summer and through the fall. The temperatures fell, and dirty snow and ice covered the ground. Nine days before Christmas, William, tired of wrestling with the hawk in Chicago, decided it was time to return to Richmond.

***

William had plenty of time to think on the long drive back to Virginia. He hadn't called to tell Goldie or his father that he was on his way. Two of his fellow clergy rode part of the way with him. He dropped one of them off in Detroit. The other preacher, Marshall, insisted that William spend the night at his house in Cleveland. Marshall and his family were overjoyed when the car pulled up to the house. Seeing the welcoming hugs and kisses he was greeted with only made the hollowness inside William grow bigger. He hesitated to guess what kind of reception he would get when he got home.

He had only been away from home for 18 months, but it seemed longer. Goldie had visited him a couple of times in Chicago, but it was evident that the connection between them had been strained by the distance. She'd stopped asking him 20 questions about whom, what, and where things were going with the movement. She was polite and smiled at all the right moments, but they didn't laugh. He missed her wry sense of humor. Then there were the times when they were socializing with the group, he would catch her looking at him as if he were a stranger.

Goldie even responded to William's touch differently. He wondered if he had lost her trust, even though he didn't deserve it. He wondered if Mamie had revealed their secret. There were so many unspoken things between them, accusations and confessions. He knew he was flawed and that his foot had slipped more than once in Chicago, but he was determined to strengthen his marriage.

The sun was going down, although it wasn't late when William stopped the car in front of his house. Most of the other houses were adorned with lights and Christmas decorations, but their house was dark inside and out. Goldie was probably in Hampton with her folks. He thanked Jesus when his key still turned the lock. The house was cold; and the familiar smell—a mixture of pot roast, baked bread, and Goldie's perfume—was gone.

William left his bag in the foyer and went into the kitchen. The refrigerator was practically empty. Still wearing his coat, he walked into the bedroom, lay down across the carefully made bed, closed his eyes, and fell asleep.

***

There was a long list of things William planned to do before he drove down to Hampton. He wanted to make things right, and that included a lot of shopping. He needed to buy groceries and a Christmas tree, and hang Christmas lights outside the house. He got an early start and was finished before noon. He was tired of driving, but he couldn't relax until Goldie was back home. Turning onto Bay Street in Hampton, he wasn't sure what he was going to say or how she would react to seeing him.

William thought about the first time he stood knocking at the Davises' door, and how much he had wanted that pretty girl to be in his life. He remembered how he used to live for her kisses. He hadn't given her the life he promised; he'd been selfish, thinking only of his own needs. It was probably because for most of his childhood, there hadn't been a woman in the house. He knocked again. Then he saw her coming through the sheer curtain on the door, and his heart began to beat faster.

"William, I didn't expect to see you," Goldie said apprehensively. "Is everything okay?"

"I missed my wife, so I came home."

"Come in," she said casually. "Let me take your coat."

He handed her his overcoat. "How's your daddy doing?" he asked, being sure to show concern.

"He's much better. He went with Mama to run errands before they go to Bible study," she answered, hanging his coat on the hall tree.

"I'm glad to hear that."

Goldie nodded. "Do you want something to eat?"

"No, pumpkin, I came to take you home."

"Home is where there are people who love you."

"I love you, Goldie, and that's where I am."

"For how long, Will? How long before you get bored and run off again?"

"I wasn't running from you, sweetie. I was trying to find something, the meaning or purpose of life, of my life."

"Did you find it?" she asked offhandedly.

"I can't say that I did," he answered humbly. "But I felt better for trying."

"So how long are you in town for?"

"I don't have any plans to go anywhere else; and I promise you that if I do go anywhere, I won't leave without you by my side."

Those words finally got her to smile. "Now that's the Christmas gift I wished for," she said happily, putting her arms around his neck.

"Get your stuff. Let's go home," William said, relieved and thankful he hadn't ruined everything between them.

"I can't leave now. I have to tell Mama and Daddy I'm going first."

"Leave them a note. You can call them later. I'm ready for us to live our life together."

Goldie loved the words she was hearing; she had waited a long time to hear them. She gathered a few things, wrote a note, and rode back to Richmond.

***

On the first Sunday in 1967, William stood up to preach. The congregation gave him a standing ovation, welcoming him back. W. J. stood beside him and clapped, too. William smiled graciously as he looked out over his congregation, relieved to see that Mamie wasn't sitting in the pew two rows behind Goldie. He was determined that this would be a fresh start for him.

"Brother and sisters, there are many battles for God's people. Our faith in the Lord is tested over and over again. Even after reaching the Promised Land, the people of Israel were tested many more times. Undoubtedly, there were reasons for their trials. First and foremost, they hadn't been faithful, so on the West Bank, they were invaded by the Midianites every year after the harvest. They were run out of their homes and robbed of their crops, leaving them to starve. But even in their disobedience, the Lord remained faithful to them.

"The Lord sent an angel to Gideon to save them from starvation. Gideon, a humble man, asked, 'O LORD, how can I save Israel? Mine is a poor family in Manasseh, and I am the least in my father's house.' The Lord told him to have no fear, for He would be with him to drive out the Midianites. But there was one thing Gideon was required to do before he would be ready. The Lord told him that before he could set his people free, he must first set them free from their worship of false idols.

"Gideon's first order of business is our lesson for today. There are great things for us to accomplish in the months ahead, but we have to ready ourselves. We have to remove those things from our lives that distract us and separate us from God, because when we are estranged from God, we're weaker and more vulnerable. We are that one sheep that has drifted from the fold that needs to brought back into protection.

"So, church, I am back home. There is much work to be done here in Richmond before we can help with the work of another city, another state, or throughout the country. I'm so thankful that God still has a job for me to do, so I'm going to give Him the praise He deserves!"

Tambourines clamored, and shouts of praise filled the room. The organist joined in, and the whole church leaped and danced with joy.

***

William was steadfast in his commitment to the church and his marriage; it was the world around him that was changing. A shift was taking place in the thinking of young blacks just as the Civil Rights Movement was losing its momentum; it was called Black Power. He used a similar premise in his messages, that the people must unite in solidarity, close ranks, and recognize their heritage before they ventured into open society. He joined a new organization in the city called The Richmond Crusade for Voters to mobilize the people to gain political power. It excited him and renewed his belief that the time would come for the people to rise up, and that time was now. It would be as it was when Gideon led 300 Israelites to defeat the Midianites. Instead of horns, their votes would do the blaring.

William spent most of the year community organizing, feeling that he was back on track with a legitimate purpose besides preaching. His relationship with Goldie was also back on track. Nevertheless, W. J. didn't like the direction his son was going in. W. J.'s health was going downhill, and he wanted to be sure that William was firm in his commitment to leading the church and that there was another Freeman male child to follow him. He started nagging William about it.

"I know you've got yourself busy with these voting campaigns and things, son, but you're not a boy anymore. You're about to be 30 years old in a few months. Where's your family? You've been married for almost ten years, and you don't have a child or a chick to call your own. There's something wrong with Goldie."

William exhaled loudly. "Goldie has been to the doctor, and he says that there is nothing wrong with her. It'll happen when it's supposed to happen."

"I warned you about marrying her; the Lord hasn't seen fit to bless the union. You need to divorce her, son."

"I don't know how you could tell me to do that! Goldie has been a good wife to me. It's in the Book, 'For I hate divorce! says the LORD, the God of Israel. To divorce your wife is to overwhelm her with cruelty, says the LORD of Heaven's Armies,' Malachi 2:16. I'm not like you, Pop. You divorced my mama after you made her run away."

"Don't sit there and try to judge me, boy! Finish the verse, 'So guard your heart; do not be unfaithful to your wife.' Maybe she'd leave you if she knew what you did!"

"I had a weak moment, but it's in the past. You're so miserable, you can't stand to see anybody happy, not even your own son!"

"That's not true. You're the only son I got left. You mean everything to me, and I want to see you happy. I want you to have all that life has to offer. It seems that Goldie can't give it to you."

"I didn't marry Goldie to have babies. I married her because I love her."

"That sounds good, but tell me this, and tell the truth. Would you have married her if you knew she couldn't have children?"

"I can't answer that. I don't know."

"Then you have something to think about," W. J. said, walking out of the door.

***

Progress at last! Midway through the year, the Supreme Court finally handed down a ruling on Loving *v.* Virginia, overturning laws against interracial marriage. A few months later, Thurgood Marshall became the first black man appointed to the Supreme Court. By the time Christmas rolled around, William and Goldie had the gift they had been praying for for such a long time. Goldie was pregnant. All the questions and criticisms were put to rest. At last, things were coming together. The New Year, 1968, should have only brought more reasons to celebrate, but it didn't.

On January 12, the coldest day of that winter, Sister Eleanor, found W. J. sprawled outside his greenhouse covered in frost. She said he'd been working to get his seeds started. The doctor said he'd had an asthma attack, probably brought on by the frigid air.

William was still in mourning, sitting in his father's office, when he heard that Martin Luther King Jr. had been shot by an assassin's bullet. If that wasn't hard enough, Goldie lost the baby. They say death comes in threes. The first two were heavy blows, but the third one was a knock-out punch. How could God have been so cruel? Sacrifice after sacrifice, and the devil could still hit his target.

Responsibilities at the church grew heavier, and there was less time to spend working with The Richmond Crusade of Voters. William became sullen and sank back to depths he'd sworn never to fall into again. W. J.'s words would replay in his head, and William blamed Goldie for losing the baby, doubting that she was the right woman for him. He lost his focus, and his eyes began to stray. He would see an attractive woman and wonder if she were the one for him.

Then there were the evenings where he had a "meeting" to go to. Goldie could always tell if he was going to do wrong because he couldn't look her in the eye and he didn't have an appetite.

"Maybe you should let the deacons handle these extra meetings," she said, staring at him across the table. "If you keep burning the candle at both ends you're going to get burned out."

"Being busy keeps my mind off of other things."

"Other things like what?" she snapped.

"Things that I don't have power over."

"Humble yourselves before the Lord, and he will lift you up, James 4:10."

"That's all I've ever done, and you see where that has gotten me."

"Is it really bad, Will? Maybe you should look at yourself for a second and not blame someone else for the wall that you have built."

"What difference would that make? There's plenty of blame to go around," he said, getting up from the table.

The pattern had become familiar, like the rerun of an old TV show. She knew the script and the outcome. He would come home guilty and remorseful and beg her forgiveness, and in less than a week, he would repeat the same scenario.

Goldie got on her knees and prayed for her husband and for herself, yet it seemed her prayers were falling on deaf ears. She watched him become more attentive to other women and less considerate to her needs. Sadness veiled the beauty of her face, and grief rounded her shoulders. It was her mama, Sister Sarah, who stepped in and kept her beautiful butterfly from reversing into a caterpillar and curling up to die.

"I'm gonna take Goldie back to Hampton for a few weeks," she told William after Sunday dinner. "It looks like she needs a change of scenery."

"I've got a lot on my plate right now," William said, sounding like W. J. "I don't have time to have a pity party for me and Goldie."

"Sometimes a girl needs her mama to take care of her for a while," Sister Sarah said, rubbing her daughter's shoulder.

Goldie didn't have the wherewithal to agree or to object. She had given all she had to give and was getting nothing in return, no child from her womb and no comfort from her husband.

"You don't ever stay where you're not wanted," Sister Sarah said, as she packed her daughter's suitcase. "Put Isaiah 31:10 in your mouth, child: 'Fear not, for I am with you; be not dismayed, for I am your God; I will strengthen you, I will help you, I will uphold you with my righteous right hand.' You don't need that man right now. The devil is using him. All you need is Jesus."

"I can't run away every time we have a problem."

"That's true. Believe me, I know that for myself. I would stay here with you, but your daddy can't do much for himself anymore."

"William isn't perfect, but he's a good man, Mama. He's gone through a lot. He don't know it, but he needs me, too."

"You can't save nobody if you're drowning yourself. Besides, you don't stay nowhere you're not cared for and appreciated. If the man is going to hurt you with other women, there's nothing you can do to stop it. But you don't have to sit here and let him smack you in the face with it."

Goldie watched her mother push down her clothes and zip up her suitcase. There was nothing else in the house that she wanted to take from her marriage. The drapes that she had so carefully chosen to hang from the windows were meaningless. The furniture held no special place in her heart. There was nothing there from the floor to the roof that could fill the emptiness in her heart or in her belly.

***

William's sermons vacillated. Some were from Psalms where he cried out in sorrow like David, full of regrets, and feeling forsaken. Others were from Isaiah where he preached of the salvation of the Lord and the greatness that lies ahead. He explained Goldie's absence telling the congregation that her father was sick and she was in Hampton to help care for him. While she was away, the fact that he was married didn't discourage some of the women from seeing him as a prize catch. There were quite a few who were constantly trying to get their hooks in him. Still a young man of 31 years, he jumped at the bait they dangled in front of him.

The elders of the church weren't ignorant to all the carrying on, but William's spirit-filled sermons kept the pews filled as well, so they turned their heads. William himself was torn. He justified the multiple affairs as an unorthodox way of having a child. He needed to prove to himself and to W. J. that he was a man in every sense of the word. He wasn't sure how he would handle the situation if it happened, but at least he could show the world that he wasn't the one to blame.

After two months in the house alone, William became angry and contemplated divorce. The way he rationalized it was that he may have been unfaithful to her, but she had been unfaithful to their marriage. She had chosen to leave the house and their bed. Furthermore, the word running through the church wasn't coming out of the Bible; it was gossip running out of the mouths of its members. It got so bad that after a conference between the elders, they sent two members as envoys to Hampton to urge Goldie to come back.

***

"Sister Goldie, I know that you have your reasons for being here; but as the first lady of the church, we need you back in Richmond. Pastor is being tested, and we can't let the devil win. He's a good man, the same man he was when you married him. He's being overrun by the Jezebel spirit. The survival of the church is at stake."

"Maybe you need to take this up with the Lord," Goldie told them. "I don't think it's within my power to change him."

"You're a righteous woman. If you stand at the gate, Satan's hounds will have to go hunting somewhere else."

"I'll pray on it, gentlemen. Whatever the Lord tells me to do, that's what I'll do."

Goldie watched as the men got back into the shiny Cadillac. Standing there in the doorway, she prayed silently. "What would you have me do, Lord?" She'd been in the church her whole life, and she was a witness that the devil is always busy, seeking to steal, kill, and destroy. There was no doubt that he was trying to destroy her marriage. Her problem was, she held William responsible for being weak and allowing the devil to manipulate him like a puppet. She wasn't sure if she could forgive William for that. She didn't even know if he wanted her to come back. The only thing she did know was that she wasn't about to let the devil win without a fight. William may be weak, but she was strong as hell.

It wasn't easy, and there were days when Goldie thought that neither William nor the church were worth the evil she had to contend with. Luke 17:4 was the verse she leaned on: "Even if they sin against you seven times in a day and seven times come back to you saying, 'I repent,' you must forgive them."

It was only after Goldie's father passed in 1971, and Sister Sarah moved in with them, that William reigned in some of his extra activities. Under her watchful eye he became a more faithful husband and Goldie began to shine again.

***

It's difficult to say who was the most blessed when Goldie found out she was pregnant again. William stood before the congregation and began to sing, "'Oh happy day, o happy day, o happy day when Jesus washed, He washed my sins away!' This is a great day sisters and brothers! The Lord has sought to bless me in spite of my unworthiness. My heart is full this morning. I am reminded of Hannah's story in the Book of First Samuel, where she prays for a son and vows to the Lord that if He gives her this son, she will return him back to Him.

"As you all know, Sister Goldie and I have had our struggles with having a child. But this morning, my wife, the love of my life, told me that our prayer has been answered, and we are expecting a child."

Praises of joy filled the room and turned to shouts and dancing. Every member of the church celebrated, quite a few of them with relief.

"Thank you, Father!" William shouted from the pulpit. "Thank you for being a merciful God, thank you for Your grace, for we are not worthy. We are but filthy rags. Yet You are faithful, O Father, 'No matter how deep the stain of your sins, I can take it out and make you clean as freshly fallen snow,' Isaiah 1:18."

This new life that Goldie carried in her belly was a new beginning. It was a new beginning for their marriage, a new beginning that would carry the church into future generations.

The hopelessness William had harbored for so long was replaced with optimism, for God had smiled on him. The church lavished Goldie with gifts for the baby, and a committee was formed to help set up the baby's nursery.

***

The contractions started on a muggy July afternoon. Goldie waited for as long as she could before she told William. His excitement was beyond words. But she knew that if they went to the hospital too early, she might be sent back home. He paced the floor of the waiting room, anxious to meet his namesake, William Edward Freeman IV. His father had to be looking down at him with pride today.

Goldie was under twilight sedation during the birth. When she woke up, William was sitting at the side of her bed, hanging his head between his knees. Something must have gone wrong with the baby. Her throat filled with tears, and she almost choked before she could ask what happened. William stood up alarmed, just as a nurse came into the room. She smiled at them, and Goldie was more confused.

"Did your husband tell you already, Mrs. Freeman?" the nurse said, patting her gently on the back. "You have a healthy baby girl. I'll go get her and bring her in to see you."

"Thank you," Goldie said before she collapsed back on the bed with relief. But why was William looking so down in the mouth. "What's wrong?" she asked him.

"I thought it would be a son," he told her, disappointed.

"The nurse said our baby is healthy. Isn't that the most important thing?"

"I'm thankful for that. I was just hoping it would be a boy."

"We can try again for a boy later. Today, we have a daughter!"

"I'm sorry, pumpkin, I'll love our daughter, no matter what. I was thinking so much about the church and having a son to carry on the legacy of my family."

"That's the weight your daddy put on you, Will. He's gone now. You can be your own man."

"I am my own man, but this is bigger than me. This calling on my family was ordained by God many generations ago."

"I don't want to hear about that right now. I want to see my baby girl, the baby I prayed for and the Lord blessed me with. Are you going to help me think of a name, or are you going to sit there and moan about something you can't change?"

"You can choose the name. I'll name the next one," he said, forcing a smile.

"I was thinking about Priscilla. She was a woman who kept God's word. Priscilla Lorraine Freeman."

"Who is the Lorraine after?"

"It's after the motel where Martin Luther King was shot, the day I lost the baby."

William paused and thought about all that had happened since that day. That was definitely a low point in his life. Things could only get better from now on.

"I like it, pumpkin. I like it a lot," he said as the door opened and the nurse walked in with their baby.

***

Priscilla was such a sweet and beautiful child. She charmed her daddy, and any misgivings he had had when she was born disappeared. William took comfort that the birth of a son was in his not-so-distant future. Now that it was proven that they could produce a healthy child, he gave Goldie little rest in his mission to get her pregnant again as quickly as he could. His efforts kept him pacified until Priscilla's third birthday. Then he became discouraged again. Why couldn't Goldie get pregnant again? Whose fault was it? Goldie refused to listen to his concerns anymore. As far as she was concerned, the Lord had blessed them, and they needed to be thankful. She couldn't have been happier with Priscilla running through the house.

William would stare at his wife when her back was turned and when she was asleep. He could see how she had changed over the years. Her breasts were fuller, but they didn't stand as high as they once did. Her waist was thicker and her hips wider, but he couldn't deny that she was just as beautiful as the day he met her. Yet, there was a truth he couldn't escape: They were getting older. He would be 40 years old on his next birthday, and Goldie was only one year behind him. Time was working against them. They didn't have another 20 years to wait.

William thought about the men in the Bible with second wives when their first wives were not able to bear children: Abraham and Sarah, Jacob and Rachel, and Elkanah and Hannah. It wasn't about loving their first wives any less. It was more about being prudent and practical. William's eyes began to wander right along with his mind. He had fantasies about bringing a younger woman into his home, her having his child, and he and Goldie raising it as their own. He broached the subject early one Saturday morning as they laid in bed.

"Have you ever thought about us adopting another baby?"

"No, I haven't," Goldie said, dismissing the thought. "I was an only child, so I know that if we don't have another, Priscilla will be fine."

"If you look in the Book, there are several men of God who had more than one woman in their lives to bear children."

"You must still be sleep, Will. You're not living in the Old Testament, you're in 1978. I am not about to let another woman come into my home for any reason. If you need another woman to help you fulfill some ancient obligation you think you have, then go get her. But rest assured that I won't be here with you. I have gone through enough trials and tribulations on this with you, and I won't go through anymore. Make up your mind once and for all on this so both of us can have some peace in our lives."

"I don't want to lose you, Goldie."

"Don't answer so quickly. Take your time, and think this over. I want you to be prepared to stick with whatever you decide."

***

Six weeks later, William stepped to the podium. "I am content today, brothers and sisters. It has taken me more than half my life, but I have finally learned what it means to surrender all to Jesus. Most of you in here knew my father, Bishop W. J. He taught me how to be a strong, independent man in this world, that you have to be in control. The lesson I have received from my heavenly Father is to submit to His will.

"I've tried in vain to exert my will in countless situations, even on my wife. Now I know we have to trust in God wholly. The Scripture says, 'And we know that all things work together for good to them that love God, to them who are the called according to his purpose.' This is important to me in my ordained mission to preserve and declare God's word. Even though I can't see how I can fulfill my commitment to Christ, the Scripture says, 'We are saved by trusting. And trusting means looking forward to getting something we don't yet have—for a man who already has something doesn't need to hope and trust he will get it. But if we must keep trusting God for something that hasn't happened yet, it teaches us to wait patiently and confidently,' Romans 8:24-25. Therefore, that is what we need to do, church. We need to wholly lean on Jesus. 'On Christ the solid rock I stand, all other ground is sinking sand, all other ground is sinking sand.' "

The choir joined in singing and shouting. It wasn't William's most earth-shaking sermon, but the sincerity of it rang loudly in the hearts of his congregation. They knew his struggle, even if he never spoke it aloud.

At the end of the service, the line to give him a handshake in fellowship was long. He didn't even notice that his baby, who they now called Prissy, was standing there, having somehow gotten free from her mama.

"Daddy, I'm gonna stand up there with you," she told him. "I'm gonna preach God's word, too."

William picked her up, wrapped her up in his robe, and held her close to his chest. "If only you could, sweet pea, that would be so good."

"I can, Daddy, and I will."

Chapter Five
Priscilla

"**I** don't know if you remember the day you first told your father that you were going to preach God's word, beloved," the stranger said, gazing toward the trees at the edge of the yard. "He would have given anything for things to have turned out differently. Regrettably, his own child felt as he once did, that she was a disappointment to her father. It wasn't his intention to make you feel this way, but nonetheless, that's what happened. William burdened his child with the same cross that his father had placed upon him, something neither he nor you could control, that being the circumstances of your birth.

"The difference was you, his daughter, wanted nothing more than to take on the awesome task of standing in the pulpit, even though everything that he believed said it wasn't possible. Your passion for the vocation made him feel ashamed, for it was the one thing he'd lacked. William could see that he'd made some of the same mistakes with his daughter that his father had made with him, and he suspected that he would probably lose you as well.

"You know how your father disappointed you and the consequences of that disappointment, and now you know the story of his disappointment. I hope that hearing your father's story and his father's story will help you understand the foundation of beliefs that he was raised on and the pressure he was under. Now, it is time for you to tell me your story."

***

My daddy always looked at me with sad eyes. I didn't fully understand it at first, but it became clear to me on my thirteenth birthday. That's when he had his second stroke. He and my mama had been arguing all morning.

"You can ignore it all you want, Will, but the child says she's been called," Mama said, scrubbing on a plate in the sink.

"It doesn't make any difference, Goldie. You know that."

Mama turned around to face him, her hands covered in soap suds. "All I know is that you ain't God. You or no other man can say who can preach His word."

That got Daddy indignant. "I can tell you this, surely no woman will stand in the pulpit at Thompson Boulevard Church of God in Christ, not even a child of mine!"

"I know you're not gonna take that 'holier than thou' tone with me," Mama fussed. "All of you men standing up there have feet of clay, and you know it. You don't have the right or the record to sit in judgment of who can speak for God."

"The word is plain. First Timothy 2:12 says, 'I do not permit a woman to teach or to assume authority over a man; she must be quiet.' I won't condone my child in sin."

"I've got a word for you too, Will. John 8:7: 'He who is without sin among you, let him cast the first stone at her.'"

"Don't stand up here in my house and disparage me, woman! I fell short, but I've repented. The Lord has forgiven me for my transgressions."

"This is my house, too, and the Lord is not the only one who had to forgive you. I forgave you, too, but I haven't forgotten, so if it's all right for you to climb up there and speak, it's alright for Priscilla to do the same."

"You're asking too much, woman. The elders and the deacons won't allow it."

"I know about all those men. There's not one in the bunch who hasn't wallowed in sin. Times have changed, and it's time for the church to change."

"This conversation is over, Goldie!"

"No, it isn't! You're being stubborn."

"I failed. That's all there is to it," Daddy said, shaking his head.

"That is ridiculous! You haven't failed. You've been a faithful servant—even if you've not been a faithful husband."

"We don't have a son to lead," he said, keeping the conversation on the matter at hand.

Unable to remain crouched in the shadows eavesdropping, I stood up and walked over to the table beside Daddy's chair. "I'll lead. I can do it, Daddy."

"No, baby, that's not the way God planned it," he said, smoothing the hair of my ponytail.

"What do you self-righteous men know about God's plan?" Mama asked, still upset. "Seems to me, you use God's word to justify controlling everybody else!"

Daddy got up from his chair and walked to the doorway. He turned back with his hand raised and pointed a finger in her direction. "Every generation in my family was charged with the responsibility of protecting God's word and His laws, and that's what I'm gonna do until the day He calls me home."

He turned his back to walk away, but before Mama could respond, he dropped to his knees and fell forward on his face.

Mama screamed and ran to him. I rushed over behind her to help.

"Call for an ambulance, Prissy!" she said, waving her arm. "Willie, what's wrong?" she asked frantically, as she loosened his tie and unbuttoned his shirt. "I'm sorry for pushing so hard!"

It seemed like an hour passed before we heard the sirens. Two men wearing white shirts came in and lifted Daddy onto a stretcher. They wheeled him out of the house, with Mama trying to hold his hand.

"Stay here, baby. I'll call you after I get to the hospital."

***

It was a mild stroke, and Daddy made a full recovery. Mama never brought up the subject of me preaching after that. In less than a month, Daddy was back in the pulpit preaching. Out of respect for Mama, I kept quiet about my calling. It was my soul that continued to cry out. Every Saturday afternoon, as Daddy prepared his sermon, I prepared one of my own. But instead of preaching it the next day, I wrote them in my diary.

During the Sunday morning service, I would sit on the right side of the sanctuary on the end of the fifth pew and read my message while Daddy professed his from the front. It wasn't obvious to me at first, but after a few months, I noticed that Daddy drew most of his messages from the Old Testament. Maybe that was why we couldn't see things eye to eye. I had the same affinity for the New Testament.

For the next four years, not much changed, except the subject we all avoided became a river that ran between us. I went through high school as if it were a way station, waiting for the time when I could cross that river or dive in and see where the tides would carry me. The only common ground between us was my decision to enroll at Hampton University after graduation.

***

Walking onto the campus at Hampton University gave me life. It was like being born again. I breathed in deeply, taking in the air like a drowning person brought up to the surface of the deepest waters. Being the quiet dutiful daughter was stifling. Daddy always took all the oxygen out of the room and left everyone else gasping.

"I'm sorry your daddy wasn't able to come and help you get settled in your dormitory," Mama said regrettably after we had gotten all my boxes and luggage into my dorm room. "He's got the revival starting in a few days."

"It's no big deal," I told her. "Besides, I'm only a little more than an hour away from home anyway."

"I guess we better get started unpacking."

"That's all right, Mama. I can do it by myself."

"I know you can, but that's what I'm here for."

"Really, Mama, I want to do it. I'm not a little kid," I said, standing guard over my suitcases.

That's when her hand flew to her hip. "You expect me to come here and drop you off and turn right back around and go home. I haven't even met your roommate. You're my child, and I'm here to make sure you get settled properly."

"I don't want to have a long goodbye scene with both of us crying. I'm fine. Daddy needs you more back at the house."

"You might think you're grown, but you're still my baby. That's never gonna change."

"I know that, and I love you, but I want to do this on my own."

Mama could see I was determined. She nodded in acceptance. "Before I go, do I need to remind you of how you were raised?"

"No, Mama, I know how to act."

"One other thing: Don't go spending too much time at the beach and socializing. You're here to get an education, not a reputation."

"Okay," I said, sighing. "You don't have to worry." She needn't have wasted her breath. My agenda at Hampton would be strictly business.

Mama dug into her purse and pulled out a pen and a piece of paper. "What's the number on that phone over there? I'm going to call you later on."

I shuffled my feet to the phone, copied the phone number, and gave her the paper and the pen.

"I'll walk you back to the car," I said, moving toward the door. I figured that that was the only way to get her to leave.

We walked to the parking lot in silence. I opened the car door for her.

"I love you, Prissy."

"I love you, too, Mama." I gave her a hug. "I'll be fine."

***

I was surprised when the doorknob turned and the door swung in against the wall with a bang. My eyebrows shot up when I saw my roommate on the other end of a luggage cart. She wasn't at all what I had expected. She was wearing a turban of brightly colored Kente cloth, a matching sleeveless blouse, baggy jeans, and a pair of Chuck Taylor's. She was dark-skinned with a lovely face, classic looking, with large brown, almond-shaped eyes and prominent cheekbones. She was petite, but with a commanding presence.

She wheeled the overloaded cart to the unoccupied bed, stopped, and looked me over from head to toe.

"Hello, I'm Tamela, Tamela Hunter. I go by Tamu. It's Swahili. It means sweet. I'm guessing that you're my roomie."

"You don't have an accent," I said, surprised again.

"Excuse me?" she asked, puzzled.

"I thought maybe you were African," I said, suddenly feeling embarrassed.

She started laughing. "I wish. No, I'm from Philly, but I'm very Afrocentric."

"My mistake. That's why they say 'Don't assume,'" I said, laughing, too. "I'm Priscilla Freeman from Richmond. Most of my friends call me Prissy."

"I can see why," she said, checking out my sleeveless button-down shirt, khaki capris, and huarache sandals.

I had to laugh again. "Touché! You got me back."

"Philly folks are not to be messed with," Tamu said, throwing a heavy suitcase on the bed.

"Did your family come with you?" I asked, wondering why she was alone.

"Nope. They dropped me off at the train station. It was easier that way. I'm the oldest, I've got two younger sisters, so I'm pretty independent. What about you?"

"My father had to work, so my mother drove me. I told her she didn't have to wait. I wanted to get settled by myself."

"Great minds think alike," she said, nodding.

"So, what's your major?" I asked.

"History and pre-law. I'm all about fighting for our people. What about you?"

"Sociology. It's just the beginning of my master plan."

"Okay, so what's the plan?" she asked, finishing up with the first suitcase.

"I want to start my own ministry, go to divinity school, and then go international."

"Big dreams!" Tamu said, unfolding her mattress cover.

"Oh, yeah, and I want to go back and preach at my daddy's church."

"Oh shit! A preacher's kid," she said, chuckling. "I might need to repack my bags!"

"Stop tripping. It's not that serious."

"Just asking, but are you some kind of religious fanatic? I don't want to cause problems, but I like to get my groove on from time to time—a little sip, a little smoke, and a little sexual satisfaction."

"God is the judge, not me. The Bible says we all sin and fall short."

She smiled. "That's cool. I can deal with that. I think we're going to be all right."

"I agree," I said, smiling back. "Now hurry up so we can get to orientation on time."

"I'm on it!" Tamu said, flipping a fresh sheet in the air above the bed.

***

Surprisingly, Tamu and I got along great. She was "more power to the people," and I was "God has the power for the people." We were both driven to work toward specific goals, and we respected that in each other. We joined the forensic debate team to be more comfortable making points in front of an audience.

We were walking back to the dorm after a meeting when we passed a group of guys hanging out in front of Harkness Hall.

One of them shouted, "Hey, dog, check out the fresh meat!"

"I see you, shorty!" another yelled out. "What's your name? I want to go to the mother country."

Then another added, "Hey, come over here! I wanna holler at you."

Tamu rolled her eyes at them. "I don't understand why these young brothers don't know how to treat black women with the respect we deserve. That's why I don't deal with boys. I prefer a mature man."

"Leave the ladies alone, man. Show some respect," the tall one said, bouncing a basketball.

"Come on, Tamu. What are you talking about?" I said with a smirk. "You are only 18."

"Age is merely a state of mind. I have dealt with a couple of older guys, and they know how to act better than these fools."

"Hey, hold up," the tall one said, running to catch up with us. "I'm sorry about my guys over there. They didn't mean any harm."

"They need to learn some manners," Tamu said.

"That's true. I'm not gonna lie. I want to apologize for

them," he said, staring at me. "My name is James Sinclair. Let me take you two lovely ladies out to get something to eat to make amends for their behavior."

"No, thank you," I said. "We've already eaten."

He kept walking with us. "It doesn't have to be today. We can go whenever you want. Give me your number, and I'll call you."

"I don't think so. I'm real busy with all my classes."

Then Tamu interrupted. "You don't even know our names. I'm Tamu, and this is my roommate, Priscilla."

"It's nice to meet you, Priscilla," he said, still staring at me.

"Most people call her Prissy," Tamu added.

"I'd like to call you, Princess," he said, grinning.

"We might be able to make some time to go out," Tamu said, taking a pen out of her backpack. "Do you have a piece of paper to write on?"

"Write it on my shirt," he said, leaning his shoulder over.

"I don't mind if you don't," she said as she wrote the phone number on his shirt.

"I'll see you ladies real soon," James said, nodding his head at me before he jogged back to his friends.

"Why did you do that?" I asked, perturbed.

"It's not that serious. Anyway, he was kinda cute, and he was really feeling you. What'll it hurt to go out sometime and have some fun?"

"Running around with some dude is not part of my master plan."

"All work and no play will make Prissy a dull girl. Besides, you have to make friends to get people to come to your little Bible meetings."

***

I got permission to use a study room in the library, and I made some flyers announcing a Bible study hour on Wednesday nights. I was apprehensive about the first meeting, so I begged Tamu to be there with me.

"Why do I have to come to this thing? You know I have to study for my first chemistry test," she said, complaining.

"Don't I go to all your 'unite the people for progress meetings' when I have better things to do? I need you just in case not many people show up."

"I'm sure James will be glad to come if you're worried about that."

"I'm not trying to hear that. I'm not going to lose my focus."

"It's not your focus that he wants you to lose," she said, pushing me on the shoulder and laughing.

Nervous about what I was going to say and whether there would be anybody there to hear me say it, I was somewhat relieved to see four people already waiting in the meeting room when Tamu and I got there.

"Welcome, fellow students, and thanks for coming," I said, taking a seat at the head of the table. "I wanted to start this group to connect to God's powerful source of strength and ignite our success as students and Christians. This group can evolve into whatever we want it to be. But I want to start out with reading Scripture, move on to questions and discussion, and then end with prayer."

Then the door opened with a loud squeak. It was James, wearing a track suit and carrying a basketball.

"Excuse me. Sorry to be late," he said, easing into a chair at the end of the table.

"No problem. Join us," Tamu teased. "There's always room at the Lord's table. Isn't that right, Princess?"

I was trying to stay in a correct frame of mind, but I still cut an evil eye in Tamu's direction.

"Since this is the beginning of the semester, I chose a passage that will encourage and motivate us. I'll be reading from Matthew 6:25-34. If you brought your Bibles, you can follow along with me.

"'Therefore I say to you, do not worry about your life, what you will eat or what you will drink; nor about your body, what you will put on. Is not life more than food and the body more than clothing? Look at the birds of the air, for they neither sow nor reap nor gather into barns; yet your heavenly Father feeds them. Are you not of more value than they? Which of you by worrying can add one cubit to his stature? . . . Therefore do not worry about tomorrow, for tomorrow will worry about its own things. Each day has enough trouble of its own.'"

After I read the passage, I asked, "Are there any questions?" I looked around the room and got the same blank look that most professors get in class when they rattle off too much information, so I started the discussion. "What this passage means to me is that God will supply all our needs if we trust in Him."

"Do you mean that God will help me pass my calculus exam?" one of the students asked.

"No, it doesn't mean that we don't have to study. It means that we should first seek His wisdom. He will help us in all things, but we have to pick up our books and study. Read the first page, then another, and He will be faithful and give us the stamina to read the whole chapter and then the whole book.

Any more questions?" Everyone looked at one another before looking back at me with that same blank stare, so I pushed forward. "Before we pray, are there any prayer requests?"

"I still think I'm going to need some prayers for me to pass that calculus test!" the student said, and everybody laughed.

"Anybody else?" I asked.

James raised his hand. "I'm having trouble making a connection with somebody who I think is very special. If you all could pray that she would open her mind and see that I'm a decent guy and let me take her out."

"In that case, I need y'all to pray that I will lose weight!" another student chimed in.

"Let's bow our heads," I said, tuning out their jokes. "Heavenly Father, we thank You and praise You for Your many blessings in our lives. We humbly ask that You grant us the wisdom and knowledge we need to excel in our classes. We ask that You would give us the willpower not to give in to temptations. And we pray for Your guidance in all that we do. We pray this prayer in Jesus' name. Amen."

Murmurs of amen echoed in the room.

"Thanks for coming, everybody! Next week, bring a friend," I said, closing the meeting.

James hung around after the other students had left.

"Umm, Princess, I didn't hear you pray for me, or will you do the work of the Lord and answer my prayer tonight?"

"I think I need to catch up with you later," Tamu said, moving toward the door.

"Wait right there," I told Tamu firmly. "Look, James, I don't know why you won't take no for an answer, but I'm not interested."

"How do you know, if you haven't given me a chance?"

"I'm not attracted to jocks. I go more for the intellectual and spiritual type."

"What makes you think I'm not intellectual or spiritual?"

"Prissy tends to judge people by appearances sometimes," Tamu interjected. "It's something that she needs to work on."

I cut my eyes at her, but she laughed and stood up to leave.

"I only want to take you out to dinner or a movie. Is that a sin?" James asked.

"C'mon, Prissy! Give the man a chance!" Tamu yelled from the doorway. "What would Jesus do?"

"Okay, whatever. I'll go," I said, giving in.

"I call you," James said, rushing out of the room.

Tamu held the door for me while I gathered up my stuff. "I don't know why you're playing so hard to get. That brother is hot, and you know it."

"With my classes, the debate team, and this Bible study group, I don't have time to be running around with a jock. They're all players anyway."

"I don't know. He seems like he's stuck on you like glue."

"I'm through talking about him. What did you think about my first Bible study?"

"It was boring."

"How are you going to diss me like that? You didn't even open your mouth to participate."

"The only way to grow your group is to be relevant. You have to relate your sessions to things that are going on in the world or what affects us as students."

"Like what?"

"Girl, like HIV and AIDS, crack, no jobs, no money, drive-by shootings, Ronald Reagan, and government cheese. The Bible is full of plagues and crisis. Tie it together, and that *might* make it more interesting. If you do all that, I'll even come back and bring a friend."

"You hurt my feelings, but you made a good point."

"I know, and I'm right about James, too. It won't kill you to have some fun. There's nothing in that Good Book against it."

Tamu was right about connecting my class to current issues. I read the newspaper every day, listened to the radio, watched the news, and started watching this program called the *Oprah Winfrey Show*. I was learning more than I was teaching. My Bible study group grew so large that we had move to a bigger room. By the following year, we were having Sunday morning services in Ogden Hall.

***

James and I became good friends. We started going out every other week. It wasn't until I saw him hugged up with another girl after we beat Howard, our rival HBCU, that I realized I wanted him for myself. I made a conscious effort to at least go out once a week. That was all I could stand. There was a lot of chemistry and heat between us. Being near him was becoming more of a temptation than any virtuous woman should have to contend with. Things reached a boiling point at the end of his senior year.

"I never met another girl like you, Princess," James said, putting his hand under my blouse and rubbing my breast. "I think you're beautiful, sexy, and we have a lot of fun together. I'm ready to move forward and take this to another level."

"I can't get up in front of people and preach to them if I'm not living right, James. That's why I made the decision not to have sex until I'm married."

James pulled away, angry. "Man, it's like I'm back in high school trying to sneak a feel! My lips are damn near raw from kissing. This is nonsense! I know you want to be with me."

"I was honest with you about how it would be from the beginning. The first time you asked me out, I told you that I was committed to God and to building my own ministry."

"Then why did you deal with me anyway," he said, shaking his head and looking away from me. "What you need to do is tell the whole truth. You only started giving me a little play because you didn't want me getting busy with any other chicks."

I pulled my blouse down. "So, you're going to look me in the face and pretend that you haven't been ducking around on me on the sly!"

"You have always been the one I wanted. I've waited for you, Princess, because I love you and respect the fact that you want to wait, but I'm a grown man. Why am I wrong for wanting to have a woman in my life and in my bed?"

"I can't allow anyone or anything to get me sidetracked," I said, shaking my head, unable to answer his question. "My ministry is very important to me."

"Is that all you want out of life, having your head stuck in a Bible or standing up in a pulpit every day? What kind of life is that? It seems kind of empty and boring to me."

"That's because you don't understand my mission. It's bigger than I am. I can't just live for myself. It's a God-appointed responsibility for my family. It goes back for generations."

"If everybody in your family was so dedicated to God and serving Him, how did you get here?"

"It's not that simple, James. It's different for a man. By me being a woman, expectations are higher. I have to work twice as hard."

"Don't you owe it to yourself to be happy, or is that a sin, too? If you're not trying to be a nun, you can be with a man."

"Believe it or not, I'm happy and satisfied with what I'm doing."

"What about being happy and satisfied with me? I know I haven't been perfect, but you know I'm crazy about you. I'm about to graduate in two months, and I want us to get married."

"I feel like you're asking me to choose between you and my calling."

"No, that's not what I'm doing. I'm asking you to open your eyes and see what we could have together. Both of us can make some compromises."

"It will end up with me being the one who makes all the compromises. That's not fair. My ministry has grown so fast. I can't throw it all away and follow you to who knows where."

"That's not what I'm asking, Princess. I know you want to finish and graduate. I can get a job close by, and we can still be together."

"I don't think I'm ready for that. I'm going to be carrying a heavy load for the next two years with my classes and the extra courses at Wave College to get an associate minister degree. The pressure from trying to divide myself between you and my commitment to God would be too much. I can't tell you what to do or where to go after you graduate, but I don't want to lose you. All I can ask is that you be patient with me."

"Everything can't always be about you and what you want. What I want matters, too."

"You have to know that God comes first in my life. If you can't live with that, then maybe you need to find someone else."

"My mother made me go to church when I was a kid. To me it was something to help you live your life better, to learn how to treat other people the way you want to be treated. With you, it is your whole life, and there isn't room for anything else. So, I guess I will find somebody else."

That hit me hard, harder than I thought it would. All that brave talk, and I was so hurt that I could barely get out of the car. I stood there with the door open, praying he would say something. Our conversation couldn't end there. I wanted him to ask me again, but he kept looking straight ahead. My pride wouldn't let me speak. I closed the door, and he drove away.

James didn't call me after that night. I saw him around campus, at mixers in Holland Gym, and with Tamu a couple of times before the semester was over, but we acted as if we had never met. There were many lonely moments when I picked up the phone and dialed a few of his numbers, but I never followed through. I decided to channel all my hurt and disappointment into fuel to propel my message. I had been humbled. Tamu said it helped me come across as more genuine. What a high price to pay for sincerity.

***

At the end of my junior year, Mama convinced Daddy to buy me a car. I had gotten an internship for the summer, and she knew I was getting more invitations to speak off campus at Women's Day celebrations and revivals, and it would surely make it more convenient for me to come home more often. The responsibilities of my nondenominational campus ministry grew along with it. Two other students came on board, and we took turns preaching.

Before I knew it, it was the spring of my senior year. Those four years had passed so quickly. Since I'd gotten a car, my favorite thing was hanging out at the beach. I could think clearly there, and it was time to make serious decisions about my life. The only thing I was sure of was that I was going back to Richmond. Whenever I had doubts, I could hear God speaking to me in the rumbling of the waves. The time for me to confront my future was fast approaching.

Dressed in our caps and gowns, Tamu and I walked over to Armstrong Stadium for our commencement ceremony.

"I'm going to miss you," I told her, scrunching up my nose to disrupt the burning that signaled tears were forming.

"You don't have to. You can always come to the Chocolate City with me; Howard has room for one more. You can work on your master's while I'm in law school."

"I don't have any more years to waste in school. It's time for me to do what God called me to do."

"Who says you have to do it in Virginia? There's a big world out there."

"That's true, but my father's church has been in our family for generations. I'm not going to be the one who breaks the chain."

"Girl, I'm sorry I didn't get a chance to meet your daddy, because he's got to be the man. That's all you have talked about for four years."

"You can meet him today if you want to. We're going to take Mama to brunch for Mother's Day. Your folks can join us too, if you want, before y'all drive back."

"No way. We're hitting the road as soon as I walk out of here. My brother said he's going to be loading my stuff in the truck while George Bush is running his mouthful of bullshit. I would have protested the commencement because of him, but I've paid my dues to march across that stage today. I wish I would have graduated last year when Dick Gregory was the speaker."

"It doesn't matter who speaks, as long as we get our piece of paper."

"You've got that right!" she said, holding her hand up for a high-five.

"It's going to be hard to leave my ministry here," I said, gazing across the campus. "I birthed it; it's like my baby. To walk away from it is heartbreaking."

"I don't understand you, Prissy," Tamu said, shaking her head. "You're getting all misty over some church service, but you let that fine man go without a thought."

"Not really. That was a heartbreaker, too. I'm not even going to pretend it wasn't. The problem was that he wanted more than I could give."

"How do you know that if you never tried to give him anything of yourself?"

"You just don't know what my mission means to me."

"I think I do. I just don't think it's worth everything that you're willing to sacrifice."

"God sacrificed everything for us. How can I limit my sacrifice to do His will?"

Tamu threw her hands up. "I'm out. You just go too deep for me. I prefer to keep my goal on very shallow and very satisfying experiences."

"You are too crazy!" I said, laughing.

"And you are too rigid. I could say frigid, but I won't."

We could see that the parking lot was already full. The stadium was packed, and graduates were forming the lines to march in. I thought about the other graduation ceremony that I had missed yesterday. I had earned my associate in ministry from Wave College, but I wasn't able to participate in the ceremony. Daddy didn't know I had started or completed the biblical and theological program. Mama had secretly paid for my tuition. Neither of those revelations would have been celebrated.

"I guess I'll see you afterwards. You're ahead of me in the line," I told Tamu, feeling emotional.

She opened her arms wide. "Come on and give me a hug now. Once this thing is over, I might not be able to find you with all these black folks."

"I was hoping to say goodbye to you and your folks before you leave."

"Stop tripping, Prissy. Nothing's going to happen to telephones after this. Any time you want to talk, just pick one up and call."

That pesky tear found its way out and rolled down my face. "I know, but you were like the sister I never had."

"Look at you getting all mushy and messing up your eyeliner. When I first met you, I didn't think I would be able to room with a self-righteous Bible-thumper, but you were cool."

"If it wasn't for you, I wouldn't have had half the fun I did."

"And that wasn't half the fun you should have had," she joked, nudging me.

"I mean it. Seriously, you opened up a new world for me."

"It wasn't the world that James wanted to open up."

"Stop it. You gave up enough free love for the both of us."

"You're probably right, and I have no regrets. Life is to be lived, my friend."

"Every life is different. I've got my path, and you've got yours."

I raised my hand for a high-five, and she grabbed it and held it. "Like I said, if you ever get tired of the straight and narrow, you know where to find me."

"We'll talk," I said, pulling my hand away. She nodded and walked ahead to find her place in line. "Bye, Tamu," I whispered as I stepped in line.

***

Back in Richmond, I returned to my role as the dutiful daughter. Living at home again with my parents made me feel as if the last four years hadn't happened. I was back to speaking at Women's Day celebrations and teaching Bible classes. At least once a week, I thought about moving out or even leaving town. The one thing that stopped me was the paltry paycheck I earned as a social worker for the city. It wasn't enough for me to take flight and try my wings.

The job required me to place the children of homeless families in schools close to shelters and public housing. I was at Thomas H. Henderson Middle School in North Richmond when I saw a guy in a conversation at the end of the hallway. It was his tall back and broad shoulders and the way he leaned on one leg that was so familiar. I kept watching until they finished talking. When he walked away, arms loose and swaying with the lithe, lanky gait of a giraffe, I knew it was him.

"James!" I called out in urgency, refusing to let him get away again without saying anything. He turned around slowly, without any look of surprise. It made me wonder if he had noticed me before I saw him and if he wanted to avoid running into me.

He just stood there. I hurried with long strides toward him, ignoring the apprehension rising in my belly from the expression on his face. There was no smile and no embrace to greet me at the end of the hallway, even though it had been almost three years since I'd seen him.

"How are you?" I asked, reaching out to squeeze his arm. It was impossible for me to stand next to him and not touch him.

"I can't complain," he said nonchalantly. "How have you been?"

I sensed hostility. I rubbed his arm affectionately, hoping to smooth it away. "I'm doing okay. I thought you went back to Baltimore."

"I did for a while. So, what brings you to this school?"

"I'm a social worker. I try to place homeless families and help get their kids back in school."

"Still saving the world I see," he said sarcastically.

"Come on, James, cut me some slack. It's good to see you. Are you a teacher here?"

"Yeah, I am."

"I thought you might have gone pro."

"Nah, I didn't have that kind of talent. I'm happy coaching the basketball team here."

"Wow, that's great."

"Well, nice seeing you. I have a class to get to."

"Wait, James. Give me a minute. I know I wasn't the

easiest person back at Hampton. I was selfish, but that wasn't because I didn't have feelings for you."

He snatched his arm out of my grasp. "I've got to go," he said angrily. "I don't have time to stand here listening to you say you had feelings for me. What are feelings anyway? I loved you, Princess. I wanted you to be my wife."

"Please, James. I loved you, too. I should have told you. I shouldn't have let you drive away that night."

"Maybe so, but that's behind us now. Take care, and good luck to you," he said, walking away.

I practically had to trot to keep up with him. "I want to talk to you. Let's not leave it like this again. Tell me what time you get off work. Let me buy you dinner, please."

He stopped, but he didn't turn around. "I'll be off at 4:30."

"I'll be here," I said as sincerely as I could.

Back in my car, I called Tamu for some advice, but she didn't answer the phone. For the rest of the day, I was preoccupied with thoughts of James and how I could get him to forgive me for being so self-centered and give me another chance. There had been no one else that interested me even a little bit. I was lonely and needed more in my life than work and teaching Bible study. I was a woman and could finally admit that I truly wanted him in every sense of the word. I prayed that I wasn't too late. Why would the Lord have allowed our paths to cross if it weren't for our good? Or was it the devil taking an opportunity to torment me?

***

"You can trail me," James said when he walked out of the school gym.

I was standing outside my car, too nervous to sit. I nodded, got back in the car, started the engine, and watched him walk to his car. It was a sporty black Nissan 300ZX. He circled to the exit of the parking lot and paused so I could catch up.

I chuckled to myself as I rolled up behind him at the stop sign and then at the traffic light. I was doing what I swore I would never do in college: follow this man around. Now I was determined to keep up with him. He signaled a left turn to an Irish pub that wasn't far from the school. He parked, and I pulled into the parking space beside him. He opened my car door after I switched off the ignition. He had always been a gentleman.

We walked into the restaurant without any words passing between us. The hostess welcomed us with pleasantries, led us to a table, and gave us menus. When the waitress came over, we ordered drinks.

"I'll have a draft beer," James told her.

"Water for me," I said.

James ordered the buffalo wings, and I got a salad. I wasn't there to eat. He took a big gulp from the frost-covered glass and then picked up one of the wings. He wasn't going to give an inch, much less meet me halfway. I guess that's what I deserved.

"I missed you after you left."

"That's hard to believe," he said, wiping the sauce from his hands on a napkin.

"It's true. For a long time, all I wanted was to replay that night. I would have reacted differently."

"It doesn't matter," he said, gulping down more of his beer.

There wasn't a ring on his finger. "Are you married or seeing anybody?

"What difference does it make?" he asked, irritated.

"I want you to give me another chance."

"What's going to be different this time, Princess?"

Hearing him say my name gave me hope. "I'm different. I want what you wanted. I want to be your wife."

"It took me a long time to get that idea out of my head. I'm not trying to go through those changes again. I've got my own game plan now."

"I'm not asking you to change anything for me. I just want to be in your life again. Don't be so cold to me."

Finally, his eyes softened. "You look beautiful."

"You look very nice yourself."

"I'm not interested in a girlfriend. I've already had my share."

I smiled. "That sounds good to me."

"Then it's time for me to meet your folks."

***

Mama and Daddy were more than happy when they met James. To me, it seemed like we were rushing things, but they were right behind me, pressing me on. They thought he would settle me down and tame some of the wild ideas in my head. I think James wanted me obligated to him before I found something else to be obligated to. For me, it was much more organic. I was a grown woman, almost 24 years old, and tired of being overrun by my fantasies and desires for the man I was in love with. First Corinthians 7: 9 says, "But if they cannot contain, let them marry: for it is better to marry than to burn."

The wedding was a grand affair because I was the only child and daughter of William Edward Freeman III, bishop of the Thompson Boulevard Church of God in Christ. James came from a big family, so he had a lot of family members come to the wedding, along with some of his former teammates, and several of his frat brothers stood up with him. Of course, Tamu was my maid of honor; but aside from her, I wasn't very close to any of my bridesmaids. It was then that I realized that I hadn't nurtured any relationships. I wasn't enjoying my path; I was too concerned about arriving at my final destination. I decided that that would have to change.

James and I couldn't go on our honeymoon until school was out. I didn't mind. The only thing I wanted was to lie in bed beside my husband and make love to him with a clear conscience. As a gift, the church gave us the weekend at the Jefferson Hotel.

"Slow your roll," James said, as we headed toward our room. "You're not going to get in there without me carrying you over the threshold."

"You don't have to do that," I said, laughing. "That is so old-fashioned."

"Are you serious? You're the one who wouldn't give me any loving until you got that ring on your finger."

"I promise you, it was worth the wait."

"Believe me, I'm not worried about that."

Making love with James was everything I had hoped it would be. It gave me moments of regret for the lost nights that we could have spent together. I was mesmerized by him, unable to think of anything else when he held me. I slept peacefully, free from all the responsibilities that drove me in all my waking hours.

***

The double lines on the test were a blessing and a burden. I was pregnant before I wanted to be. Not one item on my secret list of goals had been crossed off, and I knew that it would only be harder with a baby to care for. I couldn't wait any longer, even though Mama had asked me to let it go. She had witnessed Daddy and me have this battle before, but now I was backed into a corner. I had no choice except to throw down my gauntlet and fight as hard as I could.

On Wednesdays, Daddy usually ate dinner at church and then prepared for the midweek Bible study, so I left work early and arrived at the church before he could get into his studies. I knocked on his office door and waited.

"Come in."

I opened the door slowly.

"Prissy!" he said, standing up to greet me. "Sit down and talk to me. How are things going? Are you happy?"

I sat in one of the chairs in front of his desk. "Things are well, Daddy, but my soul isn't at peace."

"What's the matter, baby girl?"

"I need you to make a way for me."

"I'll do whatever I can, sweetheart. What do you need?"

I took a deep breath. "Let me preach the early morning service, just every other Sunday. I had my own ministry at Hampton, and I earned my associate degree in ministry at Wave. I need you to believe in me."

"Why do you continue to ask me the impossible? I can't interpret what God's call was to your heart, but the harvest is plentiful, and the workers are few. There is much you can do to spread the word of His goodness."

"This church has been in our family for generations. Your great-grandfather built it from nothing. Who would say you're wrong?"

"There is tradition in this church and in my family long before this place even existed. It is not up for debate. A son must carry on the responsibility of leading the church. It was God's mandate to His people. I failed in my service to the Lord. I don't have a son to carry His word."

"Daddy, I'm your daughter. I've been trained to lead the congregation. In my heart and soul, I've received the call. How can you stand in the way of that?"

"It's not me, baby. I've explained this to you so many times. That is not His plan. We must be obedient to Him."

"Daddy, that's antiquated thinking. Theology changes like everything else under the sun. Don't you think the elevation of women is God's desire? Anything other than that doesn't make sense. Why it is okay for me to work a job outside of my home to help support my family, but it's not okay for me to preach God's word?"

"The family is a woman's first responsibility. She is the stability of the household. If she abandons her role, we'll all cease to exist."

"All of nature is here to praise God's glory. The sun, moon, the planets, and the stars speak His word. The wind and the rain speak His word. The flowers and the trees speak His word. The blue whale and the elephants speak His word. Even the hummingbird speaks His word. And, yes, women can, too."

"I only know what my father instructed me, and his father instructed him, and his father before him, and his before him. That was God's will. We must be submissive to His authority."

"For the church to stay relevant, it has to evolve. The needs of the people have changed. We are about to go into the twenty-first century, the new millennium. How can you still be against women in the pulpit?"

"You have a husband to think about now, and soon you'll have a family to take care of. Wives are to submit to their husbands out of their reverence to God. Those responsibilities of a woman subtract from her ability to serve as a leader for God. That is something that is out of my hands. I wouldn't deny you anything within my power."

"The church can't bury its head in the sand and hide from the horrors of genocide, terrorist attacks, drug wars, and hunger around the world. It has to use its collective power and be political again, like it was during the Civil Rights Movement. We were all there—men, women, the youth, and the children. That's the only way progress is made." I could almost hear my Tamu clapping after I said that.

"As an American, I believe in the separation of church and state. Yes, there are terrible things happening around us. The prophecy is being fulfilled. Second Timothy 3:1 says, 'But know this, that in the last days perilous times will come.'"

"Daddy, the Bible has example after example where the Lord changed, where He rewarded and punished. He wasn't always fixed. Keeping me from answering my call is cruel. God is not cruel; He's merciful."

"You have to stop torturing yourself over this, Prissy. You have to accept the way things are. Don't ruin your life or your marriage. There've been times when I have neglected my family and their needs, concentrating on the needs of my congregation. I've given them words that I never spoke to my own wife or child. I've come to terms with my lot. I don't want you to be the son I never had. You're my daughter, and I love you."

"How can you say you love me and tie my hands? Why didn't you just send me away, put a pillow over my face, or pay some woman to have the son you prayed for? Are you above Abraham or David?"

Daddy's face contorted as a roar grew from deep in his gut. I could almost see it as it rose to his chest. The rumbling grew louder, and then it stopped. His eyes rolled back in his head. I'd seen it before. I screamed.

"I'm sorry, Daddy! Please forgive me!" I said, gripping his shirt as I kneeled over him. "Help us!" I screamed again. I pulled the phone down from his desk and dialed 911.

The office door flew open. "Oh my God! What happened?" the assistant pastor shrieked. "Bishop, can you speak?"

The secretary rushed in. "Lord Jesus!" she hollered. She snatched the phone from the floor and called Mama. "Sister Goldie, Bishop's suffered a stroke! The ambulance is on the way. Meet us at the hospital."

I prayed and prayed there at my father's side. I begged the Lord to heal and deliver. I pleaded for forgiveness. It wasn't my intention to be proud and rebellious against my father. I would never do anything I thought would harm him.

***

Daddy recovered, and I was so thankful. The irony was that I had to let my dream and my passion for preaching the gospel die. Neither Mama nor James knew what had been said in that room before Daddy collapsed. I wasn't sure if Daddy even remembered because he never spoke of it again. As for me, I wanted to forget it.

When my son was born, I had a new mission. I named him Timothy. I focused all my energy on my marriage and my son. James was ecstatic. Every ounce of joy and happiness that was drained out of me was poured into his cup. Daddy embraced him, the church embraced him, and the community where I grew up embraced him.

It wasn't jealousy that I was feeling; it was more like insignificant, more like an extension of my husband and a mere facilitator for my son. That wasn't the life I had planned or the one I believed God had planned for me. Then it all changed.

It was Timothy's third birthday. A feisty toddler, he sat fidgeting between James and me on the second pew where I sat next to Mama. Daddy was preaching when he read from Nehemiah 2: "'Sir, why shouldn't I be sad? For the city where my ancestors are buried is in ruins and the gates have been burned down.' The church has been damaged, brothers and sisters. The faithful have to come together to rebuild it to God's glory."

"Amen," Mama said, waving her hand in the air.

"Are we ready to do God's will?" Daddy shouted.

A loud yes echoed through the sanctuary.

"We have been through some things; the devil has attacked us from every side. Our bodies, our finances, our marriages, our children, and even our hopes for tomorrow have been under assault. We have to renew our faith and our trust in the Lord. He is my strength and my redeemer. Through Him all things are possible."

Daddy didn't know it, but his words restarted the fire in me that had fizzled three years ago when I pushed the child sitting next to me from my womb. The life I wanted had escaped me. I had surrendered. Sitting there, the courage of my convictions was reignited. I opened the Bible in my lap and turned to the Book of Nehemiah. It was there in the words before my eyes. Whenever you try to do the will of God, you will be criticized. Opposition will rise up against you.

I had allowed my wall of faith to be chipped away and broken down because of my fears and insecurities. That wall was my faith. I realized that I had turned away from God with attempts to lose myself in everyday activities. Those words found me and reclaimed me. I was going to follow my vocation, and the Lord would be my guide. I was filled with joy at the prospect.

"Hallelujah!" I shouted, rising to my feet. I wanted to dance I was so happy. "To God be the glory for all He has done and will do in my life. Praise Jesus!"

The congregation kept praising, and Daddy kept preaching. Mama patted me on the back while Timmy pulled on the hem of my dress. I was so full of emotion, emotion that came from the answer I had been waiting for. Tears of sheer happiness rolled warm down my cheeks. It gave me such peace at that moment. All I could do was thank Jesus and praise His holy name. The joy I felt must have been contagious, because praises erupted throughout the sanctuary until we were all shouting and thanking God for his goodness.

"Bishop sho nuff preached this morning!" Sister Morgan said to Mama, coming over to take a closer look at me when service was over. She was by far the nosiest women in the congregation.

Mama nodded in agreement. "Yes, he did. I could feel the presence of the Lord moving today."

"Looks like Prissy did, too," Sister Morgan said, wishing she could read my mind.

"Yes, ma'am!" I said, smiling.

Timothy squirmed in James's arms. He wanted to get down and run and let go of the pent-up energy from sitting for two hours.

"I'm going to take him out to the parking lot," James said, easing around us.

"I'm right behind you," I said, giving Mama a kiss.

"Are you coming by the house later?" she asked. "I haven't seen Timmy all week."

"Not today. I put a chicken in the crock pot. I'll call you later."

"Okay, sugar, take care. I love you."

"I love you, too."

I made my way out of the sanctuary, passing by more than a few curious smiles and inquisitive greetings. James was waiting for me in the car.

"What's going on with you?" James asked curiously, as we drove out of the parking lot. "I haven't seen you smile like that in a long time."

"I was blessed with a breakthrough this morning," I said, still smiling.

He glanced over at me again. "Wow, if it makes you this happy, then you need to give me a praise report, as your mama would say."

"I've been struggling and stressing over my life and the feeling that I'm stuck, going nowhere fast. It was like I was in some kind of prison where in order to make my family happy, I had to be miserable."

"I didn't know you were miserable."

"I don't mean it like that. What I mean is that I was losing myself and my purpose. It doesn't have anything to do with me being happy with you."

"I beg to differ. I don't see how you can say you're miserable and that it doesn't have anything to do with me. You and Timmy are everything to me, all that I need to be happy."

"I can't help that I felt empty inside. I couldn't control it, but it's going to be okay. The Lord revealed something to me today in the message. He spoke to my heart, saying that I have to move forward in my ministry again. John 4:34 says, 'Jesus said to them, My food is to do the will of him that sent me, and to finish his work.'"

"So, what are you saying? What does that mean?"

"It means that I'm going to start my ministry again."

"That was a big problem between us when we were back at Hampton. That took most of your time and energy, and there was nothing left for me. We can't go through that right now. Timmy is still a baby, and I was hoping he might get a baby sister who looks just like his mama."

"God wouldn't put this on my heart if He wasn't going to make a way for me to accomplish it. I've been supportive of you and held things down while you were coaching and volunteering at the community center. Having another baby right now would only make things harder for me. It's like you want to clip my wings before I even try to fly."

"I was going to talk to you about this after I got more information, but I'm thinking about running for city councilman for the ninth District. I've been putting together a team to work with, and I think I can win. I was hoping you would get on board with me on this."

The first thing that came to my mind wasn't anything I could let come out of my mouth. Intellectually, I knew anything that would help James further his dreams and his career wasn't the devil; but emotionally, anything that would keep me from doing God's will was from Satan himself. This was something I was going to have to get on my knees and pray about. I decided to respond cautiously. Starting an argument would only ruin my good mood and wake up Timmy, who was napping peacefully in his car seat.

"That's sounds like a great opportunity. I didn't know that was something you were even thinking about."

"I was kind of drafted into it. Douglas Bolton is ready to give up his seat for health reasons, and he wants to endorse me as his replacement. He says the timing won't ever get any better."

"For whom? The timing definitely isn't good for me."

"How do you know, Princess? Maybe that revelation you got this morning was about your role in helping me get elected. I'm going to need all the help and hands I can get."

"First of all, I know what God placed on my heart and soul with no uncertainty. Second, I should not have allowed the opinions of Daddy and the church elders to sway me from the calling God has on my life. It was never their decision."

"I never stood in your way, and I'm not now. You have to decide what's important to you. If starting your own church comes before your family, there's nothing I can do about that anyway."

"Don't put it in that context, James. It's not that cut and dried. Nobody says a man has to choose between his family and his work. It's not fair."

"You're right, it's not fair; but it is what it is."

"I not giving up on you and our family, but I'm also not giving up on my ministry again. The Lord will make a way. I believe that."

"I hope you're right," he said.

***

Initially, I planned to establish another Bible study like the one I started at Hampton. I could use the community center and try to slowly grow a following before I looked for a building to meet. I fasted and prayed for guidance.

After a week, it was clear what I had to do. I had to make a clean break from the only church home I had ever known. Easing the bandage off the wound between Daddy and me would only hurt more, so it had to be removed as swiftly as possible.

Everything in and around me was pushing me to step out on faith. Sitting in front of my computer, going through a list of affordable housing listings for a client, I changed my search to retail spaces/storefronts. Scrolling down the list, most were retail spaces for stores or restaurants. And then I saw it. It was a small warehouse on Green Noble Road. It was 5,000 square feet, and they wanted eight dollars per square foot/year. I clicked on the calculator and did the numbers. It came to $40,000 for the year. I had that in my savings from the two years I lived at home with Mama and Daddy. I picked up the phone and called the number listed.

I felt like a criminal when I signed the lease, as if I were breaking some kind of law or unspoken rule; and I knew there would be hell to pay when my deed came to light. My defense was an irresistible compulsion to pursue my lifelong purpose. Who would believe I was compelled by God to write that check without consulting a single soul about the risk that I was taking? I began to wonder if maybe I did need some type of psychiatric evaluation.

After the fact, sitting in my car, and reeling from my own actions, there was only one person on earth I felt would understand. I prayed there was some battery life on my phone.

"What's up, girlfriend?" Tamu answered cheerily.

"I've done something that you won't believe," I whispered as if somebody else could hear.

"Excuse me! I lived with you for four years. I'll believe it."

"I signed a lease on a building that will be my first church, a church without any members, and I didn't discuss it with James or my folks."

There was a pause on the phone, a silence I didn't know how to interpret.

Then she hollered. "Boom! You better go, Prissy! That was bold as hell! You have got more balls than Batman. I need you on my team!"

"What if I made a mistake, Tam? I'm shaking so badly I can't even drive."

"No sense in shaking now. What's done is done. You've committed yourself. Now you have to follow through. Erase all those doubts, and get your ass to work. You have to fill that building with some bodies and a few fat wallets."

"I haven't even thought that far."

"Well, now you have to. You know this hustle. You did this before, and you can do it again. It's time to step out of the Jimmy Choo's and into some Chuck Taylor's or Timberlands and pound the pavement."

"That's not the part that's scaring the hell out of me. It's telling my family. James will probably leave me, and my father will probably have another stroke."

"James isn't going anywhere. That brother is certifiably insane when it comes to you. And your daddy has been a pain in your ass since you were born, so now you'll be a pain in his. He'll deal with it. Y'all are blood."

"It's more complicated than that. James has his own agenda now; he wants to run for city councilman, with me as the woman by his side—and a pregnant one at that! He thinks I'm selfish for wanting to establish this church."

"Yeah, you're right. That deepened the plot. All I can tell you is that we're all selfish to a certain extent. I think you both can work together and mutually benefit each of you." Then she laughed. "Y 'all can knock on doors together—him with the 'Vote for Me' flyers and you with the 'Visit Our Church' flyers. Girl, this can work!"

I laughed with her, and her positivity and humor calmed me down some. Then I thought about Daddy.

"This is not the way I wanted things to be between my father and me. I wanted to be his protégé. I wanted to sit beside him on the platform. I wanted to preach in his pulpit, with him shouting amen behind me. I wanted him to be proud of me."

"I understand why you can't let that go. You idolize that man. But if you're gonna do this, you're gonna have to let it go. At some point, you have to stop living for the approval of other people and live your truth, right or wrong. You know me. I'm not about regrets; I'm about experiences. This is going to be an exciting experience for you."

"In my head, I know that. I'm just not looking forward to the walk through the fire that I know is waiting for me."

"Walk on through it, child. You're not going to get burned. Go back to that story you told about the three men in the fire and God in there with them. They survived, and you will, too. That's not to say I wouldn't pay for a ringside ticket to see that show."

"I can send you a plane ticket. I need somebody in my corner."

"You'll be fine. I have faith in you, and you have faith in God. Just don't hurt anybody; I haven't passed the bar exam yet."

"Thanks, Tamu. I think I can at least get myself home now."

"Okay, well, call me after the showdown; I want a blow-by-blow of what happened."

"You know I will. God bless you, Tamu. You always bless me."

"Bye, Prissy."

***

I folded a towel on the floor of the master bathroom beside the tub to cushion my knees before I began to pray. Having the courage of my convictions wasn't enough, I needed the Savior to intercede on my behalf. The jury would not be unprejudiced or impartial.

"Lord Jesus, please grant me Your mercy and Your grace today. I don't believe You would have put this calling on me and not provide a path for me to follow. Soften the hearts of those who would judge and condemn me, and fill me the peace that passes all understanding. In Your precious and holy name, I pray."

My emotions vacillated during the morning service from sadness, guilt, and then relief. Breaking away from your upbringing is traumatic and heart-wrenching. At moments, I had to turn away from the sight of my father as he preached from the deception I felt. My comfort was in knowing that I finally had implemented a plan. I wasn't hanging and twisting at the end of my rope; I had taken the big leap, and I was airborne. Only God would know my fate; but at that moment, I was soaring, buoyant with the hope of the future.

Sitting at the dinner table that Sunday afternoon, I felt like Judas Iscariot. The bubbling in my gut signaled to me that I should have told James about the lease before I told my parents, but I didn't want to go through the impending punishment twice. I was torn between dropping the bomb before we ate and ruining everyone's appetite, or waiting until after we ate and causing indigestion and heartburn. Thinking about all the work Mama had done to prepare the meal, I decided that it would be better not to waste good food.

After dinner, I took Timmy out of his highchair and let him sit in my lap, hoping that the full-on assault might be gentler if he were there in front of me. I shifted Timmy to the crook of my left arm and began to plead my case. "There's something that I have to share with everybody, and

I hope you all will be happy for me; and if not, I hope you can understand my actions."

James and Daddy stared at me with stone faces.

Mama, already sympathetic, spoke nervously. "We all love you, Prissy, and we're here for you."

"There's no way I can say this easily or make it more acceptable, so I'll be straightforward. Last Sunday, the Lord spoke to me and revealed that it is time for me to go out on my own and start my own ministry."

"Prissy, please don't!" Mama said, her eyes pleading with me.

Neither James nor Daddy spoke.

"Please, let me finish. It is not my intention to hurt anyone. This is something that God has put on me. I have to be obedient to His will. This week, I found a building that will serve as the church for my ministry, and I signed a lease."

James threw his napkin down and almost knocked the table over when he stood up and stomped out of the room.

"Child, how could you do such a thing without discussing it with us first?" Mama asked, shaking her head in dismay. "Do you think you can cancel it and get your money back?"

"I don't want to cancel it, and I don't want my money back. I want your blessings on my ministry."

"Let me take Timmy out to his daddy," Mama said, pulling him from my arms and hurrying out of the room.

Daddy finally spoke. "I can't give you my blessing on something I know is not right. Why do you insist on defying me, young lady? This is nothing but the devil trying to destroy our family. I won't stand for it."

"You're wrong, Daddy. I'm not defying you; I'm being obedient to God."

"God is good, God is love. He wouldn't direct you to dishonor your father and deceive your husband. That's from the pits of hell!"

"No, Daddy, there is no ill will in my heart. I honor you, and I have been honest with James. God called me to preach the gospel; I told you that a long time ago. You won't let me stand in your pulpit, so I didn't have any other choice. Preaching God's word is what I was born to do."

"If God wanted you to preach, you would have been my son, but you're my daughter. I can't change that, and you can't either."

That riled me up out of my chair. "If that's what you want to believe, I can't change that! I've made peace with who I am after spending my life torn up because I was born female. I'm sorry for being a disappointment to you, but it's time for me to live my life, the life God has preordained for me."

"Don't disrespect your father in this house!" Mama said, coming back into the room.

"I'm sorry. I didn't want it to be like this."

"Enough has been said about this today," Mama said, ending the discussion. I knew she was worried about Daddy getting upset and running his blood pressure up.

"I love you, Mama," I said giving her a hug. On my way out, I put my hand on Daddy's shoulder. "I love you, too, Daddy." He didn't respond.

"We love you, Prissy," Mama called out as I stepped out the door.

***

James gave me the silent treatment all the way home, and I was grateful for it. It gave me a chance to calm down after talking to Daddy and time to gather my thoughts for Round Two. My jump out of the starting gate might have been questionable, but I was positive I had done the right thing. I had to make a strong move before I told them, or they would have put up barriers to slow me down or get in my way.

Anyway, I was feeling encouraged. Daddy had survived my announcement without having to be rushed to the hospital. Getting James to give me a pass on this was the most important hurdle I would have to leap over; he's the one I had to sleep with.

There was no doubt that James was pissed with me. When we got home, he got out of the car, no waiting or holding doors, and walked in the house like I wasn't even there. The gentleman in him was definitely on hiatus. I got Timmy out of his car seat and carried him straight to his bedroom, praying he would stay asleep until after the showdown. James was in our bedroom changing clothes. I opened the door, walked in, and stood in the middle of the floor, ready for my second tongue-lashing.

He shook his head before he looked in my direction. "You know, when I met you, I thought you were an angel. You certainly looked like one. You were innocent and sweet, something I hadn't seen much of. That's what I wanted in my life; that's what I wanted in my wife. After today, it looks like you were the devil in disguise."

"What are you talking about, James? I'm not going to stand here and let you call me a devil."

"Don't forget I've been sitting in church beside you for four years while your Daddy preached about the devil, and

I've heard the description from your own mouth. You said he moves like a thief, deceives you, and wrestles against you like an enemy. That's what you do, Princess. You're always going against me. You took our money, the trust I had in you, and you betrayed me without any consideration to how I would feel or the damage it would have on our marriage."

"James, you are being super dramatic. That's not what happened. I didn't use the money from our joint account; I had some money saved before we got married."

"So that makes what you did all right."

"I'm not saying that."

"What are you saying then, that you were honest and upfront about it?"

"It wasn't like that. I wasn't sneaking around behind your back trying to undermine you. I wasn't even looking for a church. I believe that finding that building was some kind of divine intervention. I just stepped out on faith and claimed it. There was no evil intent."

"When you first mentioned starting your ministry again, I told you that I wanted to run for the city council. Don't you think we should have talked more about it before you signed anything? That's the consideration I gave you when they asked me to run. I told them I would have to discuss it with my wife."

The conversation wasn't going the way I had planned. James was making more sense than I was. Maybe I had been too hasty.

"I can't understand why the men in my life can't get behind me and support me on this!" I said in frustration.

"My place isn't behind you, Princess. We are supposed to be partners who support each other. Except, this marriage isn't a partnership. We're on two different sides."

"That's not true. I'm on your side. I heard you when you said you wanted to run for city council. I support you on that. I wouldn't do anything to stand in your way, and I hope you feel the same about me and my ministry."

"I know how you get when your mind is set on something. You go full throttle, and anything in front of you is going to get rolled over."

"All I'm asking for is that you not fight me on this."

"It doesn't make any difference how I feel. You're going to do what you want anyway."

"We can work this out," I said, remembering what Tamu told me. "We can canvass the neighborhood together—you for votes; me for church members. It'll be fun. I'll be there for whatever you need: rallies, meetings, and fundraisers. I promise."

James's shoulders relaxed, and he exhaled. He was out of attack mode. He still wouldn't look at me, but thank the Lord, he was listening again and was thinking about my idea. If Tamu were here in my corner, she'd tell me that it was time to use the secret weapon and end this fight. I moved in closer, close enough to touch his back. I stroked it lightly, hoping to soften his resolve.

"I know I should have talked with you first. The way I went about it was wrong, and I'm very sorry for that. I love you, and I don't want to do anything that would jeopardize our family." He didn't answer, but he didn't move away. I put my arms around his waist and moved around to face him. I stood on my toes to kiss his lips and pulled him closer. "I don't want to lose you, baby. You're everything to me."

"This was your last time to do something like that," he said, staring straight in my eyes. "It was disrespectful, and that's not the way I want to live."

"Don't worry. I won't," I said, pulling him over to the bed.

***

I kept my word and canvassed the neighborhood with James. From the first door we knocked on, I knew everything was going to be all right. James knocked on the door, I stood next to him holding Timmy's hand.

"Good afternoon, sir. My name is James Sinclair," James said, extending his hand. "This is my wife, Priscilla, and my son, Timmy. I'm running for councilman in this district, and I would love to have your support."

"Yeah, I know you," the man said. "You coach the basketball team over at Henderson."

James handed him a flyer. "That's right, I do. I'm a teacher there as well. I'm hoping to fill Councilman Bolton's seat, and I need your vote to do that."

"Oh sure, you can have my vote. You're a good man working with those boys. We need more like you in the community."

"Thank you, sir, I appreciate that."

"Hold on a minute. I want my wife to meet you. Honeybun, come here," he said, calling over his shoulder. "This fellow here is running for the councilman's seat."

"Hi there. You are a tall, handsome one, aren't you?" she said, stepping into the doorway.

"Thank you, ma'am."

"Pretty wife and baby, too," she said, smiling at me.

"My wife is starting up a church over on Crescent."

"Yes, ma'am," I said, taking James's cue and moving

forward. "It's the Tabernacle of Grace Nondenominational Church. I would love it if you would come and visit. We're having a grand opening in two weeks."

"We don't have a car, so we don't get around much," the woman said.

"We both need your support. If you need a ride to church or to the polls to vote, call me," James said, handing them a card.

"I'll definitely do that," the man said.

We paced ourselves and knocked on doors for a couple of hours after work every day. James went with his campaign supporters on Saturday. In the meantime, I was interviewing for a musician to play my second-hand piano and making a few renovations to turn my building into a church before the first service. Luckily, I had several clients who needed extra money, so I hired them to do clean-up, painting, and landscaping. It was a far cry from the grand building and grounds of Thompson Boulevard, where I grew up, but it was a start. And nobody could keep me from preaching and teaching the goodness of God.

More out of habit than anything else, I sat on the pew next to Mama on Sunday and listened to Daddy preach his sermon. I was there physically, but my mind and heart had already left the building. The whispers and gossip had become uncomfortable, so I was glad that this was my last Sunday at Daddy's church. With James and me canvassing the neighborhood almost every day, it was no longer a secret that I was leaving and starting my own church.

***

Finally, it was the day I had prayed and waited for, the day I would preach my first sermon in my own church. My sermon had been prepared for weeks, but the finishing touches on the building weren't completed until after dark the night before. It had to be spotless. Tamu had come to town to help me and to be a seat-filler just in case I found myself having to preach to an empty room.

I slowly eased out of bed, trying not to disturb James, who was still asleep. I wasn't rested by any means, but I had been awake for hours. Wrapped in a towel after my shower, I gazed at my reflection in the mirror, staring at the only person who knew how much this day meant to me and the trials I had gone through to get here. There was a hint of tiredness around my eyes. It was strange to be exhausted and exhilarated at the same time.

I hadn't had time to get to the beauty salon, so I twisted and pinned my weak curls into a nice up-do. With make-up done and ready except for the new cream-colored suit I bought especially for today, I went to the kitchen to make coffee before Timmy woke up. I was too anxious to eat, but I knew I should put something in my stomach. It would be a while before I got another chance to eat. I was peering in the fridge, trying to decide what to eat, when Tamu, wearing her robe and carrying the newspaper, came dragging her feet into the kitchen.

"What are you rambling around in here for?" Tamu asked, tossing her newspaper on the table. "I know you're not getting ready to cook."

"I need to eat something; I just don't want anything too heavy."

"Go on over there and sit down. Keep your mind relaxed. I'll scramble some eggs and throw some of that turkey bacon in the microwave."

"Thanks, girl. I have enough to think about. I hope everything goes well."

"Everything is going to be fine. It's not that serious. You're not going to man a spaceship and orbit the earth. You're going to lead a worship service. You've done that many times."

"I know. But I've burned a few bridges, and there's no turning back."

"You've never turned back in your life. If I know you—and I do—this is only the beginning for you and Tabernacle of Grace."

"Amen, Tamu, you're preaching to me this morning."

"Yes, girl, and if you need me, I'll be sitting right in the back row."

"Stop it," I laughed, remembering how she always sat in the last row. "I wish my folks could be there today."

"Don't even go there, Prissy. They have their business to tend to and so do you. Now do you want some toast with these eggs?"

"Yes, please, and some jelly if you don't mind."

"I don't mind," she said, dropping four pieces of rye bread in the toaster.

I poured myself a cup of coffee, sat down, and browsed through the newspaper, looking at pictures and ads. James walked in holding Timmy, both of them dressed and ready to go.

"Good morning, ladies," James said, sliding Timmy in his booster seat. "I knew I smelled something cooking."

"It's not much, but it will fill the void," Tamu said, putting the food on the table. "What do you want to drink?"

"A cup of coffee for me," James answered.

"I want juice," Timmy said, chiming in. He was at the age of repeating everything he heard.

"All right, little man," Tamu said, reaching in the cabinet for one of his sippy cups. She filled Timmy's cup with apple juice, poured James a mug of coffee, and placed them on the table. "I'm going to finish getting dressed while you all eat. I've never been much of a breakfast person myself."

"Well, we have to thank you, Tamu. We're all on edge a little this morning," James said. "Lunch is on me, whatever you want."

"Now that's what I'm talking about!" Tamu said, strutting back to the guest room to get dressed.

"How do you feel?" James asked, touching my hand.

"I'm excited, but I'm nervous. I've wanted this for so long."

"You've always known what you wanted to do, and you made it happen. I'm proud of you."

"I'm proud of you, Mommy," Timmy added, echoing his father.

"It's about time for us to get this show on the road," James said, looking at his watch.

"You're right," I said. I stood up and put my arms around James and hugged him tightly. "I know I make a big deal about God being first in my life, but you two guys are my life. Thanks for your patience and understanding. I know I'm not the easiest person to live with."

"Tell me about it!" James chuckled. "But you're worth it."

"I love you, baby."

"I love you, Princess."

"I love you, Mommy," Timmy added.

***

When we pulled up to the parking lot outside of the church, my heart sank a little. There was only one car there. It belonged to Kenny Price, the man I had hired to be the musician and choir director. He got out of his car and came to meet us. For a moment, I was embarrassed by the empty parking lot. Something in me wanted to go back home and hide; but when James opened the car door for me, I didn't have a choice. I had to get out and face the music.

"Good morning, Pastor Sinclair," Kenny said, smiling widely. "It's a beautiful day to open your church."

"Yes, it is a beautiful day," I said. "I hope we have a few more folks come out to share it with us."

"It's still early," Kenny said, still smiling.

I nodded and led the way to the front door. "Remind me to give you a key so you can open up when you get here."

"All right," he said, holding the door for us.

I walked past the door of the sanctuary without looking in. At that moment, I couldn't bear the sight of 250 empty chairs.

"Aren't you going in?" James asked, confused.

"You all go ahead on in and sit down. I'll be back. I've got to go to my office for a minute," I told them, needing a few moments to pray and gather my emotions.

In my office, I closed the door behind me and considered locking it for some reason. I would have fallen on my knees and cried to the Lord, but the dust would have shown up on my light-colored suit.

"My God!" I called out to Him in a hushed shout. "I know You would not have brought me this far to leave me. I need thee, O Lord. I have sacrificed so much for this moment. I have turned my back on my father. I just wanted to do Thy will. Help me, Jesus."

I heard a voice inside me speak. "You are only worried about appearances. You haven't suffered anything. It is only your pride that is hurt. Stop licking imaginary wounds, and go deliver God's word. Remember Matthew 18:20: 'For where two or three are gathered together in my name, there am I in the midst of them.'"

I straightened my back and raised my chin. I had nothing to be ashamed of. I would preach the word given to me. It didn't matter how many people were there to hear me. Kenny was playing the song "He Is Able" as I walked to the sanctuary. My heels clicked loudly on the linoleum floor, and I made a mental note to get a carpet runner before next Sunday. I took a deep breath and pushed open the doors to my makeshift sanctuary.

All I could say was, "Thank you, Jesus!" I hadn't failed. There were almost 100 people sitting in that sanctuary. I even recognized several people from Daddy's church. I walked up the short center aisle, making eye contact with everyone I could, shaking hands, and thanking them for coming.

At last, I stood in my own pulpit. "Glory be to God, who has brought us all here today. Good morning, and thank you for sharing this grand opening of the Tabernacle of Grace. I'm so privileged to have you here. I want to thank God, who is my Savior, and my husband, James, for all of his support. This is an informal service today, and we'll go wherever the Spirit carries us.

"I'd like to call you to worship with these words. In the Book of Exodus, God instructed the Israelites to build a 'place of dwelling for him' a 'tabernacle.' When Christ was born, everything changed. Second Corinthians 6:16 says, 'And what agreement hath the temple of God with idols? For ye are the temple of the living God; as God hath said, I will dwell in them, and walk in them; and I will be their God, and they shall be my people.' Please stand with me as we sing."

The room wasn't big enough to require a microphone; and the sound of those voices—some off key—hit the walls, bounced back from the ceiling, and filled my heart with joy. I glanced over toward James and saw Timmy, clapping and grinning. I sang louder, feeling the sentiment of every word. If this makeshift church would have been the Sistine Chapel, I could not have been happier.

"I want to talk for a few moments about 'Stepping Out of Your Comfort Zone.' Isaiah 42:16 says, 'And I will lead the blind in a way that they do not know, in paths that they have not known I will guide them. I will turn the darkness before them into light, the rough places into level ground. These are the things I do, and I do not forsake them.'

"Christian friends, fear is a basic human emotion. We have natural built-in instincts of fear: fear of heights; fear of water; fear of mice or spiders; and my personal number one, fear of snakes. In many ways, our fears protect us from certain danger. We retreat to places of safety, our comfort zones. Then there are other kinds of fears: fear of public speaking, fear of heartbreak, fear of failure, and fear of success. These fears can block us from God's greatest blessings if we choose to stay in our places of safety.

"When the Israelites arrived at Canaan, the land promised to them, they were afraid to cross over into the land. They had lost their trust in God. Because of that, they weren't allowed to enter the Promised Land. Because Caleb trusted the Lord, free from fear, he was allowed to enter into Canaan and was given a portion that would belong to his descendants forever.

"I want to challenge you, as I challenge myself, to come out of your comfort zone, to take chances, to step out on faith and witness the miracles that God has to offer. Go back to school, apply for that new job, go out on that date, or audition for that part. God cannot move in our lives unless we move. Sure, it's scary, but our God is faithful. He will never leave you nor forsake you. Put your trust in Him, Christian friends.

"Please stand with me. If there is anyone here today who would like to join me in this new journey, anyone who is ready to put their trust in Jesus Christ and throw away their fears, please come forward. I offer you my hand in fellowship."

Kenny started to play. I wanted to shout and do the holy dance when I saw someone move toward the front, then another and then another and then another. I couldn't count them as I took their hands in mine.

"Thank you, my sister; thank you, my brother," I said, acknowledging a couple from my daddy's church. "Welcome to the Tabernacle of Grace." The atmosphere was so genuine, a feeling I hadn't experienced in a very long time. "This is a very young church, and I need your support. I'm going to pass around a basket for offering to keep this ministry alive and growing. I thank the Lord, and I thank you all."

I gave the benediction to end the service. James was there and took my hand as I stepped down onto the floor. I grabbed him in a hug and held on in relief.

"You did it, Princess," he whispered in my ear.

"I give God all the glory," I said, holding back my tears of joy.

A line formed to speak to me and shake my hand. They gave me the support and the encouragement I needed that day. Someone offered to form a clean-up crew; another person said she wanted to join the choir. Others volunteered to print our church programs, care for the children during the services, and cook food. It was so beautifully overwhelming that I didn't even notice when James drifted away. Before long, the group had dwindled down to the five of us who met in the empty parking lot earlier that morning: James, Timmy, Tamu, Kenny, and me.

"I'll see you next week!" Kenny said, walking toward his car.

I hurried over to speak with him. "Thank you for doing such a wonderful job."

"It was my pleasure. I didn't know how this was going to work out, but when I heard your message, all my worries disappeared like hot steam."

"I'm glad to hear that," I said.

"I don't mean to rush you but I'm about to starve," Tamu yelled out from the backseat window.

"Go on and have a nice lunch with your family," Kenny said, "You earned it."

"Thanks, I couldn't have done it without you," I said, squeezing his hand before I headed over to the car.

He smiled and waved as he drove away.

"Sorry for holding up the progress," I said, sliding in the front seat.

"It's your moment," James said. "I guess I can forgive you."

"We forgive you," Timmy chimed in.

"Speak for yourself, Timmy," Tamu added. "Your auntie needs some food."

"I'm going to feed you whatever you want," James said with a quick glance over his shoulder as he pulled out of the parking lot.

"I'm so glad you could come, Tamu," I told her. "For a minute, I thought you were going to be sitting in that back row by yourself."

"You don't have that to worry about. For a first Sunday in a brand-new church, you did a fantastic job."

"I have to say that the canvassing I did with you, James, really helped me get the word out."

"Well, the election is not for six weeks so we'll have to keep it going," James said, stopping at a red light.

I rubbed my hand on his leg. "I'll be right there, believe me. I have to thank you again for your patience and understanding . . . and for not leaving me!" I added, half joking.

"You tried me," he said, chuckling, and gave me a quick kiss. "I've always been a sucker for a pretty face."

"Do you all need to get a room before we eat?" Tamu asked, teasing us. "This is too much for me, what do you think, Timmy?"

"It's too much," Timmy squealed, and we all laughed.

"Seriously though, Princess," James said after we calmed down. "I know you're not going to act like you didn't see those people from your daddy's church there today."

"I know. They were probably just curious. Word gets around in this city."

"A few of them joined and filled out membership cards," James added.

"What can I say? The doors of the church are open to anybody who wants to come in. There's nothing I can do about that."

"Maybe not, but it means you have a problem, Prissy," Tamu said. "That's all about loyalty right there."

"What am I supposed to do? Should I tell them they can't join my congregation because my daddy might get upset? This isn't the way I wanted things to go. I wanted to sit up there next to my daddy and be his right hand, but he said no."

"Let's forget about all that and celebrate this day," James said, changing the subject. "Who wants to eat at The Roosevelt?"

"Yes, indeed, I do," Tamu said happily.

"I do," Timmy repeated enthusiastically.

***

Over the next six weeks, the membership at Tabernacle of Grace grew like wildflowers. Each Sunday, it seemed like it was double the number of the week before. I had to buy more chairs, and we were running out of space to put them. We now had a choir and a secretary. If things continued to blossom as they were, I was going to have to find a larger building. It was also time to appoint additional leadership to help handle the business of the church.

I had been so busy with the church and campaign activities with James that I hadn't been able to make Sunday dinner with Mama and Daddy for a month. When she called and asked me to meet her for lunch the day before the election, it was bad timing; but I felt so guilty for not seeing her for several weeks that I cancelled two appointments so I could meet her.

She looked older or tired when she walked into Morton's Restaurant downtown. I stood up to greet her, we hugged, and she kissed me on the cheek.

"It's good to see you, Prissy. I've been missing you and Timmy."

"I know. Things have been so hectic lately. After tomorrow, it should ease up some, and we can get our schedules back close to normal."

"I wanted to talk to you about your father." Before she could say anything else, the waitress came over to the table. "Could you give us a few minutes?" Mama told her with a strained smile.

I sensed that might be the subject of the lunch, quite a few members from his church were now members of my church, but I was surprised that she got to it before we even ordered. She was usually more diplomatic in her approach. That's when I knew it was serious.

"Is Daddy okay?" I asked, concerned.

"No, he isn't. Your church is causing a rift at Thompson Boulevard, and it's breaking your father's heart. So many members have left, people who had been there for years. Some grew up there, just like you did. This can't go on."

It hurt me to see my mother so upset. "I never set out to take members from the church I grew up in. I would never do that."

"But that's what has happened, child."

"I don't have any control over that. What do you want me to do?"

"I want you to unite these people into one church, your daddy's church. This split is tearing him down."

"Mama, how can I do that? I have financial responsibilities to Tabernacle of Grace. The church doesn't just belong to me; it belongs to the congregation. I can't shut it down and say never mind."

"You are young. You can start another church in a few years. Give your father this time. This is weakening him. I can see it."

"Why is this my fault? I am a pastor, but Daddy wouldn't let me preach there. I accepted that. I left without causing any problems or protests. The people at my church don't have a problem with a woman preaching the word of God. I couldn't even guarantee that they would come back. Maybe they have their reasons for leaving."

"Don't be disrespectful."

"I'm sorry, Mama, but there isn't much I can do."

"Don't you love your father?"

"Of course, I do. You know that."

"Then you have to know that this is killing him."

"Maybe you should be talking to the elders at the church. They are the ones who have a decision to make. I don't have a problem uniting our churches as long as I can stand in the pulpit just like any of them."

Mama shook her head in dismay. I could tell this wasn't the response she'd hoped for. She looked at her watch and reached for her purse.

"Prissy, I won't be able to stay for lunch. I've got to get back and check on your father."

"Okay, Mama, I love you; and I love Daddy."

"We love you too, baby," she said and hurried out of the restaurant.

****

James won Douglas Bolton's seat on the city council. The blessings that were pouring on us forced us to make more changes. James hadn't thought he would have to give up teaching at Henderson or coaching the basketball team, but the obligations of being councilman in the Ninth District were more demanding of his time. I empathized with the internal struggle because I was having one of my own. The inevitable conversation that we had been avoiding couldn't be put off any longer.

One evening after I put Timmy to bed, I joined him on the carport, where he liked to sit and drink a beer at the end of a hectic day.

"What's on your mind?" I asked, sitting on the wall next to him.

"I'm wondering how I got here. I never set out to be a politician. I didn't have big dreams like some people; all I wanted to do was teach kids and coach basketball. I loved what I was doing, and it's all changed."

"You have an opportunity to make a difference in those kids' lives, James. You can help make sure that they have more resources, better housing, and better schools and programs that will benefit many more. You can have a real impact on the community."

"I understand that, but I don't like the feeling that I've abandoned them for my own gain."

"You haven't done that. You're still there for them; it's just in another capacity. You can still spend time at the school and help out with the team. If being councilman isn't what you want to do, then after you serve your two years, you don't have to run again. You can go back to teaching."

"I know that, but all my life, I've been a team player, and now it seems like I've left the team out of the game. One of my frat brothers called earlier, and he can't catch a break."

"Don't ever feel guilty about the doors that God has opened for you. That's the only way you can help someone else come through."

"I can't argue with that," he said, taking a swig of beer.

"I'm having a similar problem," I told him, brushing my foot against the pavement. "I think the time has come for me to leave my job and pastor full-time."

"It's only been a few months. Don't you think that's rushing things?"

"The church has grown so fast, we've already outgrown the building we're in. I didn't expect this to happen so soon. I'm hoping that we can find a larger church that's for sale close by, or we may have to build a new one from the ground up."

"You're talking big money and a big commitment."

"Absolutely, and there are so many things to deal with that it's becoming too hard for me to work full-time and handle the rising responsibilities. We need to have a permanent staff to maintain the business and the building of the church. I can't keep asking people to volunteer."

"What do you want me to say, Princess? I have accepted how much this means to you. What is hard for me to accept is that it all comes before our family. You never mentioned us in your future plans. It's always about you and the church."

"That's not fair, babe. If I were a man, this would not be

an issue. My dedication wouldn't be questioned. It would be praised and admired."

"That may be true, but you are a wife and a mother, positions you voluntarily took. Don't you think we deserve the same dedication as your ministry?"

"Family and a career or a vocation is a balancing act for every woman. I'm not perfect. No one is, but I do the best I can."

"With both of us going full speed in different directions, where does that leave Timmy?"

"We can make it work if we support each other. That's how we've made it this far."

"Okay, Princess, we'll see," he said, draining his beer.

***

A few months later, I was sitting in the pulpit when I saw an older man in a dark suit who looked vaguely familiar rush in the sanctuary and head straight for James in the front pew. He leaned over and whispered in his ear. I watched James's facial expression change as he listened, his brow furrowed and a frown appeared. Something was wrong. Wild birds instead of butterflies took flight in my stomach. When James got up and moved toward me, I knew it was Daddy. I whispered to my assistant that I would have to leave the service and began to pray.

We left Timmy in the church nursery, and James broke every speed limit driving me to the hospital. He was dodging and changing lanes so erratically, I closed my eyes. While I was praying for Daddy, I prayed for the Lord to get us there safely. I was a nervous wreck by the time we pulled into the emergency room parking lot. There was a group of church members in the waiting area praying in a circle, but I didn't see Mama.

I burst through the door that read "Do Not Enter," searching every window until I found the room where my father was located. I pushed it open. Mama was sitting next to the bed hunched over and humming a song I didn't recognize; it almost sounded like moaning. Daddy had tubes and wires all over him that were connected to a machine beside his bed. His face was twisted as if he were in pain.

"Mama, what happened?" I asked, gently touching her shoulder.

"Prissy, I'm glad you're here. Your father had another stroke. It was a bad one this time. He was preaching, and then all of sudden, he fell down right there in the pulpit."

"Is he conscious? Did he say anything?"

"No, he hasn't come to yet. They did a brain scan. The doctor says we have to wait and see what the damage is," she said, taking my hand in hers and holding it.

I felt helpless standing there. Silently, I asked God to forgive me because I knew that I owned some of the blame for him lying there. I don't know how long I stood there, but my feet had gone numb. Mama kept on humming her sad song. Then I saw James at the window. I eased my hand from Mama's and stepped out.

"How's your Dad?" James asked, concerned.

"We don't know yet. We're waiting for the tests to come back, and he hasn't woken up yet."

"I'm going to have to pick up Timmy, but I'll be back as soon as I can."

"Don't worry about me. Take him home, and get something to eat. I'm going to be here for a while. I'll call you when I get any news."

"Okay, I'll be at the house. If you need me, call," he said, wrapping his arms around me in a hug I didn't want to let go.

"I will," I said, going back into the room.

***

The doctors told us that Daddy had a massive stroke and that they couldn't give us a set prognosis. After a week, he was transferred to a rehabilitation center for long-term care. My mother and I were praying at his bedside when three elders from the church came to visit. Brother Harold was the leader in front with his Bible in his hand. He took off his hat as he approached Daddy's bed. Mama raised her hand and motioned for them all to wait outside.

"I'll be back, Prissy," she said, getting up. "Your father doesn't need to be disturbed." Then she tiptoed out to talk with the elders in the hallway. Quietly, I got up to peep and listen to them through a crack in the door.

"Sister Goldie, he's paralyzed on his right side this time. He can barely speak. There's no way to know how long it will take for him to recover. We can't leave the pulpit empty indefinitely. We've got to put someone in his place."

"No, Brother Harold, we need to wait on the Lord. He's always answered my prayers and healed William. Where's your faith?"

"I'm praying for the bishop, too, but it's been three months without any change. You know if he recovers that there won't be a problem with him taking his rightful place in the church."

"You mean *when* he recovers, and don't you forget who built that church," Mama said, pointing her finger at him.

Brother Harold didn't back down. "The church doesn't belong to any man. It's God's house. The congregation has to have leadership."

"Priscilla can come back and take his place until he's able to get back up there. She's an ordained pastor, and she's respected in the community."

"As much as I love Prissy, we can't allow that, and you know the bishop wouldn't approve."

"Half of the congregation is already over there at Tabernacle anyway. Maybe we can put the church back together again."

"It's not our place to try to please the world, sister. We have to stay true to God's teaching and His holy word. We didn't come here to trouble you; we came to put you at ease. There's nothing for you to worry about except getting the bishop well."

"Thank you for coming, Brother Harold," she said harshly.

"The church is praying for you all," he said, putting his hat back on.

Mama came back and sat down without a word. I knew she wanted me to come back to the church and help unite the congregation again. She'd hinted at it a couple of times. Somehow, she thought it would spark the miracle to Daddy's healing, except I knew it would never happen. Those old men were stuck in their ways and would never let me preach, and there was no way I could sit in a pew in my father's church and see another man standing in his place. It would be too much to bear. He was the only man I'd seen there, and I was the only one who should take his place.

"Is everything okay?" I asked, knowing it wasn't.

"The devil is busy as usual," she answered.

***

Three years later, so many things had changed, and some things had remained the same. James learned to play the game of politics and discovered he was pretty good at it. He ran again for his second term and was reelected councilman. I resigned from my job as a social worker and worked full-time as pastor at our new church. We were able to purchase a larger building that held over 2,000 people, and it was full every Sunday. Our choir had grown, and we had added additional ministries for youth, singles, and seniors.

Daddy had improved some, but he was still a patient at the rehabilitation center. His speech was slurred, and he remained partially paralyzed on one side, unable to dress himself. Mentally, he had all his faculties, thank God, or at least most of them. He'd sunk into a deep depression. Some days when I visited, he made no secret about wanting the Lord to take him home. Mama had spent a whole year by his side until her doctor warned her that if she kept it up, she would soon be in a bed next him. We agreed that she would go visit twice a week, the church mothers would go twice a week, and I would go once a week.

When the elders hired a new pastor, Mama refused to go back to Thompson Boulevard until Daddy was back in the pulpit. In the meantime, she was sitting on the front pew on the other side of Timmy at our church.

"I believe in your calling, Prissy," she said to me after she heard me preach for the first time. "Your daddy was blind and is set in his ways."

"Thank you, Mama. It makes me feel better seeing you here. Sometimes I think I'm responsible for Daddy being sick."

"Stop thinking that! Your father has his cross to bear as we all do. There's nothing you can do about it. God is in control, and that's what gives me peace at night."

"I wish he could come and hear me preach. Maybe it might change his mind."

"Your daddy is an old man. Don't ask or expect the impossible from him. Thank the Lord that you have this beautiful church here. You have so many blessings to count."

"Not everything is perfect, Mama. Things aren't so good between James and me. He's out late most of the time; and when he comes home, we don't talk. He used to share all the things that happened to him during the day, the things that he's working on, the meetings he went to, and what people were saying. We're drifting further apart."

"When you're the leader of a church, whether you intend it or not, your family comes second. That's easier for a woman to understand than it is for a man. Don't treat him like your housemaid or your nanny. You have to do everything you can to let him know how important he is in your life. Men have to feel needed. If you act like you don't need him, he'll find someone else who does."

"I'm doing the best I can, but it's hard trying to be in two places at once."

"You made your decision to accept the call. Now you have to live with the sacrifice. We all have to pay for everything we do. The best you can hope for is that the price is worth the reward. James is a good man and a good father, but he's human. He loves you, that much I know, or he wouldn't have hung around this long. But you have asked a lot from him."

"Men don't have to choose between a family and serving God."

"They do in the Catholic Church; they don't want their servants to be divided by family. This was the reason for limiting women in the first place."

"Women's roles were different then. Women work now and have demanding careers of all kinds, and nobody punishes them for it. Why should leading a congregation be any different for women?"

"I can't answer that, except to say, I know how James feels because I've been on the short end of that stick for 35 years. Constant prayer is the only reason I'm standing here today."

"What are you telling me to do, Mama?"

"I can't tell you what to do. Take it to the Lord. In the meantime, you need to do what Titus 2:5 tells all wives, 'to be sensible and pure, to manage their households, to be kind, and to submit themselves to their husbands. Otherwise, the word of God may be discredited.'"

***

It seemed like whenever things fell into place for the church to move forward and thrive, things between James and me fell apart. My faithfulness to the church made me feel as if I was being unfaithful to him. I didn't feel comfortable sharing good news about the church with him because he would probably see it as bad news. It hurt to be the rope in a tug-of-war between my husband and my commitment to God. The tension never let up, and I could feel my patience unraveling. This wasn't how it was supposed to be. My success should be his success; my joys should be his joys. I'd promised him no more surprises, so we needed to talk soon.

Later that night when he was relaxing, watching a basketball game on TV, I sat down on the couch beside him. I thought that it might be easier to have this conversation with him while he was a little distracted. For almost half an hour, I watched the players running back and forth on the court, trying to score for their team. It was a relentless competition to win. The similarities to my situation were blatant. James and I were like two star players on one team who hadn't figured out how to play together.

A commercial came on, and I seized the moment. "The elders and I met the other day, and we decided that it's time for us to build our own church from the ground up."

"You've only been in this building for two years. Don't you think you are moving a little fast?"

"It is fast, but there is a prime spot of land less than a mile away from where we are now. If we don't make an offer, somebody else will. Besides, we can do so much more for the community with a bigger space. It's a possibility that we may be able to add an assisted-living unit on the property. We might even have a buyer for our current building."

James's lips moved as if were chewing on something. That's what he did when he was trying to choose his words carefully. "That's a huge project. As usual, the timing is off. I've been having some discussions of my own with my staff. I'm considering throwing my hat into the mayoral race."

"That's awesome, James! Why didn't you tell me?"

"I didn't say anything because we were just getting things settled down for a change. I was also thinking it might be the right time to have another baby. Timmy is almost eight years old."

That was a slam-dunk over my head. "Wow, babe, I don't know what to say."

"Say you want us to have another baby. I was an only child, you were an only child, and I don't want that for Timmy."

"You always make me feel so selfish."

"Maybe because you are."

"That's not fair! I'm thinking about you, too. You have a great opportunity to make things better for the whole city.

"I can put off running for mayor. I have time to do that later."

"This is your time, James. I definitely think you should go for it."

"That would require more of my time, family time, and I would have to give up coaching my team. With both of us running around, who's going to cover the bases at home? One of us has to stay here and step up more for Timmy."

"This is a critical point for both of us. The reality is that we're a power couple in this district, and we have the ability to expand citywide. There's so much more we can accomplish if we don't lose our focus."

"I thought our family was the focus."

"It is, but we have obligations and responsibilities to a lot of people."

"What about our son? Doesn't he come first? Isn't he more important than talking the ears off more and more people?"

"It's my talking people's ears off that pays for Timmy's tuition," I said, slightly offended.

"He doesn't have to go to some expensive private school as far as I'm concerned. He can go to a public school just like I did."

"It's small-minded thinking that keeps us from progressing as a people."

"Is that what your goal is, to help us progress as a people, or is it to build a bigger church and then another bigger church? Is it to drive expensive cars or wear designer clothing? Whose glory is that for? Is that what Jesus would do, or would He be out on the front lines fighting gangs, drug abuse, and creating jobs?"

"Excuse me, but aren't those things on the agenda of politicians."

"That proves my point completely! We aren't on the same team, and we don't want the same things."

"Everything is a competition with you, James. I don't see it that way. What is so wrong with wanting to enlarge God's church and spread the word of His goodness? You make me feel like I'm some kind of charlatan. I'm not. I want to do God's will. I'm trying to fulfill the purpose that He gave me. I told you that the day you met me, and I've never changed."

"You're right, Princess, you're always right," James said with disdain. "I can't imagine what it is to be perfect."

"Don't do that. You're putting up a wall to shut me out. I want us to come to some resolution, some type of compromise."

"All right. How's this for a compromise? You can do whatever you want; the only thing I ask is that we don't keep waiting to have another child."

"I don't have a problem with having another baby."

"Well, let's get started," he said, standing to his feet.

That was the moment I should have been honest, but I was too scared. I should have told James that I had had a copper

IUD put in shortly after Timmy was born, the kind that lasts
for ten years. I wasn't prepared to suffer the consequences of
dropping two nuclear bombs in one day. The collateral damage
would have been devastating. I knew I was wrong, but I counted
it as an act of self-preservation. Right now, I just wanted to live
and have the chance to come back and fight another day. So, I
followed him into our bedroom without saying a word.

***

James decided not to run for mayor or reelection to the
city council. He claimed his decision was based on his desire
to keep our family first, that he wanted to be there for Timmy
and another child, and that he missed the human reward he
got from teaching. I thought he did it out of spite, that he was
being self-righteous to make me feel like the villain. If that
was his plan, it worked perfectly. On one hand, I saw myself as
someone dedicated to serving the Lord and His people; on the
other, I was a greedy, self-centered egotist.

I refused to see myself in that light and threw myself into
my work. I wrote a book about the sacrifice of leading and
recorded tapes of inspiration during the two years that the
new church was under construction. Working long hours at
the church became my haven. At home, I was scrutinized and
criticized, with James believing the stress on me working
so hard was the reason I wasn't getting pregnant. So, we
gravitated to different rooms without much to say to each other,
tired of breathing the same air.

Daddy wasn't any happier with me either. There was a split
in his church; and with him out of the pulpit, half of his loyal

members looked for refuge in the Tabernacle. That wasn't my fault, but I had to bear the blame just the same. At least once a week, I uttered the same plea, "Lord, why am I in such conflict with the people I love. I'm only trying to do Your will." I'd prayed and fasted, waiting for God to move in my marriage, and my patience was waning. I needed a miracle.

I got a reprieve when I received an email about a women and chaplains retreat in California. I registered without hesitation. Tamu had moved out to San Francisco a few years back, and I could get the chance to visit with her.

The retreat was God-sent. It was renewing to have a chance to share and converse with other women who were dealing with the same obstacles and experiences that I was. For so long, I thought I was alone; and now it was clear to me that strong women are always challenged, professionally and personally. Some of the burdens I'd been carrying were lifted, except one, the crucial one, my secret sin. That one could only be shared with someone I trusted, the only one I knew on earth who wouldn't judge me.

Tamu picked me up at the airport, looking younger than she did seven years ago. Her hair was wrapped in Kente cloth just as she wore it back when we were at Hampton.

"Take me to that fountain of youth you're drinking from," I said, grabbing her in a hug.

"If I had one, I'd be selling bottles from it on the corner!" she said, laughing.

"I can't tell you how good it feels to get some time off and visit with you," I said, throwing my bags in the trunk of the car. "Your girl needs this break badly!"

"What's going on with you?" she asked, looking me in the face. "You looked stressed."

"You should have seen me before the retreat. I was a total wreck."

"You just built a megachurch, and you're rolling in the dough. Life should be good."

"It should be, but it's not. I'll tell you about it later," I said, waving it off. "Let's talk about you and what you have going on out here on the West Coast."

"Well, I can't complain. I've started an activist group called Political Black Women Pushing for Progress, and I absolutely love it. I work with two other attorneys, several doctors, educators, and mothers who have lost children to violence or drugs. We have a powerful coalition going."

"That's what you always wanted to do, Tee. I'm happy for you."

"Girl, thank you. I'm happy for myself. Now, I have to tell you, I met this fine brother about six months ago. He's a lawyer, too. He works for the public defender's office. I'm coo-coo crazy about him!"

"Like I said, I'm happy for you! I'd love to meet him."

"You will meet him sooner than you think. We live together. I wanted to give you a heads-up just in case that's a problem for you and you want to get a hotel."

"Come on. You know that's not a problem for me. We've always respected each other without judgment."

"That's true. I was just checking. We live on the other side of the Bay Bridge in Oakland. It's not far from San Francisco, but it's about $3,000 a month difference."

"Sounds like it's worth the trip over the bridge."

"No doubt," Tamu said, laughing.

I stared out the window as she drove. The city streets were a perfect example of life. There were steep hills all around, with people on both sides. It was either a long trudge uphill or smooth sailing downhill. You were either climbing to the top or falling to the bottom. One minute, you're up; and the next minute, you're down. It all depended on your perspective, which changed from one intersection to the next. I was approaching an intersection in my life, and there was no telling which way things would go as I moved forward. The only thing I was sure of was that I wasn't turning around.

***

Tamu's guy was great. His name was Derek. Wearing a dashiki and faded jeans with long dreads pulled back in a neat ponytail, he welcomed me like a long-lost sister when I walked in the door.

"I cooked a special meal in your honor," he said, hugging me with a kiss on the cheek. "Make yourself comfortable and come on to the kitchen."

"You won't have to ask me twice. It smells delicious," I said, following Tamu down the hallway to the guestroom.

"So, what's going on with you?" Tamu asked, sitting on the bed while I unpacked my things.

"After dinner," I told her, wanting to enjoy the meal first. Our talk would probably ruin my appetite.

She gave me a puzzled look and said, "Okay."

Derek made us chicken and beef stir-fry, with vegetables over rice. He poured us glasses of wine and asked me to bless the food. His deep laugh warmed the room as we ate dinner. It was crystal clear what attracted Tamu to him. The relaxed atmosphere struck me as I thought about the strain that James and I lived under.

"I hope you ladies will excuse me. I have some work to do for tomorrow," Derek said, getting up from the table.

"Anybody want coffee or dessert before I go?"

"No, thank you," I said. "I couldn't eat another bite."

"Mission accomplished," he said, kissing Tamu on the forehead on his way out.

"Time to spill the beans," Tamu said as soon as he was out of the room.

"Can we go outside on the porch?" I didn't want to take a chance that Derek might overhear our conversation.

"Sure, it might be a little chilly though. I'll get a couple of throw blankets to keep us warm."

"All right."

I stepped out the front door onto the porch and into the night air. There was a cool mist settling on the city that I assumed brought the chill. Visibility was low as the cloudy mist blurred the houses and cars across the street. A similar blur clouded my thinking. I hoped that talking with Tamu would give me the clarity I needed.

"This should help," Tamu said, coming out and handing me one of the blankets.

I wrapped myself tightly and took a breath. "I've been dishonest with James for a long time, and I can't take it anymore. It's slowly killing both of us."

"What are you talking about?" Tamu asked, slightly alarmed.

"Shortly after Timmy was born, I got an IUD, the copper one that lasts ten years."

"So, what's the problem with that?"

"I never told James."

"That's deep," she said, nodding her head. "Why don't you just tell him?"

"About two years ago, I agreed that we should start trying to have another baby, but I haven't had the IUD removed. He's wondering why I haven't gotten pregnant after all this time."

"Prissy, this is over the top," she said, throwing her hands up out of the blanket. "You should have come clean the day you agreed to try to pregnant. Now it only gets worse every day."

"Tell me about it," I said hopelessly. "Do you know how hard it is to stand up there and preach to people with my own sin growing bigger and bigger? It's hell."

"You've got to tell him. You know I have your back, but this isn't right."

"I'm damned if I do and damned if I don't. Either way, he's probably going to leave me."

"He's going to be off the chain, no doubt, but you have to deal with it."

"I know. I can't put it off any longer. I just wish it could have been different. Why am I wrong for wanting to have my ministry and my family too?"

"It's not that you are wrong; it's practically impossible to do two things in a big way. Your ministry is all-consuming. It even consumes you. That leaves crumbs for James and Timmy. You may be one of those people who doesn't need or want the confines of a family."

"I'm not; I need and want my family. I just don't want to have another baby."

"Even if the Good Book says you must submit to your husband."

"We all sin and fall short of the glory of God."

"Then I guess it is true that you can't serve two masters."

"I should have stopped you from coming to my Bible class."

She laughed. "And you thought I wasn't listening. Anyway, you're in a tough spot. If you want me to, I'll come to Richmond and hold your hand while you tell him, or at least hold him back from strangling you."

"No, I appreciate that, but I made this mess. I'm going to bare my soul and accept the consequences."

"I feel for you," she said, staring toward the sky. "In the words of Buddha, 'Three things cannot be long hidden: the sun, the moon, and the truth.'"

My eyes followed hers in the direction of the shrouded moon.

***

I chose my moment of truth on Good Friday after the church service of "The Last Seven Words of Christ." Hopefully, if this revelation killed my marriage, through God's grace it could be revived in a few days, having new life on Resurrection Sunday.

Timmy was going home with Mama and spending the night there with her and Daddy. James and I walked them to the car and gave Timmy a hug.

"Behave yourself, champ," James told him, giving him a high five.

"You don't have to tell me that. I'm not a little kid," Timmy replied with a bashful smile.

"I'll pick you up in the morning," I said, planting a kiss on his cheek.

"Okay, Mom," he said.

My mama gave me a goodbye wave with her fingers as they pulled away.

"You about ready?" James asked once they were out of sight.

"Almost," I said, avoiding his gaze. "Would you make sure all the doors are locked and meet me in my office before we go?"

"Sure, no problem."

While he made the rounds, I went to my office and got down on my knees to pray. "Heavenly Father, I come humbly before Your throne of grace in contrition, asking for Your forgiveness. I have not been the wife I should have been; I have been dishonest and selfish. Lord, I ask that you give me the words to speak that will soften James's heart toward me. Wrap us in Your Spirit of peace. In Your precious name, Jesus, I pray. Amen."

I heard James's footsteps. I got up from my knees and sat on the couch.

"Everything is good to go," James said, entering the office.

"Sit down for a minute," I said, touching the place beside me. "I need to tell you something."

The wrinkles formed between James's eyes. I knew he was bracing himself for whatever news I was about to blast him with. I knew he was battle-weary from the barrage of bombs I had dropped on him over the years. He sat down without any comment.

"I don't know how to sugarcoat this or break it to you gently, so I'll just say it. After Timmy was born, I had an IUD put in for birth control. It is the kind that lasts for ten years." He stopped looking at me and looked down at his hands. "When we agreed that we would start trying to have another baby, I should have told you. But I didn't, and I'm sorry for that. I wanted to be honest with you, but I knew it would cause problems, and I was afraid of losing you."

The silence in the room was like quicksand. It was dragging me down, and I felt like I couldn't breathe.

"Please say something," I begged, needing him to give me a word to hang onto.

"There's nothing to say," he said evenly.

"Yes, there is. I want to fix things between us."

His voice still calm, he asked, "Why now? You've been lying to me for years."

"I know that, and it's been hell for me."

"I never noticed. You may have missed your calling; you're a damn good actress."

"Don't be cruel, James."

"Me be cruel? You've cornered the market on that, Princess. You never wanted a husband. You just wanted another dutiful member of your congregation to worship you."

"That's not true! I've always loved you. I admit that I've had bad judgment as far as our relationship is concerned. It's because all my life I've felt like I had to prove something to my family and to myself. It drives me, and it drove a wedge between us. I don't want anything to come between us anymore."

"So, have you proven whatever it is that you felt you had to prove?"

"What I've learned is that it doesn't matter."

"But it does matter, because you've proved to me that you have never cared about our family; that you don't give a flying freak about what I wanted in this marriage; and that I can't trust you, even while I'm looking at you."

"I was wrong. Please, please, please forgive me."

James stood up and walked to the door. He turned around staring at the ground, unable to look at me. "I will forgive you, but I can't forget how you made a fool out of me. I'm out, Princess. I should have left this sideshow a long time ago."

He walked out the door and closed it quietly behind him. I wanted to run after him and beg him not to leave me, but I knew it wouldn't help.

***

James didn't come home that night, but he was there the next evening when I brought Timmy home from my parents' house. He smiled when we came in and gave Timmy a hug like he always did. Timmy showed him the Easter eggs that he and his grandma had colored. It all seemed natural, even peaceful, except he refused to look me in the face. I had no idea what was going on in his head, and that made me feel uncomfortable. I left them alone in the great room and went to our bedroom. I took a shower and got in bed early with a book.

I had no idea when I fell asleep, but I woke up before dawn, alone. James had probably slept in one of the guestrooms. I resisted the urge to wake him and try to talk with him because it might stir up a negative vibe that I didn't want to carry into the pulpit on Easter morning. I decided to go through the day as normally as possible. It wasn't unusual for James and Timmy to skip the Easter sunrise service, so I dressed and headed to church by myself.

When I arrived at the church, daylight was creeping through the clouds, but the sun hadn't taken its rightful place yet. As always, Kenny was the first person there.

"Praise the Lord, Pastor!" Kenny said with the warm smile that never seemed to leave his face. It was a great comfort to me at that moment. People have no idea how something so small can change the tenor of the day.

"Great morning, Kenny," I said, getting out of the car. "This is a day to rejoice and be glad in Him."

"Hallelujah! I can feel the presence of the Lord already," he said as we walked in the side entrance. "Easter Sunday is the most meaningful Sunday of all."

"Amen. If it weren't for Christ rising on this day, we would all be condemned for our sins," I said, thinking about my own transgressions. "God sacrificed His only Son so that we might be redeemed. I thank Him for His mercy and grace. I could shout about it right now!"

"Save some for the pulpit, Pastor," Kenny said, doing a quick dance into the sanctuary.

I went into my office and prayed, changed into my robe, and headed into the sanctuary to bring a message of praise and salvation.

The sunrise service was easier than the main service of the day. The number that attended was smaller, and James wasn't there. During the main service, seeing him and Timmy sitting down front made me feel like a hypocrite. It was difficult to uplift the name of Jesus with the burden of the problems between James and me dragging my soul down. I wanted to fall on the altar and confess, but I had already done that. Still the spirit of the Lord was alive as the choir sang and church rejoiced in the Resurrection; me, only half-heartedly, because my marriage was still dead.

***

Mama cooked a dinner that was fit for the heavens, and she did most of the talking as we ate. Daddy was there, sitting at the head of the table in his wheelchair, but he didn't speak. James was there, but he didn't speak directly to me. He was pleasant and congenial, talking around me as if nothing were wrong. I had never seen him behave like this. Usually, when he was angry, there was no doubt about it, everyone around him knew it. I don't think Mama even noticed that we weren't speaking.

After we got home and Timmy went to bed, I was determined to make James talk to me. He was in the guest bedroom watching the nightly news.

"You've ignored me all day. At dinner, you sat there right in front of my mom like you didn't have a care in the world."

"I discovered that you're not the only one who can act," he said.

"I know you're upset, but we can talk it through."

"There's nothing we can say that can change the past."

"We can talk about going forward."

"I'm not sure I want to go forward."

"We're family. That means something."

"To whom? It certainly didn't mean anything to you."

"Okay, let's jump to the bottom line then. Are you going to leave me?" I asked, tired of the games.

"I can't even deal with that right now. Our son is my first concern."

"That's fair. I'll leave you alone then."

"That's probably best," he said, staring at the TV screen.

***

Over the next five years, my ministry continued to flourish. We filled every pew in the sanctuary that had seemed so large when we built it. The years passed quickly, as I thrust myself deeper into my mission. I was basically buried in it.

Needless to say, the money was plentiful, so much so, that it was no longer an issue for us. The messages became more about God granting favor for the faithful. It was never my intention to preach prosperity; it was more as a result of the church prospering. We had television and radio spots, DVDs, and the choir recorded several CDs. I conducted workshops and published another book. The church had a life of its own; it became like a living, breathing entity. There were times when I didn't feel like the leader but more like a caboose being dragged along by a powerful train.

My home life was another story entirely. It was painfully obvious that James couldn't bring himself to forgive me, although he remained respectful and polite. It was almost as if we had transformed from man and wife to business associates. I heard rumors of him and other women, but I dismissed them. I had given up on making my marriage better. There was no time for sincere personal relationships; the church staff filled the void of friends.

To maintain things at home, I hired a housekeeper, Sofia, to help with the cooking and the cleaning. I didn't have to worry about Timmy, who was growing up and now wanted to be called Tim. James was completely devoted to him and never missed any of his games or activities.

I began to travel for speaking engagements and held my own retreats. The empty hotel rooms always reminded me of how alone I really was. Out of desperation, I asked James to come with me to one retreat in Detroit.

"What's going on? I don't get it," he said, responding to my request.

"It's been a long time, James. How long are you going to continue to punish me?"

He laughed. "Is that what you think I'm doing? I should have known. In your mind, everything is still about you. I'm not trying to get back at you. I'm trying to raise our son. If it weren't for him, I would have left this place seven years ago."

"You said you loved me. I can't understand how you could throw away our relationship without trying to put yourself in my shoes for a minute."

"It was never about me wanting you. You didn't want me. You didn't want the trappings of a marriage, the obligation to your husband, or being a mother to my children."

"That's not true! You have no idea the inner turmoil that I've been in over this. If I could turn back time and do things differently, I would."

"That's what you say now because you've gotten everything you want. I'm surprised a woman of the word like you wouldn't realize that there are sacrifices to be made to get the desires of your heart."

"What do I have to do to get you to forgive me? Living like this is hell for me, and I know it's no picnic for you. I want us to be happy. I want to be happy."

"I don't know, Princess. That'll give you something to pray about while you're in Detroit."

***

If James couldn't forgive me, I definitely had to forgive myself. The burden of my wrong was dragging me down. It was time to take it to the Lord and leave it there.

As the host of the Detroit retreat, I was scheduled to do the welcome at the meet and greet session on the first day. During the time of fellowship, it was nice to see familiar faces, and it felt good to talk with Roberta Daniels and Charlotte Smith, good friends I had made over the years. Just being in a different environment was refreshing.

I called the room to attention. "Good evening, ladies. I want to welcome every one of you to the Detroit Spiritual Retreat for Church Leaders. The theme for this year's retreat is "Rebirth Through Redemption." This retreat is going to be somewhat non-traditional. By definition, a retreat is when the army withdraws or pulls back from a dangerous or difficult position. As leaders in the church, we are on the frontlines under attack and often take enemy fire. This doesn't mean we are any less than or more than any other soldier, for all have sinned and fallen short of the glory of God.

"As leaders, we administer to the injuries of our troops and leave our own wounds unattended. Jesus asked, 'How can you say to you brother, "Let me take the speck out of your eye," when all the time there is a plank in your own eye.' So, during this retreat we are going to focus on those parts of our lives that we have slapped Band-Aids on. We're going to pull off the covering and allow them to heal.

"What I hope to have, and what I hope for you all to have is restoration and redemption. What will be different about this weekend is that some may want to attend seminars and meditations, some may need to commune with nature, the answer for someone else may be to lie in bed the whole time. It is up to you as an individual to choose the best way to renew your strength to return back to the battlefield. You will not see my name on the list for the seminars as I have chosen to commune with nature this weekend."

***

I got up early the next morning; dressed in jeans, sweatshirt, hiking boots; and left the cabin armed with my Bible, a pair of binoculars, and two bottles of water. I saw a hill not far off, so I figured the view would be worth the trek. The distance was longer than I thought, and the sandy earth beneath the tall grass required more energy for each step. As I moved up the hill, the muscles of my thighs burned; but the earth under my feet became firmer and the density of the trees around me increased.

I went higher toward a bright spot where the sunlight was intense. By the time I reached the clearing, I was covered in perspiration. Standing on the peak of the hill, I gazed across the landscape. It was beautiful, the mixtures of the earth's vivid colors blended perfectly. The first thought in my head was, "How Great Thou Art."

The blue water below rushing past with a froth of white foam over it was soothing. I sat down on a rock and opened a bottle of water and drank in the peace around me. For a while, I used my binoculars to observe the birds flying overhead and the ants crawling along near my feet. God's creations were miracles within themselves.

I opened my Bible and scanned through the pages. Then I saw the words that changed my perspective up on that hill, Isaiah 44:21-22, "Remember these things, Jacob, for you, Israel, are my servant. I have made you, you are my servant; Israel, I will not forget you. I have swept away your offenses like a cloud, your sins like the morning mist. Return to me, for I have redeemed you."

I surrendered it all at that moment, my sinful wrongs, my painful regrets, and my relentless guilt. I gave it all to Jesus, thrown down like a shield that I once believed protected me. I could see now that it had only served to imprison me. I was set free. The words of the song "You Must Be Born Again" filled my head, and I began to sing, "I looked at my hands, and my hands looked new, I looked my feet, and they were new too." A lightness filled my heart that I had never felt before, and I didn't want to lose that feeling. I stayed up on that hill until the grumblings of my stomach were audible.

****

I had reclaimed my joy that day. Over the evening meal, I laughed, not a forced or surface laugh, but a laugh from deep in my belly. I ate and enjoyed the food, allowing myself the pleasure of the flavors. The next morning, I took another therapeutic walk. It began to drizzle, but instead of running for shelter, I embraced every drop. I needed the Lord to rain down on me. I didn't need the spectacular view; I needed my soul to be cleansed.

When I got back to my room to get ready for dinner, I caught a glimpse of myself in the mirror and didn't recognize the reflection there. My clothes were soaked, my hair was drenched, and the little makeup I had on was gone. I looked like a younger and messier version of myself. I had to smile at the crazy-looking woman staring back at me.

"Priscilla, I know you found something out there in those woods," Roberta said, when I joined them for dinner. "You look like you saw Jacob's ladder, Ezekiel's wheel, or the burning bush out there. What is going on with you?"

"Do tell!" Charlotte added. "You're absolutely glowing."

"Let's just say, I saw the light," I told them, taking a seat.

Roberta kept looking at me. "Well, we need to stay another day so you can take us all out to see that light, honey. It has worked a miracle on you."

"You don't know the half of it, my dear. I wish I could stay another day. This retreat has been so beneficial for me. I guess I came in the right spirit this year."

"Amen," Charlotte said. "That makes all the difference."

After the meditation later that evening, we had Communion together. And this time when I took those sacraments, I knew without any doubt that my sins were forgiven.

I packed my clothes that night, anxious to get back home to my family.

***

The house was empty when I got home. Sofia came in the door a few minutes after I did. I told her to take a few days off. I figured that if I wanted to get all of my life back, I needed to take my house back first. I unpacked my suitcase and then cleaned up the mess left by James and Tim over the weekend. Next, I went to the grocery store. Checking out the prices, I realized it had been a long time since I had been shopping for food. Back home in my own kitchen, I felt like a stranger; everything had been rearranged.

When James and Tim walked in that afternoon, I had dinner waiting for them.

"Hey there, guys," I said, welcoming them home.

"What's up, Mom?" Tim said, giving me a hug.

James was stunned into silence for a moment before he said, "Welcome back. How was your retreat?"

"It was the best ever," I answered with a genuine smile. "You two can wash your hands, and then we can eat."

Tim rushed back to his room to drop his gear.

James was still looking confused. "Don't you have to go to the church to make sure they didn't burn it down while you were gone?"

"It will be fine; I just want to spend some quiet quality time at home."

I could see that James didn't seem to know what to think about me or what to say. There I was, with my hair pulled back in a ponytail, no make-up, and wearing a sundress instead of a power suit. Even when we sat down to eat, he had a suspicious look on his face, as if I were an impostor trying to pull off some strange ruse. I could have tried to give him an explanation for my behavior, but it wasn't my intention to try to influence him in anyway. The change in me wasn't for him or my marriage; it was for my soul.

Dinner was relaxed, and after I cleaned up the kitchen, I sat down and watched James go over Tim's homework. I watched them play a couple of games on the Xbox before I went into my bedroom to watch TV. After the news, I turned it off, and knelt to pray. I thanked the Lord for His mercy and grace. I thanked Him for my family, prayed for their continued health and strength. I prayed for my father and mother, for my congregation, for the city of Richmond, the country, and for love and peace to abound all over the world. I wanted to shout and do a holy dance for the Lord at the foot of my bed, but I held it in and opted for handclaps of praise and arms flailing in thanks for His goodness.

I stayed at home all week, and on Friday, I went to the school to see Tim play in one of his basketball games. Neither James nor Tim would have seen me there, except there were several church members at the game who were emphatic in their greeting. The bewildered expression was still on James's face, but Tim took it all in stride with a wave in my direction. After the game was over, I texted them both that I would see them later. When they got home, I was already in my room reading a book. I didn't come out. I wasn't campaigning for a vote of approval from them; I just wanted to be in their lives again.

Saturday morning, I got up early to spend a few hours at church preparing my message. I didn't really need the time, because my message had been ready more than a week ago. I was more curious to see how I would feel being at the church after my experience at the retreat. Sitting behind my desk at the office, I could see things clearer. The awards, commendations, and accolades that lined the wall brought me face to face with my ambition, the ambition that had consumed me for nearly 20 years. I was humbled because I had only just discovered what it cost me.

***

There were puzzled faces throughout the sanctuary when I walked in after the call to worship wearing a baptismal robe instead of my pastor's robe. After the opening selection, I stood at the podium.

"Good morning, brothers and sisters. I stand before you this morning as a woman who has been transformed. As you know, last weekend, I was away on my yearly retreat. It's not an easy task for a woman to lead a church. Your loyalties are divided between your family and the church. My father discouraged me from pursuing my ministry for that very reason, but I was determined to push forward, and here I am today." The congregation applauded, but I raised my hand for quiet so I could continue.

"In my dedication to this church, I wasn't always the wife I should have been to my husband. The Bible says that is a sin. For many years, I have been carrying that burden. So up on a hill in Detroit, I had to purge myself of the sins that I had intentionally and persistently committed. And up on that hill I was set free!

"We all know that to be set free you must be born again. It doesn't matter that I've been a Christian all my life and that I've given my life to serving Christ Jesus. There are times that we all have to stop in our tracks and recommit ourselves to the Lord. Today, I wear this baptismal robe as a symbol of God's redeeming love for me and for all of us. A change, a change has come over me," I repeated, glancing over at my family in the front pew.

I saw my mother wiping her eyes, and I saw James staring at me as if he were seeing a ghost. Kenny started to play the song, and the musicians joined in. "He changed my life and now I'm free. He washed away all my sins, and He made me whole." I sat down in my chair, and the choir began to sing.

Every time I thought about the goodness of God and his faithfulness, I threw up my hands. There was so much emotion within me I wasn't sure what would have happened if I released it. I might have shouted until I passed out, run madly through the aisles, or rolled down the stairs and up onto a pew. So many tissues were passed out by the ushers, and there were few dry eyes left in the congregation when the service ended. Members lined up to hug me. Some gave me a word of thanks; others gave me a word of understanding. Mama stood at the rear, waiting for the crowd to thin.

"Prissy, I'm so proud of you. I didn't know you and James ever had any problems."

"Everybody has problems, Mama. We were just better at hiding ours."

"Ain't that the truth," she said, shaking her head. "Well, anyway, what you did today was beautiful. Most of the time, folks get up in the pulpit and act holier-than-thou, but you were truthful today. You let people know they don't have to pretend to be something they're not, and they can always change where they are. That's what you father didn't learn in all his years of preaching, that we can change, and that we should change."

I grabbed her hand. "Thank you, Mama, I needed to hear that."

"Child, I'm so happy today. I wished I would have cooked a big dinner where we could just fellowship over this thing some more."

"That's all right. After that revelation, I should be at home with James and Tim. We probably have a lot to talk about."

"Yes, I'm sure you do."

In all the commotion, I hadn't noticed when James and Tim had left. It didn't matter though. In my heart, I had gotten right with God and was at peace. If James still couldn't forgive me, that was something I was prepared to accept. The congregation filed out, and the church grew quiet.

The volume of all the praise, shouts, and songs had faded. I changed clothes in my office, waved to the custodian, and drove home.

I was in the bedroom putting on something comfortable when James walked in. "I need to talk to you," he said, closing the door.

Unable to gauge his mood, I nodded and sat down on the bed.

"The message you gave this morning, I'm wondering why you didn't tell me about your trip when you came home. It was obvious that something was different, with you cooking, cleaning, and coming to Tim's game."

"The experience I had in Detroit was for me, to save me, not our marriage. This morning, I wasn't trying to influence you or anyone else. I just needed to give God the glory for His forgiveness. I gave up the right to ask anything from you when I lied to you."

"What you did bothered me so much, more than I can ever tell you. There weren't words harsh enough to express how I felt, and I didn't think you even cared. To me, you had left the marriage. So I did what I could to hold the rest together for Timothy."

"And I appreciate that very much."

"When I listened to you this morning, it was surreal. You were unassuming and vulnerable. I was seeing a woman I'd never met before."

I smiled at his cruel but well-meaning honesty. "I am different, James. There are no excuses, except, I'm not perfect."

"They tell me nobody is," he said, with his tone softening. "I probably could have handled the situation better, but I was so angry."

"I don't blame you."

"There is something you can do for me."

"What's that?"

"That woman up there today, I'd like to get to know her."

"She'd give anything for that chance," I said, tearing up.

And after all the hugs I'd gotten that morning, I finally got the one that I really needed.

***

It was a slow process, but James started to trust me again. Since we'd never really had a honeymoon, I suggested that maybe we should get away to spend some quality time alone. An island paradise sounded like a great place to take a romantic trip, but James wanted to go to Paris. He remembered how his mom liked to watch old movies about Paris on Saturday afternoons, and that it was known for being the City of Love.

"Maybe you'll fall in love with me there," he said as we stood in the long security line at the airport.

"What do you mean?" I laughed, thinking he was joking. "I already love you."

"I don't think you have ever been in love with me like I have with you," he said seriously.

I was stunned for a second. "That's not true. I'm just not as expressive as you are."

"I've seen you shout, dance, and cry in the pulpit. I've never seen you have that kind of emotion for me."

I thought about it for a moment, and I had to admit that he was right. I guess I never really learned how to love anybody in that way. I was taught that God was first in your life. Surely, Mama loved Daddy, was utterly devoted to him. But now that

I thought about it, I wasn't sure he felt the same about her. He certainly needed her; she filled an important position as his right hand, his assistant. Was that the way I treated James? Chills ran through me, the kind you get when you catch yourself from falling. I hadn't deserved the loyalty I had been given.

"I owed you more, James," I said, squeezing his hand. "You mean a lot more to me than you think. Give me a chance to show you."

"I'm going to hold you to that," he said, kissing my hand before he took off his shoes to place them on the scanner.

On the flight, without my cell phone, tablet, or laptop, all of which I left home at James's request, I slept for most of the traveling time. I guess you never know how tired you are until you slow down. The truth was I felt slightly awkward without my distractions. It sounds odd to say that we made love on the first night in the city, because we were a married couple, but it had been more than a year since we'd slept together.

Paris wasn't the Caribbean, but it did have a certain romance about it. The city glowed at night with its spectacular views, like the Basilique du Sacre-Couer from our hotel room and the Eiffel Tower. We visited the Louvre Museum of Art and did the romantic walks that were listed in the brochure. We ate at quaint cafes and took a night cruise on the Seine River. None of our meals were eaten at the same table.

There were so many new experiences, new foods, and new wines. My favorite activity was when we toured the fairytale castles in the French countryside. Seeing them made me feel like a girl again, maybe for the first time. I had spent most of my youth trying to convince Daddy that I could fill the shoes he would never let me wear.

Every day was beautiful; but what mattered to me most was that we were together again. It sounds weird, because we never split up, but we hadn't been together for a long time either. In the quiet of the night, I laid next to my husband, listening to him breathe and feeling the expansion of his body as he inhaled. Joel 2:25 came to mind: "I will restore to you the years that the swarming locust has eaten, the hopper, the destroyer, and the cutter, my great army, which I sent among you." The locusts were ambition, selfishness, jealousy, and unforgiveness. Silently, I thanked the Lord for restoration.

***

I made a conscious effort not to put the church before my family, delegating more duties and responsibilities to the elders and the deacons. I had more time to check on Mama and Daddy. He was still at home, but he had to have nurses to help Mama care for him. He had stopped talking, although the doctors said his cognitive skills hadn't deteriorated any further. They thought he might be suffering from depression. Mama and I had done our best to raise his spirits, but it hadn't made much difference. One afternoon, I played him a tape of one of my sermons, and I thought I detected the beginnings of a smile. After that, I always brought a tape from the weekly service for him to listen to.

Being home more, it was clear how much I'd missed while Timothy was growing up. I had built a church from the ground up, a megachurch, but James had raised our son. Sitting at the dinner table while they were having a deep debate about athletic scholarships and star athletes getting paid, I felt left out of the conversation. I couldn't remember having a significant or lengthy discussion with my son about anything. He was starting his senior year in high school, and I didn't know what he wanted to do with his life. Instead of trying to interject in their discord, I got up and went to my office.

I was checking my emails when I saw an invitation to be the key speaker at the Toronto Christian Conference in three months. I tapped my feet under the desk as I whispered, "Thank you, Jesus." This was just the mental pick-me-up that I needed. Limiting my time at work was making me feel unfocused. I jumped up to tell James my good news.

"You won't believe it!" I said, interrupting them. "I've been invited to be the keynote speaker at the Christian Conference in Toronto after Christmas. It's the largest nondenominational conference in North America. More than 25,000 people attend that event every year."

Timothy spoke first. "That's great, Mom. Canada. I'm definitely going along for the ride on that one. Dad, we might get to see the Toronto Raptors play on their home court."

"Wow," James said without much enthusiasm. "I guess we'll have to see."

"It's really a big thing," I said, trying to get James to catch our excitement. "They want me to bring the church choir with me."

"That's great, Princess," he said, taking a beer from the fridge. "I'm really happy for you."

Obviously, James wasn't really thrilled with the idea. That was fine with me because I was thrilled enough for the both of us. I rushed back into my office and called Mama.

"I have some awesome news for you!" I said after Mama answered the phone.

"What is it?" she asked cheerfully.

"I'm going to be the keynote speaker at a Christian conference in Canada. It is totally a big deal. It's a few days after Christmas. I wish you and Daddy could come and see me there."

"I wish we could, too. You know I would be there if your father was doing better. I'm so proud of you and all you have accomplished."

"I know you are, Mama. I wish Daddy could see me there with all those people."

"I'm sure James will record it, and then we can see it."

"Absolutely," I said. "I've got to make a few more calls. I'll call you back later."

***

The choir and the congregation were excited about the invitation to the conference, and several members said they were going to attend. I was like an eager little kid who couldn't wait for Christmas to come. It was a dream come true. There was only one drawback. After all the progress that James and I had made in rebuilding our relationship, after my announcement about the conference, he was starting to pull back. I confronted him after Thanksgiving, a month before the trip.

"Is something wrong, James? I don't want to lose my best friend again."

"Then don't be that woman again."

"What are you talking about?" I asked, agitated.

"The woman who only sees gains, prestige, and can't stop counting the number of seats in her head. The woman who keeps trying to prove herself worthy to her daddy."

"That's not fair. I thought we moved past this."

"I thought we had, too. When are you going to stop trying to be your father's son? You're grown and have a son of your own."

"You sound like you're jealous of my success."

"You can't handle the success. You're like an addict. Once you hear all the amens from that crowd of people, you'll be back on the wagon again. It's never enough. Then you'll want a bigger church to hold more sheep for you to gather."

"That's nothing but the devil speaking through you!" I told him. "'So to keep me from being conceited because of the surpassing greatness of the revelations, a thorn was given me in the flesh, a messenger of Satan to harass me, to keep me from becoming conceited,' 2 Corinthians 12:7. That's who you have been to me. Why can't you support me?"

"What do you think I have been doing for 18 years?"

"You don't understand what this means to me, and I can't explain it to you. Let me have this moment, and I'll let it go, I promise."

James shook his head and walked away.

I was tired, tired of running after this man who didn't understand me or what it meant for me to have a calling on my life. Why was he so threatened by my accomplishments anyway? I decided to leave it in God's hands and prepare for the trip.

***

Walking toward that plexiglass podium with thunderous applause filling the room, I felt like a superstar. This moment was worth all the scorn and criticism, all the pain and sacrifice. I would be lying if I didn't say that I felt vindicated seeing this multitude of people on their feet in front of me.

It had been a long uphill battle to get to this moment, a moment I'd only dared to envision in the wee hours of the morning before I was fully awake. The warmth of this huge crowd of eager Christians embraced me. It was an affirmation for all the work that had gone into creating and nurturing my ministry into the thriving church that it was. I was proud of myself but guilty at the same time. I was proud of what I had accomplished but guilty of the hurt I had caused the ones I loved.

"To God be the glory!" I exclaimed to the enthusiastic crowd. "It is a wonderful blessing to stand before you today and profess the goodness of Christ Jesus."

Praises rose from the audience and filled the air around me. I clapped my hands in praise along with them. After a minute, I motioned for them to take their seats.

"It has been a journey, Christian friends, and we still have quite a distance ahead of us. We live in uncertain times, and the only thing we can rely on is God's faithfulness. And as faithful as our Lord has been to us, we can't leave all the work up to him. The subject for my message today is 'Fighting the Good Fight.' Brothers and sisters, how many of you know we are in a fight? A straight-up struggle, a never-ending battle, not against one another, as it sometimes seems, but against principalities, against rulers of the darkness in this world, and against spiritual wickedness in high places.

"It is not an easy fight. There are no time limits or rests between rounds. It is a continuous arduous contest of wills. How many of you here want to do God's will?" Hands were raised, and a roar of voices spoke back to me. "I'll read from 2 Timothy 2:2-4, 'And the things you have heard from me among many witnesses, commit these to faithful men who will be able to teach others also. You therefore must endure hardships as a good soldier of Jesus Christ. No one engaged in warfare entangles himself in the affairs of this life, that he may please him who enlisted him as a soldier.' Brothers and sisters, it is so easy to get sidetracked and distracted. Our human frailties or moral weaknesses get in the way.

"Our father has given us the most effective weapon to fight the enemy. That weapon is prayer. So we must stay in prayer, Christian friends. Prayer is our strength. Prayer is the armor of God. Prayer is peace. How many of you can testify that the Lord answers prayer?" If there was one person still sitting in their seat, I couldn't see them. "It doesn't matter what your challenge is, yours may not be the same as mine, but the key to victory is the same. 'The effectual fervent prayer of a righteous man avails much.' Victory is ours, Christian friends!"

The choir sang "Victory Is Mine," and the mass of people standing in union sang with them. I was filled with joy, filled with the Holy Spirit, and filled with thankfulness.

The service was truly uplifting. The choir sang more beautifully than I had ever heard them. It was a heavenly experience. People all throughout the stadium were moved to rededicate their lives to Christ. A spirit of hope and encouragement engulfed all of us. I wanted to bottle up this moment and share it with all my Tabernacle of Grace members back in Richmond, but more than that, I wanted to share it with Daddy.

"Well, you did it, Princess," James said when we met up in the dressing room. His tone was more of resignation than congratulation.

"We did it together!" I told him. "You may not believe it, but you and Timothy made this so special. I'm so glad you guys came. If I didn't have you both here with me, it wouldn't have meant so much."

"So, what else is on the agenda?" he asked.

"There's a dinner for all the speakers, the choirs, and their families in the ballroom back at the hotel. That's the last event."

"I'm asking because Timothy wanted to try and make that basketball game tomorrow."

I frowned. I knew I was about to be the bad guy again. "I was hoping we could fly out tonight. I can't wait to show my folks the tape of the conference."

"It's just one more day, Princess."

"I'll talk to Timothy. I'll get him tickets to any basketball game he wants if he'll agree to leave tonight."

* * *

"Looks like the later flights are cancelled," Kenny said, checking his phone after the celebration dinner.

"You're kidding," I said, disappointed. "What's the problem?"

"They say a storm is rolling in later tonight."

"What if we leave on an earlier flight?"

"They're all booked."

"See if we can charter a flight. If we get caught here in a bad storm, we may not be able to leave for several days."

"I'm on it, Pastor," Kenny said, leaving the banquet hall.

Kenny came back a half hour later. There was a charter available, but it would only seat 50 people. Our whole group wouldn't fit, so I offered to pay hotel and traveling cost for those who wanted to travel after the storm.

"It's only a three-hour flight," I told them. "We should be able to beat the storm."

We should have gone back to the hotel and relaxed, but the energy of the day was driving my decisions. I had in my mind that I was going home one way or another. It was the worst decision of my life.

***

I woke up in a hospital with Mama staring down at me.

"Where am I?" I asked her, blinking my eyes and trying to adjust to the light.

"You're in a hospital in Pittsburgh. There was an accident. The plane crashed."

"Oh, God!" I screamed, terrified by the realization that it wasn't a nightmare. "Was anybody else hurt? Where's Timothy and James?" I looked into her eyes and screamed again.

Mama pushed a button, calling for a nurse. "You're going to need to calm down, sweetheart. It's going to be hard as hell, but you're going to get through this."

"Mama, where is my son? Where's James?"

"They're gone, baby. They aren't in any pain. They're with the Lord now."

I screamed and screamed until I passed out or until they gave me some drugs to knock me out. When I woke up, I was numb. I could hear people talking to me, asking me questions, but the words didn't make sense to me. I couldn't respond. All I could do was stare back at them.

I learned what happened from the words that scrolled across the bottom of a news program. "A prominent minister, Rev. Priscilla Sinclair from Richmond, was on board a plane that crashed into the Allegheny Mountains during a blizzard yesterday. Her husband, James Sinclair, and son, Timothy Sinclair, were among those killed. Fourteen passengers and one crew member perished in the crash."

They released me from the hospital a few days later. Mama hired a nurse and a limousine to drive us home to Richmond. I laid in my old bedroom, down the hall from my daddy. Both of us were in a vegetative state—his, from the long-term effect of heart disease, mine, from the mental breakdown of my heart being ripped from my chest.

Tamu flew in for the funeral. Like a rag doll, she dressed me in a black dress and jacket trimmed in purple, and pushed me through the service and burial in a wheelchair. Mama kept her hand on my shoulder, not for comfort, but to secure me from keeling over onto the floor of the church or into the grave before me.

The repass was at the church. My eyes were closed behind the dark sunglasses I wore. I didn't want to see anyone or speak to anyone. It was all useless. There was no consolation for me in this world.

After the slow agonizing day was over, Tamu suggested to my mother that it might help if I went back to my house. She planned to stay in town with me for a month to help me recover. I was ambivalent. Mama had her doubts but didn't force the issue.

I walked in my house with my eyes closed and kept them closed for days, not wanting to see the emptiness. The structure of wood and bricks that I had helped design was my refuge and stronghold in one minute and my cruel torture chamber in the next. The house comforted me with the memories we had there and then punished me with the reality that there would be no more. I woke up one night screaming and crying. Tamu rushed in and climbed in the bed with me. We both cried until the sheets were soaked with our tears.

When daybreak came, my voice was so hoarse I could barely speak. "Why did He do it, Tamu? Please tell me why."

"It was a terrible accident."

"He allowed that to happen to me. Why? Did I try to claim His glory? What?"

"There's so little in this life that can be explained."

"All I wanted to do was preach His word. I know I wasn't perfect but, God, why chastise me so brutally? Why hurt my son because of what I did?"

"Don't go down that road, girlfriend. There's no way back from it. You have read the Bible from front to back, and you know it is full of suffering. It's God's favorites who suffer the most. Their faith is challenged in the worst ways. Don't try to make sense out of this because there is none. Tragedy doesn't discriminate. What you have to do is survive. You didn't die in that plane because you were meant to survive."

"Surviving is not living. I don't want to live like this."

"I've seen you put your trust in God from the first day I met you. That's all you have to do. Let Him work it out. You said He called you and put you on your path; keep trusting Him to see you through this."

I fell back onto the wrinkled and damp pillow, too weak to talk anymore.

***

Tamu was a great friend to me. I didn't want to disappoint her or make her feel as if she was wasting her time taking care of me, so I pretended. I pretended that I was coming to terms with the accident and my loss and accepting God's will. I pretended that I wanted to shower, get dressed, and eat every day. I pretended that I was going to see a grief counselor. I pretended that eventually I would go back to the church. So, when it was time for her to go home, she did so with half a smile on her face, probably because she didn't believe all my pretenses; but at least I had given her some hope.

I'm sure Tamu called Mama and told her to check on me after she left. The doorbell rang at 4:00 on the dot, two hours after Tamu had left for the airport.

"I was out shopping and thought I would stop by and check on you on my way home," Mama said, pushing her way through the door with a bag of take-out food in her hand.

"You could have just called," I said, following her into the kitchen.

"You're my daughter, and I'm always going to come and see about you. Have you eaten?"

"I had a late lunch with Tamu before she left."

She sat down at the table and motioned for me to take the seat next to her. "I understand that you are feeling better, but I can't help but worry about you over here all by yourself. I was thinking that maybe you should come back home with me for a week or two."

"I know you want to help and you want to take care of me, but I'm a grown woman. It doesn't matter whether I'm here or at the house with you and Daddy, nothing is going to change. I have to face this on my own."

"You don't have to face it alone."

"Yes, I do. The whole thing is my fault."

"How can you say that?"

"What do you mean, how can I say that? Mama, I jeopardized the safety of all the people who loved and trusted me. The only thing I could think about at the time was impressing Daddy. That's what the whole trip was about. It was for me, not for God."

"You were starved for your father's approval, and that was your downfall."

"Yes, and I should have been the first to die."

"Child, you think too much of yourself! You don't determine the weather. You're not that powerful. What happens in this world is God's will, not yours. You weren't in control of the weather, the plane, or the pilot. And you can't choose who lives and who dies. God uses you just like He does everyone else."

"I was selfish."

"No, you were foolish. You've spent your whole life trying to please your father. You made him your idol. Good things came out of it, but bad things did, too. That's the nature of this world."

"I just need a few days to myself," I said, trying to get her to go home. "I'll think about coming back to the house after that."

"Okay, sweetheart," she said with a sigh. Reluctantly, she got up to leave. "I'll call you in the morning." Then she gave me a hug and a kiss..

"Pray for me, Mama."

"I always have, and I always will," she said.

I watched her walk to her car, and I waved goodbye. I felt sorry for her, knowing the pain she would feel after I was gone.

Priscilla and the Stranger

"Now you know my story," I said to the stranger. "Now you see why there's nothing left for me to live for."

"I'm sorry for your loss, Priscilla," the stranger said. "There is no doubt that you have been deeply and irrevocably hurt. That I cannot change. It may feel like it today, but sorrow didn't begin with you; it's been around a long time. David and Job thought their pain was unbearable and wished for death, yet they were restored. Knowing the struggles of all those before you should help you process your own pain. Psalms 71:20-21 says, 'Though you have made me see troubles, many and bitter, you will restore my life again; from the depths of the earth you will again bring me up. You will increase my honor and comfort me once more.' If you have learned nothing else from your legacy, you have seen strength and resilience in your people. The breath in your body says you have much to live for."

"I've lost everything that made my life worth living. My father was right. I shouldn't have tried to follow in the steps of all those men of God."

"That's where you are wrong, beloved. None of them were perfect or any more worthy than you. The past doesn't condemn us; it blesses us. Don't throw your life away."

"There's nothing left but trash."

"One man's trash is another man's treasure. A treasure trove of triumphs and, yes, tragedies. That's living. We suffer from similar frailties, step into the same pitfalls, and endure inescapable heartbreaks."

"Don't you get it, Mister? I am a broken person."

"Go back, find the pieces, and put them back together."

"What good will that do?"

"You will become whole again. You will find a reason to live again."

"This isn't the life I want. I want the life I had."

"Things change whether we like it or not. That is the nature of time. Your life is the time you are given. It must be valued. Because you are grieving, you have cheapened your time."

"Look, I've listened to your story, and I'll admit that it was awesome. And now you have listened to mine. So will you please go and leave me in peace?"

"I want to leave you in peace, but you haven't made it yet."

"What do you want from me?"

"I want you to wait a week."

"What difference will that make?"

"God made the heavens and the earth in less than a week. Since your time means nothing to you, you can spare it. It won't matter much in the end."

"If it will get you to leave, I'll do it."

"I have one condition."

"I knew it.

"The first day must be spent in prayer, and the second must be spent with your mother."

"Whatever," I said, getting up from the chaise. "You found your way in here, so I'm sure you know the way out."

I marched into the house without looking back. Once inside, I peeked through the blinds to make sure he had gone out through the gate, but he was already gone.

The sun was setting, and I couldn't believe I had been listening to that strange man for nearly 24 hours. Exhausted, I staggered into the den and collapsed onto the sofa.

"What in the world just happened?" I thought. The whole day had been totally bizarre. A strange man wandered onto my property and told me an extraordinary tale of my family's history. Beginning at the end of 400 years of slavery in Egypt to the wars in Jerusalem, exile in Babylon, crossing the Arabian Desert into Saba, migrating across the Red Sea into Axum, through political and religious wars, invasions, sold into 400 more years of slavery from Jamaica to Virginia, and then freedom again. I was humbled and proud all at once.

I reflected on my father's story and understood his struggle, I understood my grandfather's struggle and his father's struggle, each one before him going back all those generations. With that understanding, my perspective on my own struggle began to shift. I rolled off the sofa onto my knees and began to pray for the first time since the crash.

"Help me, Lord, please help me," I pleaded. I was so low I didn't even know what to ask. I needed so much. I felt weak in my body, mind, and soul. I was even too tired to kneel. I rolled over onto the floor, still begging the Lord to remember me.

Chapter Six

Finding the Way Back

The pounding on the door woke me up. Was the stranger back? Stiff and aching from sleeping on the floor, I leaned on the sofa to pull myself up. It was daylight, but I had no idea how long I had been sleeping. I staggered to the door, peered through the glass, and saw my mother.

"Mama?" I said, opening the door.

"What is going on with you?" she yelled, standing in the doorway, "I've been calling you since yesterday morning. Is there a reason why you haven't been answering your phone?"

I didn't have the energy to lie. "The reason I didn't answer the phone is because I took it off the hook so I could kill myself without being disturbed."

She stared at me through squinted eyes, trying to figure out if I was joking or not. Realizing there was more truth than teasing in my statement, she stomped inside and slammed the door.

"Are you that selfish and inconsiderate?"

Her response threw me for a loop. "Mama, you know what I'm going through," I said, walking back to the den.

"Yes, I do, but that doesn't excuse you," she fussed, following me. "We all got a cross to bear. How could you think about putting all the pain you feel on your mama? I'm already carrying more than my share."

"I'm sorry, Mama," I said, seeing the cruelty of my plan. "I don't know what to do."

"I raised you better than that," she said. "I've never known you to take the easy way out of anything."

I sat on the floor at her feet. "It hurts so bad," I said, letting a fresh supply of tears flow.

"Why do you act as if you have been singled out? There is pain all around you, around the whole world. It will bury you if you let it," she said, rubbing my shoulders. "Don't give in to it, Prissy, that would bury me."

"I've got to get out of this house!" I cried out. Then I thought about the stranger's story, the story he said was mine, the legacy he said I could lean on. Somehow, I needed to make it real. "I'm going away on a trip, Mama," I said, getting up from the floor.

"What are you talking about?" she asked, baffled.

"I've got to find the pieces of my life," I said, hurrying to my office with her close behind me.

I sat down in front of my computer and searched a travel website for plane tickets.

"Get two tickets, I'm coming with you," she said, watching me.

"Not this time. I've got to go alone. Plus, you have to take care of Daddy."

"I can hire a full-time nurse."

"No, Mama," I said, terrified to travel with anyone. "If something happened to you because of me, nothing and nobody could stop me from leaving this world."

"All right, then call Tamu to go with you."

"Don't worry about me. I'll call you every day."

***

With packed bags, I drove to Charles City County. It was a short drive, but for some reason, we rarely visited there when I was growing up. Most of the land had been sold, except for the 40 acres that my grandpa had insisted never leave the family. I pulled up in front of the house. Boarded up, it seemed smaller and forgotten; but the rocking chair, cracked and weathered, moved slightly in the wind.

I walked toward the shed and the shell of the barn that leaned to one side. Among the sound of the rustling leaves, I could almost hear the voice of Grandpapa W. J. and so many others who had lived there. I made my way to the fields and walked acre after acre, envisioning the healthy rows of tobacco that once grew there. The crevices in the ground told of the blood, sweat, and tears that it had taken to acquire the land and then to dig something out of it.

Back at the house, near the edge of the field, I walked the quarter-mile to the church. It had been sold to another congregation years ago. Standing at the entrance, I tried to imagine the services that took place inside there, my grandpapa preaching, and his father before him preaching. I closed my eyes and tried to picture the original church built by Grandpapa W. J.'s great-great-grandfather Jordan.

The family graveyard was about 50 yards from the church. Seeing the graves of William Sr., Anna Bell, Thomas, Blossom, and Edward Freeman, I felt the gravity of my history, the hardships, and the perseverance. The sense of unworthiness returned. I wanted to lay there in the rich soil around them and beg for the strength they had, but I had many more miles to go.

It was barely a 20-minute drive from there to the Shirley Plantation where my great-great-great-grandfather Jordan was paid to preach to the slaves and where he met his wife, Talitha. I parked my car at the gate of the place where Jordan had bought the freedom of his wife; his daughter, Joanna; and his son, Edward. This was my first time visiting a plantation in Virginia or anywhere else. Cars passed by me, eager to tour the meticulously kept grounds and mansion of the estate. I got back in the car and drove to my next stop, the Berkeley Plantation.

There were six miles between the two plantations. Much like the Shirley Plantation, the Berkeley Plantation was lovely and serene, exponentially more civilized than its history. I parked, bought my ticket, and followed a group of tourists for the guided house tour. The guide supplied us with a great deal of historical tidbits: Berkeley was the site of the first true Thanksgiving, it was the birthplace of a US president, the first ten presidents had visited there, and the first bourbon whiskey was distilled there. There was no mention of the horrors suffered by the generations of house negros who had served and supplied the masters' every need.

On my self-guided tour of the gardens, previously worked by field negros, the grounds were immaculate and quiet. No conspicuous faces filled with anguish, no sounds of chants while laboring, and no sad soul spirituals during worship. All the visible signs of the abomination had been cleaned away. There was no evidence of beaten backs, humiliations, or heartbreaks of those who had been enslaved on the plantation. There were no remnants or connections to Adio, who they called Adam; his wife, Irene; or their son, Jordan. Brought back to the second stage of grief, anger, I headed to the airport for my flight to Kingston, Jamaica.

***

Boarding the flight, I was apathetic. The worst experience on an airplane had already happened to me. I took my first-class seat and slept for the three hours. It was late in the evening when we landed. I collected my luggage and took a taxi to the Marriot Hotel. As soon as I was checked in and settled in my room, I turned my cell phone on. There were several missed calls, most from Mama. I wasn't in the mood to talk, but I didn't want her to worry, so I called.

"How are you, Prissy?" she said without a hello.

"I'm fine," I answered, placing a lift in my tone. "I'm about to eat something and go to bed. I'll call you again tomorrow, I promise."

"All right, baby, get some rest," she said, satisfied after hearing my voice.

I picked over my food and sat out on the balcony for hours, smelling the tropical air and listening to the noises of the city. Suddenly, it occurred to me that Jamaica was the place I wanted to visit for our many-years-later honeymoon. With that thought, the bed was too lonely. I slept on the couch.

In the morning, I ate a quick breakfast at the hotel buffet. After some advice from the hotel concierge, I hired a private charter to taxi me around. The driver's name was Leroy.

"Good morning, madam," he said with a heavy accent, opening the door as I approached his van. "Where would you like to go on this fine day?"

"Take me to Port Royal, and then Temple Hall, I want to see the plantation," I said, putting on my sunglassess.

"There's nothing much of the plantation left to see, ma'am. It's mostly a residential area, but we can drive to St. Andrew Parish after we leave Port Royal."

It was early, and not many folks were on the beach. The sand was rocky and darker than I had expected. I walked along the edge of the water, feeling the wind in my hair and the waves rushing over the tops of my feet. Looking out over the ocean, I imagined that the view was probably the same as it was over 300 years ago when the ship carrying Abdalla sailed into the port. I toured Fort Charles and saw a few artifacts from the days of slave trading.

Leroy was right about Temple Hall Estate. It hadn't been preserved as the plantations in Virginia had been; and the more I thought about it, that was a good thing. On the way back to the hotel, I asked Leroy to stop at a market. I wanted to buy something special for Mama. In the market, I struck up a conversation with one of the vendors sitting beside her booth.

"Your bags are very nice," I said.

"Thank you, ma'am. I'm Hannah. How are you enjoying your visit here in Jamaica?" she asked as I perused the colorful bags.

"I'm not on a vacation," I answered. "I'm from Richmond, Virginia, in the States. I came here to trace the path of my family."

"Is your family from Jamaica?" she asked, interested.

"I was told that they were brought here as slaves from the east coast of Africa."

"That's a good thing to try and connect with your family. I have family that I would like to meet."

"Where is your family?" I asked.

"I am a descendant of the tribe of Levites, the great-great-granddaughter of Hannah Glaze and James Levy," she said. Then she proudly recited a full list of her family line. "But I haven't met any of the Hebrew people."

"Well, my sister, from what I've been told, you are meeting one today. I am a descendant of that same tribe."

The woman stood up and took my hand. "I thank God for putting you in my path, sister. You have made me happy today!"

"It's my pleasure," I said, smiling. It was confirmation that I was going in the right direction.

Back at the hotel, I arranged my flight to Mombasa, Kenya.

***

The flight from Jamaica to Mombasa was 17 hours. Once I was settled in my first-class seat, I drank a bottle of water and slept most of the way there. During the few hours I was awake, I listened to my playlist of Tremaine Hawkins and Wintley Phipps and reflected on the story the stranger told me. After we landed, I took a taxi to the Sarova Whitesands Beach Resort.

Mombasa was more beautiful than I could have imagined, with its palm trees, white-sand beaches, and blue water. I didn't know where I was going or what I hoped to find. Undoubtedly, there would be no history or evidence of my ancestors to be found; but more than anything, I just wanted to walk on the land where they walked.

I checked into the hotel, dropped my bags, called Mama, and then headed out to hire a guide for a tour. The city was alive with people. Old Town was a mixture of not-quite ancient and not-quite modern. Fort Jesus, with its cracked walls, belied the significance that it had once had. This military fortification, captured and recaptured between the Portuguese and the Omani Arabs when they traded slaves, was now a tourist stop where children ran, played soccer, and climbed the wall and the stairs.

The energy at the Mombasa market got my blood flowing again. People were bustling about, and the vibrant colors of their clothes and the food of the street vendors were a feast for the eyes. More ethnicities and cultures were represented than I had anticipated. There was so much to see and to buy. I was delighted when a man chopped a coconut open and offered me the water to refresh myself. Then his young son came to help him; and, like a humongous wave, sadness washed over me. I felt so alone. I asked the guide to take me back to the hotel.

After an early breakfast the next morning, I hired another guide to drive me to the outskirts of Mombasa. I wanted to see more of the area outside the city. The view changed quickly as we drove past the warehouses and cultural centers, heading up from the coast to Tsavo National Park.

Off the road, trees were spattered along the plains, and the mountains stood majestically on the horizon. From my window, I could see antelopes grazing, birds soaring above, and elephants and zebras drinking from watering holes. The utopic scene probably hadn't changed much over the past 400 years. I felt peaceful for a few moments, until the noise of a car passing us on the road brought me back to reality.

I considered driving from Mombasa, Kenya, to Addis Ababa, the capital of Ethiopia, with the idea that I could see more of the country and the path of migration. But with so much of my journey ahead of me, I took the short flight.

***

Addis Ababa had the similar mix of the old world and the new. The traffic was heavy and confusing. I was fascinated seeing the people, the culture, and smelling the spices at the Addis Mercato Market, the largest open market in Africa. I hired another private guide to show me around the city. At the end of the day, I had seen many amazing things, except something was bothering me. I felt like a tourist on vacation, and that's not why I had taken this trip. The connection I wanted to make with my history continued to be elusive.

The next day, I took a flight to Lalibela to see the rock-hewn churches. Knowing Mama was worried after a few days, I called her to let her know where I was.

Before she said hello, she snapped, "Where are you? I thought you were going to call me every day. I was about to call President Obama and tell him my child was kidnapped in Kenya."

That made me laugh, and it felt good. I hadn't laughed in a long time.

"I'm in Gondar, Ethiopia. I'm staying at the Ghoa Hotel."

"Oh, my Jesus, where in the world is that? she asked, flabbergasted. "I thought you were still in Mombasa."

"No, I left there a few days ago. I flew into Addis Ababa, Ethiopia, the capital. I got a chance to visit the Holy Trinity Cathedral. It was magnificent, Mama. The food was a bit spicy for me, but the coffee was amazing. Then I flew to Lalibela, the place where the churches are hewn out of rock. I couldn't believe my eyes. It was spectacular. You have to take your shoes off to go down into the churches, and you can feel the coolness of the stone under the red carpet. The skill and artistry that it took to create those buildings is miraculous."

"You're going to give me a heart attack, Prissy!"

"I wish you could have been there with me. Drums were playing, and the people came to worship dressed in white. And they have real services underground!"

"Child, when are you coming home? You've been gone for more than two weeks."

"Not long, Mama. I'm searching for something that can help me keep going."

There was a long pause before she said, "I hope you find it, sweetheart."

"I won't stop trying," I said, hoping to ease her worrying.

"Well, you need to call Tamu. You have her stressed out, too. She has been calling here every evening."

"I will. I love you, and Daddy, too."

"We love you so much, Prissy, and if you're not going to answer your phone, please call me. You promised."

"I'll do better, Mama. Bear with me a little longer."

Instead of calling Tamu, I made arrangements to take a day trip to the Simien Mountains.

***

It was an hour and a half drive to get to the National Park, or Ethiopian Highlands. The view of the landscape was impressive, even more so when we drove into the park. The trees and the brush were the greenest of greens. The panorama of imposing mountains and expansive plateaus were more colorful than any painting or photograph could capture.

Following the guide on the hike was surreal; but with each step I took, I felt the actuality of God. Who else could have shaped or designed such splendor? How great thou art, almighty God.

Walking the trail, each scene was more breathtaking than the last, with perfection in every crack and crevice. Seeing the freedom of the exquisite animals as they ran, played, and basked in the richness of the terrain was pure harmony. We passed huts that were neatly fashioned, and once again, the years disappeared. We stopped on a cliff, and I was spellbound by the vastness of the earth and how insignificant we are. I thought of God looking at His creation. Then the words from the Book of Genesis came to mind: "And God saw it was good."

Thunder sounded in the distance as the temperature began to fall. As we hiked back toward the entrance, a mist began to roll and rise from the ground. Then I saw an immense waterfall. We got closer, and I could hear the power in the rushing water. It was a religious experience. The words of the song filled my head, "Oh Lord my God, When I in awesome wonder, consider all the worlds Thy Hands have made. I see the stars, I hear the rolling thunder. Thy power throughout the universe displayed."

On the ride back to the hotel, I gazed out the window and decided to stop trying to make sense of things that were beyond my understanding. From Jamaica to Kenya to Ethiopia, countless numbers of my people had lost everything and were separated from their families, but they persevered. It did not matter why or how they persisted, only that they did. I wasn't sure if I could, but I owed it to them to make the effort.

While dining in a restaurant near the hotel, I reviewed my itinerary. It included a stop in Djibouti before crossing the Red

Sea into Yemen, the ancient city of Saba. From what I could tell from the internet, Djibouti was essentially a desert, better visible from a helicopter. And with battles raging in Yemen, it was unlikely that I could find a guide willing to risk his life for a tourist. Likewise, Iraq, the ancient city of Babylon, still basically a war zone, would also be too dangerous to explore.

The next day, I flew out of Gondar back to Addis Ababa to connect to a flight to Jerusalem.

***

Relaxing on the balcony of my room at the Leonardo Hotel, I braced myself for the scolding I knew I would get from Tamu. No doubt, Mama had told her that I was on the brink of leaving this cruel world and definitely not in my right mind. I picked up my phone, took a deep breath, and called my friend.

"It's about time!" Tamu said, obviously peeved. "Put me on FaceTime. I need to see you."

Once we could see each other, I said, "Hey, girl, I know you're pissed. Cut me some slack."

"Uh, no!" she said, determined to deliver her speech. "We've known each other a long time; and in that time, I have known you to be selfish and inconsiderate, but not to the level where you would take your own life and leave the people who love you with a mess to clean up. You need to stop feeling sorry for yourself. You could have been killed in that plane crash, too. God must have had something left for your pitiful ass to do. When your mama told me what you almost did, I made up my mind to hunt you down and kill you myself."

"Okay, Tee, I get it. I'm sorry. Please calm down."

"You have a lot of nerve telling me to calm down! You have been off the grid for weeks now. Nobody knew where you were. I'm your sister, and I didn't even know."

"It was spur of the moment. I was desperate. If I didn't get away, I might not have made it."

"Well, where have you been?" she asked, still salty.

"Jamaica first, then Kenya. From there to Ethiopia, and now I'm in Jerusalem."

"What the hell?"

"It's a long story, literally. I'll tell you when I see you."

"I'm done. I'm on the floor. You have knocked me out."

"Listen, Tee, I'm near the end of this journey. I've been doing great running around the world, but I need you to help me get back home. I can't do it by myself."

"Look, hard head, you know I'm here for you. Tell me where to come."

"I bought you a ticket. Can you meet me in Egypt?"

Tamu shook her head, completely taken aback. Then she said, "I'll be there whenever you say. I'll pack my bag as soon as we hang up."

"Thank you, Tee, thank you so much. I've got to go, but I'll call you in a couple of days."

"All right, Prissy, take care of yourself. Do it for me and for your mama."

"I will," I said, trying to hang up before the tears came.

***

It was a short walk to the Old City and to the Western Wall, also known as the Wailing Wall. Only a small section of the wall remained after the Romans destroyed the second Temple built by King Herod. It was odd to think that the battle over religions in Ethiopia nearly two millennia ago is still going on in Israel. Dressed appropriately in pants and a long-sleeve sweater up to my neck, I gathered on the women's side, stuck my written prayer into a crack of the wall, and got in line to enter the Temple Mount. The Dome of the Rock was most impressive, with its brilliant color, intricate designs, and dazzling gold dome. However, non-Muslims were not allowed inside.

I hired a private guide who showed me the Tower of David and the Garden of Gethsemane at the foot of the Mount of Olives, where Jesus, in despair, prayed on the night He was betrayed. Next, we visited the Church of the Holy Sepulcher, which stands on the site where Jesus was crucified and is the site of His tomb. Then we went to Bethlehem, where Jesus was born. I was able to go down into the grotto and see the spot where Mary gave birth.

Being in Jerusalem was mind-blowing. Going to places I had only read about in the Bible all my life was incredible. I thought about Mama and felt guilty. She would have thoroughly enjoyed being in the Old City. I vowed that if I ever got my life back on firm footing, I would bring her here for a visit.

Back at the hostel, I couldn't help but feel let down. As much as I had wanted to feel a connection to the places I'd visited, I still felt lost. I had gone back like the stranger said, but there were no pieces there for me to pick up. The only thing revealed to me on this journey was that I couldn't go back and retrace the path of my ancestors; everything had changed. The other truth that I had to come to terms with was that the world didn't stop turning just because my life exploded.

***

I flew into Cairo a couple of days before Tamu arrived. I booked us a large suite at the Nile Ritz-Carlton. I needed the time to rest and to find the energy to put on a good face when she got there.

"You look better than you did the last time I saw you," Tamu said, putting down her luggage and greeting me with a hug after she arrived at the suite.

"I'm feeling better. I'm glad you could come."

"Come on, girl, you know I have your back." She stepped to the window to check out the view. "So what have you been up to?"

"Just trying to get my head on straight."

"I hear you. I can unpack this stuff later. Let's go to the rooftop lounge. I need a drink after being on a plane for 17 hours."

Tamu chose a table near a window so we could see the city. She ordered calamari and a bottle of Chardonnay. Having been roommates for four years, we never felt obligated to make small talk. We sat there for 15 minutes in silence. Once the food arrived and the wine was poured, Tamu ate a bit, took a few sips, and reached for my hand.

"We have been friends for over 20 years. I need you to know that when your heart is heavy, my heart is heavy. You are not by yourself."

I nodded. "More than my grief, it's the guilt that is so hard to bear."

"Priss, you must not know God like you profess. You don't have the power to determine who lives or dies. That crash was not to punish you. The order of life cannot be explained. Even I know Isaiah 55:8-9: 'For My thoughts are not your thoughts, Nor are your ways My ways, says the LORD. For as the heavens are higher than the earth, So are My ways higher than your ways, And My thoughts than your thoughts.'"

"I know that intellectually, even spiritually; but emotionally, I can't get past it."

"What's this trip all about?"

"You probably wouldn't believe me if I told you."

"Try me," she said, pouring herself another glass of wine.

"I was sitting on the patio at home with a bottle of wine and a bottle of pills. I was tired of trying to keep my head above water. I was ready to let go. Then this older man dressed in a caftan appeared out of nowhere. He asked to tell me a story, the history of my family going back to the Israelites."

Tamu was stunned. She couldn't reply for a minute. "You are kidding."

"No joke. He refused to leave until he had told me the whole story. It was a story of high priests and men of God that went from Aaron all the way down to my father. It crossed countries and generations and over 3,000 years."

"What kind of wine were you drinking?" she asked, mystified.

"It was amazing. When I finished the bottle, he kept pouring from it, and my glass was filled."

Tamu threw up her hand. "Okay, stop. That's too deep for me. I'm just glad you pushed the pause button."

"What I thought was that I could retrace the path of my ancestors and that it might give me the peace and strength I need to keep going."

"Have you found it?" she asked warily.

"I don't know. I'm taking it minute by minute."

"That's good enough for me," she said, finishing her wine. "Now let's get to bed. I know you made some plans for us to see Egypt."

"You know me," I laughed, feeling grateful for my faithful friend.

***

I had booked a six-day tour that took us to the pyramids and the Sphinx at Giza Plateau. We rode camels, which was a ton of fun, before we went to the burial grounds of Saqqara. In the evening, we traveled to Luxor on an overnight sleeper train. When we got there, we checked into a hotel, did some shopping, and explored the ancient city of Thebes. Later, we visited the Temple of Luxor. The grand statues, colossal columns, and the hieroglyphics were unbelievable. The thousand lights that illuminate the temple at night were spectacular.

Over the next four days, we did all the things that tourists do. We crossed the Nile River to the West Bank; saw more huge statues, sanctuaries, and obelisks; went into quite a few tombs, and visited the remains of more temples. We were exhausted when we boarded the overnight train back to

Cairo. Our final stop was to see the solid gold mask of King Tutankhamun at the Egyptian Museum.

We spent Tamu's last day relaxing around the hotel. These were my final hours of escape before I had to go back to the empty house where my grief consumed me.

"Why don't you fly back with me and stay in San Francisco for a while?" Tamu asked, while we rested at the pool. "I'm sure you can change your flight. It's only one day difference."

"I would, but I've got to check on Mama and Daddy," I lied. "I know she's been stressed out with me being gone so long." The fact was, there was no way I could fly on a plane with someone I loved.

"If you're not ready to go back home, you don't have to. No one would blame you if you decided to sell the house."

I could tell that Tamu was nervous about me being there alone.

"It's painful being there without them, Tee, but I have so many happy memories there."

"I know. Anyway, the holidays are coming soon, and I want you to spend Christmas and New Year's with me and Derek."

"That's sounds good. I would love to," I said to appease her, unsure of what I'd be doing for the holidays. I was just living minute by minute.

***

My car was in long-term parking at the Richmond Airport. From there, I drove straight to Mama's house. I thought I owed her at least that for nearly worrying her to death.

"Thank you, Jesus!" Mama said when she opened the door. "I was going crazy here with you not half-calling me like you said you would."

"I'm sorry, I know that was inconsiderate. Believe it or not, all that exploring kept me really busy. And with the time changes, it was hard to call. I didn't want to call in the middle of the night and give you a heart attack."

"It's all right, child, I'm just glad you're home now. Your Daddy is probably awake. You can go on in and say hello."

"Not tonight, probably tomorrow."

"Aren't you staying here tonight?"

"No, Mama, I just wanted let you know I was back. I'm sure I have a ton of mail and messages to go through."

"Well, thank you for coming by, maybe I can get a good night's sleep for a change."

We hugged and I gave her a kiss before I headed back home. I wasn't ready to face Daddy. We still hadn't been able to communicate for whatever reason.

The house was dark and cold when I got there. I dropped my bags at the door, turned on the heat, and started a pot of coffee. I'd left so abruptly that I neglected to stop the mail delivery. I grabbed a grocery bag and went to the mailbox. It was packed to capacity. I stuffed it all in the bag, went in and dumped it on the table, and poured myself a large mug of coffee.

I was sifting through bills and junk mail when I saw the letter from the Toronto Christian Conference. What could they possibly have to write me about? I held the envelope up to the light for a hint, unsure if I wanted to open it. I dropped several four-letter word bombs before I tore open the envelope.

It was an invitation. I was dumbfounded. How could they be so cruel as to invite me back to speak after what happened last year? Who could be that heartless? In a burst of anger, I swept all the mail onto the floor and stomped out of the kitchen.

I dug in my handbag for my cell phone and called Tamu.

"What's wrong?" she asked right away, probably because of the late hour.

"I just got back a few hours ago," I told her, almost frantic. "I was going through my mail, and there was an invitation to speak at the Toronto Conference. I'm sure they know what happened after I was there last year."

"Calm down. I'm sure they didn't invite you to hurt you."

"Why would they think I would ever come back there?"

"They probably think you have a mighty story of faith to share with the conference."

I hung up on Tamu. The whole world had gone crazy. After all the torture I had been through, they had the nerve to think I would return. How could they not know that my greatest wish is that I never went there in the first place? That conference ruined my life. I staggered into my bedroom and cried myself to sleep.

I woke up before dawn, damp and sticky from my own tears. I felt a presence in the room, and heard the words of the stranger over and over in my head: "Go back, find the pieces, and put them back together." Could it be that Toronto was the place I needed to go? I had already been halfway around the world. If I could take that trip, I could make it to the conference, even if I didn't speak. I got up, found my laptop, searched for the email that proceeded the letter, and confirmed that I would attend.

***

Mama agreed to travel with me to Toronto, even so, I bought tickets that flew us back home separately. Something in me refused to make that flight back with anyone I loved.

"Thanks for letting me be here for you, sweetie," Mama said, patting me on the arm during the taxi ride to our hotel.

"I couldn't have come without you. There was no one else I could ask."

"I'm your mother, Prissy, we need each other."

Memories were starting to flood in when got to our hotel suite. Mama wanted to go over to the convention center and check out some of the booths and vendors. I feigned a headache and told her to go ahead and have a good time. I was playing solitaire on my laptop when she got back a few hours later with the schedule of events.

She sat down quietly beside me for a minute before she said anything. Then she asked, "Prissy, do you know you are the keynote speaker tomorrow?"

"What!" I screeched. "There's no way."

She showed me the program, and I was stupefied. Instantly, I had the headache I had lied about. It took me several minutes to gather myself and figure out what to do. I had the organizer's name and contact information, so I sent her a quick email, stating that there had been a misunderstanding. For the next hour, I watched the inbox for a reply. Mama ordered me some room service, but I couldn't eat.

"Don't worry. It'll get worked out tomorrow," Mama said, urging me to go to bed and get some rest.

"You're right," I said, even more grateful that she was there. I took one of my sleeping pills, knowing I wouldn't be able to fall asleep without it.

***

It was practically noon before I woke up. I jumped out of the bed and checked my emails for a reply. There was none. I was beginning to panic. I needed to let someone know they needed a replacement speaker.

"You need to relax, Prissy," Mama said, watching me run around like a caged animal. "Get changed, we'll get something to eat, and then we'll find somebody to fix things at the convention center."

"Okay, that sounds like a good plan," I said, taking a deep breath.

I took a shower and dressed, and we had lunch in the hotel restaurant. By time we were finished, it was after 3:00, and I was scheduled to speak in three hours. On the walk to the convention center, I held Mama's hand as I did when I was six years old. I was terrified. This was where my nightmare began a year ago.

A woman at the entrance gave Mama directions to the area backstage where scheduled speakers were assigned dressing rooms. When we got there, I saw Roberta Daniels. She rushed over when she saw me.

"It's so good to see you, Rev.," she said embracing me, "I was on the organizing committee and suggested you for keynote. I know how difficult this is for you, but you have a strong testimony."

"There's been a mistake," I told her. "I can't do this."

"Oh, Priscilla," she said, looking sympathetic. "We don't

have time to change the schedule; but if you can't do it, you can't do it. Your room is on the right. Take some time alone, and pray about it. It'll be fine, whatever you decide."

"Go ahead, Prissy," Mama said. "I'll wait out here where I can listen to the other speakers."

The dressing room had a huge mirror, so I couldn't escape my reflection. Staring back, I was still standing. The Lord had brought me this way for a reason. I just didn't know what it was. There was a Bible on the dressing table. I opened it, and the pages fell on 1 Corinthians 2. I read it and realized it was the message God had brought me there to deliver. I began to pray.

"Open my mind, Lord, pour into me a stream of Your wisdom. Make me an oracle of Thy word. Tether me with Your tools, and arm me with Your weapons. Allow me to be an instrument for Your will."

***

As I walked to the podium, for a moment, I thought I was going to pass out. Then I caught a glimpse of Mama nodding at me from the side. I bent closer to the mic and opened my mouth.

"The last time I was here in Toronto as the keynote speaker, I had a wonderful revival. On my way home, there was a plane crash. I lost everything: my husband, my son, my ministry, and my will to live. Today, I stand before you as a broken person. We all are in some way or another. It's what makes us human. We suffer from the same confusions and challenges: detractors, doubts, insecurities, pride, greed, shame, illnesses, and sorrow.

"I have not preached a word since I left this building last year. I questioned God and my calling. The message that I want to bring to you today is from 1 Corinthians 2:4: 'My message and my preaching were not with wise and persuasive words, but with a demonstration of the Spirit's power, so that your faith might not rest on men's wisdom, but on God's power.' That's what I had to come to terms with, Christian friends. All the times that I worked so hard to prepare the perfect sermon, using the appropriate references, old adages, with a few double-entendres, most of the time the message was lost among all my words.

"Today, I didn't have anything prepared. I didn't plan to speak. Then I realized that simply walking out here was a demonstration of the Holy Spirit in my life, evidence that God is a Savior, an ever-present help in a time of need. So, I am thankful this evening that the Lord has not forsaken me. To God be the glory! Help me to praise him, brothers and sisters. Hallelujah. Hallelujah!"

The room erupted in praise and adoration. I was filled with joy, something I thought I would never feel again. I cried out, "Thank you, Lord!"

Epilogue

On the first Sunday of the New Year, I sat in the pulpit at Tabernacle of Grace for the first time since before the crash. I hadn't stepped foot in the building since the memorial services. I can't begin to describe the love I felt as so many members welcomed me back with warm, heartfelt hugs. I was still seated in the pulpit when, unexpectedly, Mama wheeled Daddy up the center aisle to the front pew. It was time for me to speak, but I didn't think I could stand.

"God, help me!" I whispered as I moved to the podium to speak. "As you all know, I have been on a leave of absence for more than a year. I wasn't sure if I would ever be back. I know I don't have to explain. You all know my struggles, my triumphs, and my tragedies. But I must confess that the Lord has seen me through all of them. Even when I had given up, He wouldn't leave the pitiful sheep that I was alone to die. He picked me up and brought me back into His fold.

"The message for today is 'Restoration.' Second Corinthians 5:17 says, 'Therefore, if anyone is in Christ he is a new creation; the old has gone, the new has come!' Through Him, we have been reconciled with God. The Tribe of Levi was a prime example of restoration. Aaron made the idol of the golden calf, and the tribes of Levi sinned and fell short of God's glory with the other tribes. But when Moses asked, 'Who is for the LORD?' the Levites stepped forward and were set apart. They were restored to a privileged place of priests to stand before the Lord, to serve Him and to bless His name. They served as the intercessors until Christ came, took our sins upon Himself, and died.

"Through the ultimate sacrifice, Jesus became the High Priest who intercedes for us. Hebrews 4:15-16 says, 'For we have not a high priest who is unable to sympathize with our weaknesses, but we have one who has been tempted in every way, just as we are—yet was without sin.' Jesus Christ was chosen by God, a precious Lamb with no defects, to be our Redeemer. We were purchased with His blood. We belong to Him. First Peter 2:9 says, 'But you are a chosen people, a royal priesthood, a holy nation, a people belonging to God, that you may declare the praises of him who called you out of darkness into his wonderful light.' Because of His mercy, we have been reconciled, rectified, and restored."

A deep voice shouted, "Amen!" It was Daddy.

Then Mama shouted, "Amen!" and the congregation clapped and praised the Lord.

I raised my arms. "I'm here, standing before the throne of grace, to give the Lord praise this morning for His faithfulness. Great is Thy Faithfulness! Please sing, choir."

Kenny played and directed the choir in the hymn as the Holy Spirit filled the room. Then I saw the stranger, standing in the back of the sanctuary. I rushed down the aisle toward him as he turned and walked out the door. I searched the vestibule and outside the church, but there was no sight of him.

THE END